SIX-GUN SHOWDOWN

Kid Carver stood in the middle of the street facing Frank Lowry, some thirty yards away.

"Anytime you're ready, louse!" Kid Carver cried.

"You did the calling, mister," Frank Lowery answered, placing the fingers of his right hand only inches away from his holstered gun.

Kid Carver licked his lips. He saw no fear in his adversary's eye, only a calm, steady stare. He glanced at the sidewalk where a dozen people stood immobile, like wax statuettes, staring at the drama in the middle of the street. Carver felt a nervous twinge. Perhaps he'd made a mistake, but he knew he could not back off now.

"I'm waiting, Mr. Carver!"

The Kid glanced once more at the silent crowd, and then reached for his gun. . . .

DEPUTY TRAIL

BY LAWRENCE CORBETT

ZEBRA BOOKS
KENSINGTON PUBLISHING CORP.

ZEBRA BOOKS

are published by

Kensington Publishing Corp.
475 Park Avenue South
New York, NY 10016

First printing: April 1987

Printed in the United States of America

Chapter One

After more than a month on the trail, Frank Lowery, twenty-one other cowpunchers, and two trail bosses had completed the cattle drive. They had taken a herd of five hundred cattle from the QB Ranch outside of Stillwater, Oklahoma and driven the beasts for three hundred miles to the railhead of Wichita, Kansas. But, while the other cowpunchers had splurged their pay, Frank had not spent his earnings in the glittering cow town on prostitutes, drink, and gambling. No, he had better things to do with his $100. The money would give him and Sarah a start, maybe small, but at least a start. The hundred, plus the $50 he had banked in Stillwater, would enable them to buy some furnishings and to rent a flat.

But if Frank Lowery eagerly anticipated his return to Stillwater, he would find disappointment when he got back, and the disillusionment would change the course of his life.

In mid-October of 1874, Frank Lowery and several other cowpunchers who had made the trek to Kansas started back to Stillwater on horseback. They would need ten days to cover the three hundred miles, and perhaps less if they moved fast and without dallying in some of the ramshackle clapboard towns along the way. The weather remained hot in this early fall. On the seventh day out of Wichita, with the sun still beating down with considerable warmth, Frank wiped away the sweat on his neck and took off his hat to fan himself to dry away some of the perspiration on his square face. Next to him, Jesse Meade grinned, but the grin drew a frown from Lowery.

"I don't know how you can take this heat," Frank said. "You don't even work up a sweat."

"The sun don't bother me none," Meade shrugged.

"You're a man just like me; it ought to bother you."

Meade leaned from his saddle toward Lowery and grinned. "You're all horned up, Frank. That's why you're sweatin' like a pig. You can't wait to get back to Stillwater and wed that fillie so's you can get into bed with her."

"Sure, I'm looking forward to seeing Sarah again, but not just for that," Frank said. "We promised to marry as soon as I got back from this drive, and I'm anxious to have her for a wife."

"Did she say yes?" Jesse Meade asked.

"I already gave her a ring," Lowery said. "It cost me twenty-five dollars." Then he slapped his bedroll, which was draped over the mount behind the saddle. "I've got a new suit of clothes in here. It's the only money I spent in Wichita. Before I go to see her, I'll stop at Lin Ching's bathhouse to clean myself up real good. Then I'll dress and call on her."

"Will she be at Mae's Boardinghouse?"

"That's where she's been staying," Lowery answered, "so I expect to find her there. She's been working at the Broadway Cafe as a waitress, so if she isn't at the boardinghouse, I'll probably find her at the cafe."

6

Then the two men stiffened in their saddles and reined their horses when they saw a rider galloping up the trail toward them from the south. Both Lowery and Meade knew that the man was Swede Anderson, who had been on the point this morning, staying well ahead of the other six men. The point man kept a sharp eye for possible bandits or renegade Indians who might ambush a party of riders to rob or even kill them. Lowery screwed his face, worried. Why was Anderson lathering his horse so hard? Had he seen trouble up ahead? However, when Swede reached him and stopped his mount, he wore a big grin on his rugged face.

"The Arkansas, boys; the river is jes' ahead, as muddy as ever. We can't be more'n a day or two outa Stillwater."

"Goddamn." Jesse Meade returned the grin. "Let's hit it. We can make another ten miles 'afore dark. We'll camp tonight and be in Stillwater in a couple o' days."

"Yee-hah!" Anderson cried.

"It'll sure be good to get home," Jesse Meade said. "I got a fillie o' my own I'm anxious to see."

"You mean that whore, don't you?" the Swede laughed. "That woman goes to bed with anybody who'll give her a dollar."

"It don't matter," Meade said, "so long as I'm the only one in bed with her at the time."

"Yee-hah!" Anderson cried again. Then he whirled his horse and opened the mount to a full gallop. Lowery, Meade, and the others also slapped leather. The riders moved swiftly over the last streak of plain toward the Arkansas River. They hurried on for more than two hours, giving their mounts only short rests or frequently walking the animals. Soon the snaking Arkansas River loomed into view.

"We'll rest near the bank and chow down," Swede Anderson said to the others. "These mounts could use a good rest."

On the shore of the river, some of the men gathered wood for a fire. Then Frank Lowery and the Swede placed the last slabs of bacon in a skillet and they fried biscuits in a second pan with the last of their flour. A third member of the party made coffee, but they had no sugar. The men ate and relaxed here for more than an hour, engaging in small talk, discussing what they would do when they reached Stillwater. Three of the men would go back at once to the QB Ranch to resume their work there. Swede Anderson and a fifth man, however, said they would continue on to Ardmore, near the Texas border, to join up with one of the ranches there, where the pay was supposedly better.

"They'll pay fifty a month and quarters," the Swede said.

"I have never heard of pay like that for a ranch hand," Lowery said.

"That's what they'll pay for good, experienced hands," Anderson insisted.

"That's near twice the thirty a month old man Barker and the others around Stillwater will pay," Jesse Meade said.

"Well," Frank said, leaning forward after a sip of coffee, "if that's truly what they pay around Ardmore, then maybe Sarah and me will go down there. They have cafes there, too, and I suppose she can work in one of them."

"Is that all you think about? That Sarah?" the Swede asked.

Frank Lowery grinned.

Now Jesse Meade looked soberly at Lowery. "Frank, I don't know why you waste your time cowpunching. You got brains; you're educated. You could be a banker, or at least a Wells Fargo agent, and maybe even a lawyer."

True! Lowery had been a fortunate youth who had enjoyed a good education. He had completed eight grades at the public school in Tulsa. His father's pay as a foreman had been enough so that Frank could to go school instead of working, and he had also had the pleasure of merely wandering freely about the ranchlands, to do as he pleased. He might even have gone to college to study law or medicine, but when his folks had suddenly died in an overturned-wagon accident, he had left Tulsa and its memories. He had drifted for a while and then hired on with the QB Ranch, where he had worked as a puncher for the past two years.

"I don't like stiff collar work," Frank told Meade. "I like a job where I can be outdoors a lot."

"Well, then," Meade pointed out, "if'n you want the outdoors, get yourself a job with them Pinkertons or get yourself a lawman's job to make a name for yourself. There ain't nobody as good or as fast with a gun as you are, but you jes' let that talent go to waste."

Lowery did not answer. True, he could draw a six-shooter as fast as any man alive, for he had practiced by killing rattlesnakes since he was a lad of twelve. He had then improved his accuracy shooting down speeding mountain cats or swift running deer. After years of hitting rattlers and tracking coyotes and bobcats, he had reached the point where he could knock a pine cone off a tree at two hundred yards. Some of his fellow cowpunchers wondered why he had not put his ability to use a six-shooter and a rifle to better use.

Several times men like Frank Caxton, who routed sodbusters for various cattlemen's associations, had tried to hire Lowery at high pay. Some of the wealthy Oklahoma saloon owners had attempted to employ him as a bouncer or order man, since his presence alone could deter trouble in their establishments. In fact, just before this cattle drive, a wealthy gambling saloon owner, Carl Markham of the Silver Nugget Saloon in Guthrie, had offered Frank such a job at exceptionally good wages. There was even talk that some outlaw gang leaders had once propositioned him to take up with them.

And of course, Marshal Fred Egan, who was responsible for the Pawnee County area in the Oklahoma Territory, had several times asked him to accept a job as a deputy U.S. marshal.

Folks in the Stillwater area knew of Frank Lowery's better-than-average intelligence and his prowess with guns. He had the strong physique to accentuate these talents: tall, rugged, with a square face and deep-penetrating gray eyes. But most important of all, he had a calm and quiet demeanor. He rarely raised his voice or got excited, and most people knew enough to respect this quiet man.

"Frank," Swede Anderson now turned to Lowery, "you could stay right at the QB Ranch. Old man Barker's daughter has had an eye on you for some time. If you was to marry her, why you could own the whole spread in time, and you're smart enough to do better than the old man himself. You wouldn't be working no more for a mere thirty dollars a month."

"I'm already betrothed," Frank said.

"You're crazy, that's what you are," the Swede pointed out. "A woman is a woman. Once they're layin' naked in bed, they all taste the same."

The others laughed, but Lowery glared at the Swede. "Men like you just can't understand. Sarah means more to me than just going to bed with her. She means more than money or prestige. I'll be real lucky to have her as a wife. As I told Jesse, I've got a hundred dollars, with another fifty in the bank. It isn't much, but it's enough to buy furnishings and to rent a place. It'll be a start, and if we both work for a year or two, we could save enough to make a down payment on a small ranch. I've got plenty of experience working with cattle, and I can make a go of it."

"You wouldn't have no means to move your herd to the railhead."

"I'll do the same as some of those other small ranchers do," Lowery said. "I'll pay the common fee to one of those cattle drive agencies to take my stock north for me."

"That could be expensive," Swede Anderson said.

"It won't matter," Frank Lowery shrugged. "With the price they're paying for beef in Wichita, I'd still make a good profit."

The seated men downed their coffee and cleaned up their campsite. They then remounted, crossed the Arkansas River, and continued south. By late evening they had passed the Pawnee reservation and Indian trading post at Morrison. Beyond, they again camped for the night, because the first thing in the morning they would ride into Stillwater.

After breakfast the next day, merely a cup of black coffee, they started out again. They had been on the trail about two hours, the sun had risen above the hills to the east, when Lowery and the others heard the sound of galloping horses. They instinctively veered into some trees, dismounted, and readied their rifles. Then they stared to the south where they saw several riders coming toward them, their mounts leaving a long trail of dust behind them. The cowpunchers stiffened and stood ready to fire, prepared to defend themselves. These men knew that the desolate hills and forests of the Cimarron country often teamed with outlaws.

However, Lowery and his fellow cowpunchers soon saw the sparkling reflections from the badges pinned to the chests of at least two of the oncoming riders, so they guessed that the men were lawmen. Soon enough the leader of the visitors reached the septet of men and reared his horse. Lowery recognized the man in the saddle as Fred Egan, the Pawnee County federal marshal. The others with Egan also wore stars on their shirts.

"Marshal" Lowery said, "what are you doing so far from Guthrie?"

"We've been out since yesterday morning," Egan said.

"You lookin' for somebody?" Jesse Meade asked.

"Bronco Kinney," the marshal answered. Then he straightened in his saddle. "Him and some others hit a Wells Fargo office in Enid a couple of days ago and made off with five thousand dollars. They wounded the night watchman."

"Wowee," Jesse Meade hissed. "Five thousand!"

"Are you sure it was Bronco Kinney?" Frank Lowery asked.

"It was him, all right," the marshal said. "The watchman recognized him with no trouble. He'd seen Bronco many times at the rodeos, and he'd seen him around town. But, we don't know yet who the other four were that was with Bronco on this hold-up."

"He made enough money in those rodeos," Lowery said. "Since when did he take up robbing Wells Fargo offices?"

"Since he got thrown from his mount in less than five seconds on the last two outings and they told him not to come back no more." Now it was Deputy Jack Stone who spoke up. The deputy leaned from his saddle. "Bronco was washed up. After his last fall two weeks ago, the rodeo people had enough of him, and now he's back, robbin' a Wells Fargo office."

"I've seen Bronco Kinney many times at a rodeo," Frank Lowery said, "and I'd recognize him, though he doesn't know me. We haven't seen him. In fact, we haven't seen anybody since we crossed the Arkansas on our way back from Wichita."

"Too bad." The marshal frowned. "We were kind 'a hopin' that maybe you fellows were the fivesome who blew that Wells Fargo safe, or at least maybe you saw riders on the trail." Then Egan grinned at Lowery. "Frank, that offer to work for me is still open. I can get you a deputy marshal's badge in no time at all."

"No thanks, Marshal," Lowery said, "I have other plans."

"Marshal," Jesse Meade grinned, "you're in the Cimarron badlands and these hills are full o' good hidin' places that no posse can ever find. Of course, they might have gone to Ingalls, but the people there got so many lookouts in that outlaw haven that any wanted men in that town are long gone before any lawmen can get their hands on 'em." Jesse then gestured. "They got away, Marshal, and Wells Fargo is stuck."

"Maybe," Egan said, "but we'll keep lookin' for a couple of more days. If you fellows do see anything suspicious, why you leave word with Constable Hutchinson and he can send me a telegram in Guthrie, or send one to Deputy Vic Gray in Enid. If you fellows do see these outlaws, don't try to take Bronco and his band alone. I was told that some of the men with Kinney are pretty good shots."

"Not like Frank here." Swede Anderson cocked his head at Lowery. "He can hit a cottontail jumpin' over 'a fence."

Lowery lowered his head, slightly embarrassed.

"Don't remind me." Marshal Fred Egan grinned at Lowery. Then he tipped his hat and swung his horse. The seven men watched the posse turn away and then urged their horses into a fast trot. The cowpunchers waited until the visitors were out of sight. Then Lowery and the others remounted their own animals and headed for Stillwater. As they rode, Jesse looked at Lowery.

"Can you imagine, Frank? Five thousand. My God, Bronco and those men with him can live it up for at least a year in Ingalls."

"But they'll have to stay there," Frank Lowery said.

"Who cares?" Swede Anderson now joined the conversation. "They'll get anything they want, from juicy thick steaks to the best whores on this side of the Mississippi. I could take a year o' that kinda life." Then he pointed at Lowery. "I bet Bronco wouldn't mind havin' a gun like you with him."

"That kind of life isn't any good," Lowery answered. "Always on the run, your picture on wanted posters in every jail and post office, and posses looking for you every minute. You'd even have bounty hunters chasing after you if there's a price on your head. That's no life for anybody."

14

"Hey, Frank," Jesse Meade pointed out, "maybe that's the kind of job for you, a bounty hunter. You could make a fortune with some of the rewards some of these big companies offer."

"I keep telling you, I've got other plans."

"Let's quit dilly dallyin'," one of the other riders said. "We can make at least five or six miles before dark. Then we can hit town in the morning."

Within the next hour they had left the more rugged landscape and reached the more level stretches of the Stillwater-Ponco Highway. The trek would go easier now as they entered the more populated areas of Pawnee County. Between Stillwater and the Indian reservation there was heavier traffic, because farmers and ranchers often hauled wheat, corn, fruit, and beef for sale to the Indian agent who served the Pawnee Indians.

By midafternoon the sun was hot, and Lowery took off his hat, brushing back his sandy hair and wiping away some of the sweat from his thick locks. Then he blinked his eyes and wiped the perspiration from his square face. Next he shifted his tall, muscular frame in the saddle to loosen some of the kinks in his back. He had been riding for over a week and his bones ached, while his muscles felt tight.

And Frank Lowery was filthy. He had not washed or shaved since leaving Wichita, and the dust of so many days on the trail had thickened on his trousers and shirt and had penetrated into his chest, back, and arms. His boots were heavy with dirt, gray colored instead of black. His face itched and his growth of beard felt like sandpaper on his cheeks and his chin. His kerchief, badly soaked from perspiration, no longer helped to wipe away the sweat, so he had slipped it into his saddlebag.

15

Lowery looked up at the familiar landscape of lower Pawnee County, studying the open terrain around him that stretched to the splintered peaks of rising hills that lay silhouetted in the waning daylight. Once beyond this stretch of grassland he would be close to home.

Somewhere in the hills a coyote howled, while the sun now settled into the blue sky to the west. Lowery glanced at the arroyos and gullies that snaked across some of the segments of land. Patches of cracked earth also dotted the area. The bare spots had become hard and barren, for the summer of 1874 had been unusually hot and dry. On the opposite side of the rising hills, beyond the stretches of grass, were the dense Cimarron forests, the sanctuary for outlaws from Oklahoma and Kansas.

The men, now on the last leg of their long journey from Wichita, continued on. As they reached the near end of this remote, wide patch of countryside, Frank Lowery finally saw the familiar QB Ranch spread. Moses Barker's ranch encompassed a full four square miles of territory, one of the biggest in Oklahoma. But, Frank would not go there now. He would first go into Stillwater to clean up and to make plans with Sarah Langdon for their marriage, make furniture purchases, and then rent a flat. He would go to the ranch in a couple of days to resume his work as a hand.

Lowery did not sleep well that night in their encampment within a patch of woods about two miles out of town. He had become too restless, too anxious to see Sarah after a nearly six week absence. He lay on his blanket and stared up at the dark trees, squinting at an occasional star that sparkled through the limbs. But finally, around midnight, the incessant distant howl of coyotes lullabied him to sleep.

The seven cowpunchers needed no alarm clocks to awaken them the next morning. The band of daylight and the din of chattering birds roused them at five o'clock. The septet, of course, could not cook breakfast for they had nothing left to eat; nor did they even have enough beans to make coffee for seven men. But they didn't mind. They would ride quickly into Stillwater, clean up, and then get a hefty breakfast at one of the cafes. Lowery would go to the Broadway Cafe, where he hoped to meet Sarah at work.

By seven o'clock Frank had settled into a hot tub at the Lin Ching Bathhouse, and the warm water soothed his bones, loosened his muscles, and relaxed his nerves. He felt exhilarated, and he could have stayed in the tub all day. But he was anxious. While washing up, Lin Ching had taken his dirty clothes and had promised to have them washed, dried, and ironed by noon. After his bath, Frank shaved off his thick beard with a rented razor until his face was smooth and clean. Then, carefully, he donned his blue suit over a blue shirt and black string tie. He had carried the new clothes all the way from Wichita. He then slipped on his boots, which Ching had shined until they sparkled like black marble. By seven-thirty, he and the equally clean Jesse Meade ambled toward the Broadway Cafe.

Broadway, Stillwater's main street, teemed with people: farmers in town to bring crops, merchants opening their stores and shops, cowboys meandering along the main thoroughfare, women shopping for the day's meals. The two cowpunchers found the cafe crowded, but they did locate a small table and ordered a hearty breakfast of eggs, ham, toast, potatoes, and coffee. Lowery continually craned his neck to catch sight of

Sarah, but he did not see her. Finally, when the waitress returned with breakfast, he gripped her wrist.

"Where's Sarah?"

"Sarah?"

"Sarah Langdon; she works here."

The waitress shook her head. "There ain't no Sarah workin' here, mister."

"She's been here for the past two years."

"I've been workin' here for over a month and there ain't been no Sarah here since that time." Then the girl gestured. "Say, that must've been the girl who worked here and left, and they hired me to take her place. But I ain't never seen her, so I don't know nothin' about her."

"She's probably workin' someplace else in town," Jesse Meade said. "Maybe she had some trouble with the manager and left."

"Maybe," Frank nodded. However, he felt uneasy and he ate his meal with less than a full appetite. Only his hunger kept him in the cafe dining room longer than he wanted. As soon as he had downed the last morsel of toast and the last drop of coffee, he rose quickly from the table.

"I'm going to Mae's Boardinghouse, Jesse. Will you go to McFadden's and get us a room and stable for our horses?"

"Sure," Jesse nodded.

Frank Lowery straightened his tie and pressed down his suit coat as he wove hurriedly through the throngs that crowded the plank board sidewalks of Stillwater's Broadway. Finally, he turned into 10th Street and moved quickly over the quiet avenue until he reached a large, two-story white building. Mae's Boardinghouse. The lawn appeared immaculately clean and the front porch was newly painted. But then, Mae always kept her place

18

spotless. That was why she only catered to a better class of people and she could charge up to ten dollars for a room a week and two more for stabling horses. Lowery again straightened his tie before he came onto the porch, took a deep breath, and pulled the doorbell handle until the ring echoed through the interior of the house.

Soon Lowery heard heavy footsteps, no doubt the thuds of the obese, middle-aged Mae Crawford. He stiffened when the woman opened the front door. However, she did not smile at Frank, offer a welcoming hand, or even speak to him. She merely implanted her bulky frame in the doorway and stared.

"Mae," Frank grinned, "I'm back and all cleaned up, as you can see. I came to see my betrothed."

Again, Mae Crawford only stared.

"I said I came to see Sarah."

"Come inside." The woman finally spoke.

Frank followed the Widow Crawford through the hallway and into the musty parlor that was seldom used. "They told me at the cafe that Sarah wasn't working there anymore," Frank said. "Do you know where she works now?"

"Sit down, Frank."

Lowery flopped into the soft parlor divan but instinctively gripped the arms of the piece of furniture to brace himself as he fell deeply into the settee. All of the furniture in the room was quite plush and somewhat ornate. Mae Crawford seldom allowed anyone in here, except for some special occasions. Frank Lowery had not given this idea much thought, but he would soon learn that this moment *was* a special occasion.

Lowery looked at Mae again. "Where's Sarah?"

"She ain't here."

"I guessed that," Frank said. "I assumed if I didn't find her here, you could tell me where she's working now."

"Frank," Mae said soberly, "she ain't workin' anywhere in Stillwater, and she's probably a long way from this town. As a matter of fact," she leaned closer to Lowery, "I doubt if she's even in Oklahoma Territory."

"What are you talking about?"

Mae Crawford shuffled to the fireplace, reached up, and pulled a sealed letter off the mantel. She then came back to the settee. "She left this for you." She handed the envelope to Frank. "She's been gone for about a month now."

Frank Lowery ripped open the envelope, pulled out the note inside, and read quickly:

Frank, I couldn't wait for you. You no more than got out of sight on that cattle drive, than me and Slim got married. Then we run off and no-body has been told where we was going. There ain't nobody that knows where we are, so don't try to find me. Sarah.

"She ran off with Slim Timberlane?" Frank looked incredulously at Mae.

"It wasn't my place to tell you, Frank," the woman said, "but Sarah was seein' quite a bit o' that man, even though she was supposedly betrothed to you. They was real close to each other quite often, especially after Slim come into that thousand dollars."

"Thousand dollars?"

"Some relative back East; left Slim a thousand from his estate. I suspect that Slim and Sarah are usin' that money to get a fresh start somewhere. Them two jes' got married over to the justice; no guests, no nothing'; jes' a couple of hired witnesses. Then, before anyone even knew they was hitched, the two o' them was gone, bag and baggage. But," Mae sighed, "she did leave you that note."

Frank Lowery did not answer. He rose from the settee and staggered in utter shock. His gray eyes had marbled into hard orbs and his face had stiffened into a stunned expression. He did not say a word to Mae Crawford, he merely ambled out of the parlor, through the hall, and out to the porch. He carefully closed the door behind him.

Mae Crawford waddled swiftly to the porch and stared after the man, watching him move with brisk, steady strides. She then squeezed her face. Mae well knew of Frank's ability with a gun. She hoped he would not do anything rash.

Chapter Two

Bitterness saturated the heart of Frank Lowery after this unexpected desertion by Sarah Langdon. During the year just past Lowery had suffered a series of setbacks. The owner of the McFadden Boardinghouse had once thrown him out for nonpayment of rent. He had lost his horse because he could not keep up payments, and merchants in Stillwater had suspended further credit for serious installment arrears. He had never been able to buy Sarah so much as a decent dress as a present. Lowery had blamed these misfortunes on his job as a cowpuncher, a job that offered too little money and made too much demand on his time.

Still, despite this ill luck, Frank at least had a promise from Sarah Langdon to marry him. And for the past several months, the pretty waitress from the Broadway Cafe had encouraged him to save his money and to pay off his creditors. He had given up drinking and gambling and had felt pleased with his change of habits. By two months ago, when Lowery signed up for the cattle drive to Wichita, he had not only satisfied all debts, he had even managed to bank fifty dollars. With a hundred from the drive and his meager savings, he at least had enough to set up housekeeping with his betrothed.

"We'll get some furnishings and take a flat," he had told the girl. "At least, that will be a start."

"I agree," Sarah had answered. "I'll be waitin' for you."

But the one person Lowery had counted on had now abandoned him, and the hundred dollars he had managed, with self-discipline to bring back from Wichita now meant little to him. His disappointment left a sourness in his stomach as he strode quickly up 10th Street. By the time he reached the McFadden Boardinghouse he had become quite depressed. He almost about-faced, inclined to step into the nearest saloon to drink and gamble his money away. Then the devil could take him wherever he had to go.

But Jesse Meade now hurried up the street to meet him.

"Frank," Jesse smiled, "I got us a nice room with two beds and stable room for our horses. And I saw Jed Stevens, the QB Ranch foreman. He said we could come out there anytime we was ready to go to work again. He figured we could take a few days' rest after that drive to Kansas." Then he leaned closer and grinned. "Did you see Sarah?"

But Frank Lowery did not answer.

"Did you see your betrothed?" Jesse Meade asked again. "How is she? Was she glad to see you?"

"Jesse," Lowery said soberly, "I have a mind to look up this Bronco Kinney and join up with him."

"What brought on a crazy idea like that? You been drinkin' or somethin'? I hope not; not after you promised Sarah you wouldn't touch a drop no more."

"Promises don't seem to count in this world any-

24

more," Frank said. "Some people go crazy if they think they've got a chance for a little money, even those you trust the most. He looked soberly at his companion. "Sarah's gone, Jesse. She ran off with Slim Timberlane because he came into a thousand dollars from some uncle who died back East. Now if Sarah knew that I was coming back with a thousand or even two thousand, she'd sure as hell have waited for me."

Jesse Meade did not answer.

"I'm going to the Star Saloon."

"At eight o'clock in the morning?"

"They're open, aren't they?"

"Don't be foolish, Frank," Jesse said. "Only the worst kind go to a saloon at this time o' day. You quit drinkin' a long time ago and it done real good for you. Don't go in there and drink."

"I'm not going to drink," Frank said. He forced a grin. "You said I was horny as hell and you're right. I'm just going to get me a girl and then I'll be along. Now you go to the boardinghouse and get some rest. I'll see you in an hour or two."

"If that's all you aim to do, take a girl, why that'll be fine," Jesse Meade said. "I'll wait for you at McFadden's."

When Lowery reached the Star Saloon, the place seemed strangely quiet. No clackity-clack of a roulette wheel, no piano notes, no din from crowds of drinkers and gamblers. Frank saw only two men standing at the bar and drinking, and two women, in tight-fitting, low-necked, colorful dresses and with painted faces, loitering at one end of the room near the deserted dice table. Lowery plopped into a chair at one of the tables and within a minute a waiter came over to him. He looked at the well-dressed Lowery curiously and then grinned.

"You don't look like somebody who'd come in to get drunk at this time of day, but I can bring you breakfast; better'n any of the cafes on the street."

"Just some coffee."

"Nothin' more?" the waiter asked.

Lowery dropped a dollar bill on the table. "That should cover it."

The waiter shrugged, picked up the note, and moved off. He returned a moment later and placed a pot of coffee, a sugar bowl, a creamer, and a cup and spoon on the table. "Enjoy yourself, mister," the waiter said somewhat disdainfully. Then he walked off with a shrug.

At another table, alone, a young woman sat and eyed the neatly dressed, clean-shaven Frank Lowery. For a moment she watched him drink coffee. Then she rose from her chair and sauntered to the nearby table. Frank had just taken a gulp of coffee, and when he looked up he saw the girl sitting across from him.

"Hello, handsome?" The girl smiled.

Lowery studied the visitor and then set his cup on the table. She was a woman in perhaps her mid-twenties, quite pretty, with no wrinkles on her creamy face. Her body was full and shapely, with rounded breasts behind the top of her smart blue cotton dress.

"You don't look like you belong here," Frank said.

"Don't I, mister?" the girl answered. "Who does belong here?"

"I mean like those painted harlequins over there by the dice table." Lowery cocked his head.

"No, I'm not one of them; I'm not for sale."

Frank Lowery studied the visitor's oval face, the thin lips, the small nose, the dark eyes, and the flowing brown hair. "Then I don't know why somebody like you would come into a saloon at all, especially at this time of day."

"Because the food is good here," she smiled. "They have a good breakfast and it ain't as crowded as them cafes. Besides, I'm waitin' for someone. I was gettin' lonely sittin' alone." She leaned over the table and smiled again. "The coffee smells real good. Could I have some?"

"I've only got one cup."

The girl motioned to the waiter. "Ed, bring another cup."

A moment later the waiter dropped the cup on the table and moved off. Frank watched the girl pick up the pot, pour coffee, put in some cream, and then a little sugar. "You don't mind?" the girl asked.

Lowery shrugged. But as the girl sipped the coffee, he looked at her intently. When she put the cup down, he leaned toward her. "Are you one of those who comes with a high price?" he asked her. "You know, who takes on bankers and lawyers who need to stay home with their wives at night, instead of taking on those animals who come in here during the evening?"

The girl only laughed.

"Well, if you think I'm one of those rich men, who can pay you well, I'll have to disappoint you. I'm only dressed like this because I had a very important engagement, except that it didn't pan out."

"Most men would have a bottle of whiskey in front of them instead of a pot o' coffee if a woman deserted him."

"What makes you think it had anything to do with a woman?"

"Mister, you wouldn't be dressed like you was goin' to your own weddin' for any other reason." The girl smiled and studied him again. "Whoever she was had to be real stupid to leave somebody as handsome as you."

"Miss, I may as well tell you, I'm only a cowhand."

"Is that a fact?"

"I suggest you finish your coffee and wait for whoever it is you've been waiting for. He's got to be better than me."

"Yes," the girl nodded, "that's just how a man would react when somebody jilted him—put himself down. But you shouldn't do that. After all, it ain't the end of the world."

Frank shrugged.

The girl extended a hand. "Clara; Clara Beaufort's my name. Would you mind tellin' me yours?"

"Lowery; Frank Lowery."

The girl frowned, looked hard at Frank, and then grinned. "I do believe I met a winnin' hand. I certainly heard that name. I was told that you're quite a smart man, and a man who's also quite good with a gun. Is that true?"

"I only shoot rattlers and mountain cats."

"Too bad," the girl said. "You could do real well for yourself if you were inclined to put that talent to better use." When Frank did not answer, Clara Beaufort continued. "I mean, there's money to be made."

Then, suddenly, someone tapped Frank Lowery on the shoulder. When Frank turned, he saw a tall, lanky man standing next to him. The newcomer was clad in a neat pair of chino trousers, a laced wool shirt, tan hat, and a black gunbelt and holster that hung low on the right thigh. A pair of black boots completed the man's attire. He stared, with the slightest hint of irritation in his dark eyes.

"She's been waitin' for me, mister," the man said,

cocking his head toward Clara Beaufort.

Clara Beaufort smiled. "He's just havin' coffee, Walt. Can you imagine? Comin' into a saloon for a pot o' coffee?"

A grin creased Walt's narrow face, but he did not speak.

"His girl run out on him," Clara continued, "and he's drownin' his sorrows in a pot o' coffee. His name is Frank Lowery . . . Lowery. I think maybe you heard o' him, Walt."

"Yes, I sure have heard of 'im," the man nodded. He then looked at Lowery. "They tell me you're an ace with a gun, and a man who's had some education. Too bad you let them skills go to waste and work for a mere thirty a month." He leaned closer to Lowery. "You *are* a cowpuncher, ain't that right?"

"It's my choice," Lowery said.

"This man," Clara gestured toward Walt, "is Walter Kid Carver. Have you ever heard of him, Mr. Lowery?"

"I can't say that I have," Frank answered.

"Well," the girl grinned again, "I suppose that's what happens when you're stuck on a ranch punchin' cows— you don't know what's goin' on in the world. Walt is a friend of Bronco Kinney. Do you know him?"

"I've heard of Kinney. I've seen him many times at rodeos."

"You could do well with him," Kid Carver said.

"I don't think I'd be interested." Lowery shook his head.

"Well, big man, you think about it," Carver said. Then he gestured to the girl. "Let's go, Clara."

The girl smiled and rose from the table. "Enjoy your coffee, Mr. Lowery. Maybe I'll see you again sometime."

Frank Lowery watched the duo walk off. She was certainly pretty; and he supposed this Clara Beaufort was right about taking up with Bronco Kinney: no more boardinghouses, no more shabby clothes, no more beans and black coffee. He could afford to hire the best detectives to find out where Sarah and Slim Timberlane had gone. He could visit them, wearing the finest clothes, atop a fine breed of horse, and with an expensive saddle under him. He could flash a thick wad of bills, nothing under twenty, and nonchalantly offer them dinner in the best restaurant.

Sarah Langdon would writhe with jealousy and regret because she had left Frank Lowery for the piker Slim Timberlane, and Frank could prance around town, picking up any woman he wanted, while he spent his money freely to further intensify Sarah's regrets.

However, by the time Frank Lowery left the saloon he had denounced to himself the idea of teaming up with outlaws. Even if he could pull off a robbery, and even if he could make a bundle of money, he would not want posses chasing him for the rest of his life. Nor would he want to spend the remainder of his years hiding out in the Cimarron badlands with the likes of Kinney or this Kid Carver.

Lowery hurried through the crowd of pedestrians on Broadway, turned into 6th Street, and finally reached the McFadden Boardinghouse. Here he met Jesse Meade, who led him to their room on the second floor and then grinned at his companion.

"Did you satisfy your lust, Frank?"

"I didn't get a chance," Lowery said.

"You mean they didn't have no whores there?"

"Oh, they had a couple waiting around for customers,

30

but I met a couple of people and I soon got talking with them, and before I knew it, I forgot all about taking a woman."

Jesse Meade laughed. "Who the hell could make you forget why you went into that saloon?"

"One of them was a pretty girl named Clara Beaufort. The other one was a man by the name of Kid Carver, a friend of Bronco Kinney's, and I suspect one of them that robbed the Wells Fargo office. He hinted that Bronco might be interested in having me join them."

"That would be foolish, Frank, just like you said. You'd always be on the run, and sooner or later you'd get caught. Our life ain't so bad, and at least we don't have posses chasin' after us. Anyway, maybe Bronco wouldn't want you in his gang. Your shootin' might not be good enough for him, especially if you was an amateur in the outlaw game, which you would be. You'd most likely get caught by lawmen, and surely by a smart marshal like Fred Egan."

"I suspect you're right, Jesse," Frank answered.

"You're jes' feelin' down because Sarah Langdon run off on you. Don't get yourself into nothin' stupid. The pain will go away. There's plenty o' other decent women around."

"That Clara Beaufort is sure pretty, but I think she belongs to that man she was with, that Kid Carver."

Jesse Meade grinned. "Don't let that stop you. There ain't no sense in you broodin' too long from losin' Sarah. Maybe that's what you need, another woman. She could make you forget the hurt."

"She said that maybe she'd see me again."

"Well, there you are." Jesse gestured. "Why don't you go after this girl, if she's shown an interest in you.

And you don't have to go back to cowpunchin', either. Do somethin' else. Take one of them bouncer jobs. The work is easy and the pay is pretty good, from what I'm told. That man who runs the Silver Nugget in Guthrie has been after you for a long time. Go there and take the job. Besides, if'n you get outa Stillwater, maybe you can forget Sarah quicker."

"It might be a good idea to go to Guthrie." Frank nodded. "But I'm going to stay around Stillwater for a couple of days to take care of some business and to get me some rest. How about you, Jesse? Would you want to come with me?"

"No, I'm goin' back to the QB Ranch," Jesse answered. "I ain't got your talent, not with a gun and not in education. But I'll hang around town with you until you're ready to leave."

The town of Ingalls, a remote hamlet in the Cimarron wilds of Pawnee county, north of Stillwater, included a few clapboard houses, a general store, three saloons, two cafes, a barbershop, and two blacksmith shops with stables. The town also included two bordellos and a permanent residency of no more than three hundred people. From Ingalls there was easy access to the stark, uncharted wilderness of Indian territory, some twenty miles above Stillwater, the nearest Oklahoma settlement with a lawman, although Constable Isa Hutchinson was not much of a peace officer. He was now old and quite inept, only able to deal with drunks. So, one really needed to go all the way south to Guthrie to find a capable lawman, or west to Enid, where the efficient Deputy Marshal Vic Gray was in charge.

One of the busiest places in Ingalls was Daisy Carpenter's bordello and hotel. Daisy, a grizzly, stout, middle-aged woman, offered a girl with each bed for the night if a lodger wanted one—and if he had the money to pay for her. Of course, Bronco Kinney and his cohorts had had plenty of money when they rode into town two days before, so that he and three of his companions were already enjoying the good life, one they had previously only dreamed about. The fifth, Kid Carver, was more interested in Clara Beaufort than the luxuries of Ingalls.

The town had been an outlaw haven for some years. In fact, Ingalls had prospered around the money from the outlaws—rustlers, bank robbers, express thieves, or bank embezzlers. The price for services came high here, from a cup of coffee to a woman, but those who arrived in Ingalls had nothing else to do but spend their ill-gotten gains, so they did not mind.

Besides, the outlaws enjoyed protection in exchange for the high price of goods and services. The merchants and madams of Ingalls paid for a local peace officer and two assistants whose principal job was merely to maintain order and not to harass any visitors, no matter what law enforcement agency might be looking for them. The town business people had also set up a network of paid lookouts who maintained a twenty-four-hour vigil on the trails and roads leading into Ingalls. These sentinels quickly alerted the town of the approach of any suspected lawmen, thus giving visiting outlaws time to vanish into the Cimarron wilds before the arrival of any such officers. The merchants of Ingalls merely asked these visitors to conduct any illegal activities outside the established town limits.

Kid Carver and Clara Beaufort had been riding for two

33

days, and late in the afternoon of the second day they loped into town. Since they were a man and a woman alone, the Ingalls lookouts ignored them, certain they were not law people. The pair rode into the busy main street where bustling crowds moved about, passing a crowded barbershop, two busy cafes, and a jammed saloon where even at this hour they were doing a thriving business.

Carver squinted up at the dropping sun and wiped the perspiration from his neck. When he looked at his companion he could not understand how she could look so comfortable in this heat in her high-necked dress and many layers of underclothing. Finally, the duo reared up in front of the Cimarron Saloon. A moment later they walked inside and spotted Bronco Kinney at a table with the three other members of the gang: Colorado McGuire, Rowdy Joe Wheeler, and Jim Clayborn.

The four were playing poker, and a shapely girl stood next to the outlaw leader and caressed his shoulder. Carver noted that Bronco wore a clean white hat, a neat blue shirt, and a string tie. The man had the mark of prosperity about him, and why not? He had just garnered $5,000 in easy money.

Big, burly Bronco Kinney, with a straggly mop of light brown hair, small gray eyes, and a large, weatherbeaten face, had certainly made a financially wise move in changing occupations from bronco busting to robbery. No doubt, he had left the last rodeo show in bitter disappointment when the director refused to give him a place, hinting that he was now a has been at age thirty-two and could no longer draw a crowd. In his anger, Bronco had decided to go after illicit gains, as he had done many years before when he was quite young.

34

Bronco had easily found a willing gang.

The tall, hefty Jim Colorado McGuire had been a cowpuncher for several ranches, including a stint at the QB Ranch. He had been suspected of rustling steers now and then in penny ante thefts from a few of these employers, thus losing one job after another. He had simply been drifting for the past year and he had quickly agreed to join Bronco Kinney in the Wells Fargo heist.

Rowdy Joe Wheeler, a fat-bellied, barrel-chested former trapper, had become tired of plodding through the wilderness for furs that few people wanted anymore. He abhorred the idea of working on a farm or a ranch, where he would need to work set hours every day, at hard labor and in a confined area. He preferred to drink, carouse, and live only for today. He was not a vicious man, but the idea of easy money in a simple robbery appealed to him, so he, too, had agreed to join Bronco Kinney. With quick money, he could live a free life-style.

Jim Clayborn was a quiet man, almost a loner, who had mostly drifted throughout the West for the past several years. No doubt, he had pulled off robberies several times in one-man operations, mostly to earn survival money. He could thus continue to drift about as a nomad. He liked the idea of a quick kill. So, when he heard Kinney's proposition in the Cimarron Saloon, he had readily agreed to join the enterprise. Clayborn did have a minor criminal record and he had spent short periods behind bars, so the thought of robbing an express office didn't bother him.

Perhaps the most vicious member of the gang was Walter Kid Carver, an adept gunman who had often hired himself out as a bounty hunter or as an enforcer for a cattlemen's association, or for anyone else who needed a fast gun to settle a controversy. No one knew how many men Carver had killed, but he usually killed neatly, methodically, and legally. So for Bronco Kinney's plans, Carver was an ideal asset. At the time Bronco approached him, the Kid had had nothing to do, so he had agreed to join the gang.

Kid Carver, tall, lean, and with deep, penetrating dark eyes on a small oval face, was a good-looking man. He had always groomed himself well, spoken softly, and acted cordially. So, when he met Clara Beaufort in a Stillwater store where she had been working, she had admired him at once. He had felt an attraction to her, as well, and she had taken up with him. While Clara Beaufort had had no part in the Wells Fargo caper, she had not protested Kid Carver's participation in it and had not been averse to accepting Carver's money to buy some new clothes, to eat in a good restaurant, or to sleep on a comfortable bed in a better-class boardinghouse.

Now, here at Ingalls, inside the Cimarron Saloon, Carver took a deep breath and walked up to the table with Clara trailing behind him. He waited until the card game hand was over and he saw Bronco sweep in the chips to his spot on the table, grinning widely. This was the best time to approach Kinney, for he was upbeat for the moment. Also, play had been temporarily suspended while one of the others at the table shuffled the cards.

The Kid moved up to Kinney. "Bronco?"

The gang leader, the girl caressing him, and the others at the table looked up at the visitor. "Ah, you're back," Bronco grinned. "What did you find out in Stillwater? Are they still lookin' for the guys who took the Wells Fargo office? Do they have any idea who we are?"

"I'm afraid I must tell you, Bronco, that you've been

identified as one of the holdup men, and they think that Jim Clayborn was in on it, too." He looked at his fellow outlaw. "But, they ain't go no idea about me, nor Colorado, nor Rowdy Joe."

"Damn," Bronco scowled. "How could they know that?"

"They got them artists now who make up drawings from descriptions that witnesses give 'em. Bronco, you're well known all over the Oklahoma Territory, since you've been a bronco buster for many years in them rodeos." He pointed at Kinney. Then Carver looked at Clayborn. "You've been in and out of so many jails, your photograph is well known. So, the law knows who you are."

"It don't bother me none." Jim Clayborn shrugged.

"Well, we can't worry about it," Kinney said before he looked at Kid Carver again. "What about posses? They still out after us?"

"They never did pick up our trail from what I could find out in Stillwater," Carver said, "so they ain't got no idea where we are. I also heard gossip, though, that they might give up and just send out wanted posters."

"Then the whole thing will cool down." Bronco gestered. "Still, I don't intend to simply sit in Ingalls. I got another job in mind, and I could use another good gun."

Carver leaned forward and grinned at Bronco Kinney. "Strange that you should say that, Bronco. We might have just the man you're lookin' for, a real good man with a gun, from what I hear."

"Who would that be?"

"A cowpuncher that's down and out, and who just had his girl run out on him. His name is Frank Lowery, and

37

they say he has the best gun in Pawnee County. But they also say he only uses his guns to shoot rattlesnakes and mountain lions. Me and Clara met this man in Stillwater and we hinted to him that you might like to see him, that he had a chance to make some real money. But he didn't seem to be too interested."

"I heard of 'im." Bronco Kinney nodded. "And I sure would like to see him, but I got to stay here right now, if they suspect I'm the one who held up the Wells Fargo office. That Marshal Egan won't quit lookin' for me." Kinney shuttled his glance between Carver and Clara and then spoke to the Kid. "But they don't know about you, Kid. Maybe you could see him again and talk to him."

"Well, I can say this," Kid Carver grinned, "this Lowery sure took a shine to Clara here."

Bronco now stared hard at Clara Beaufort. "Is that true?"

"It seemed that way." The girl shrugged.

"Then can I count on you?" Bronco Kinney asked. "Do you think you can see him again and get him to come here to Ingalls to see me? If I had a gun like that with me, why just havin' him would make things easy for us. Just his reputation would make a clerk or a guard or a banker give up without a fight."

"I don't know if I can persuade him. Like Walt said, he didn't seem to be very interested."

"You try; try hard. Turn on the charm. Anybody who can bring a spark into a sour face like Carver's can sure interest this Lowery. I got a new plan in mind," Bronco went on, "and it could bring us fifty thousand. You'd like a piece o' that kinda money, wouldn't you, Clara?"

Clara Beaufort did not answer, and in fact an abrupt silence suddenly struck all of them around the table.

Colorado McGuire, the man holding the cards, suddenly stopped shuffling and gaped at Kinney. The others also ogled him. What could their leader mean? Fifty thousand dollars? Where would they get money like that? Bronco did not tell them, but as he looked once more at Clara, the grin still simmered on his face.

"Well, Clara, wouldn't you want a share o' that kinda money?"

"I guess I would," Clara Beaufort answered softly.

Chapter Three

Frank Lowery spent the next two days loitering about Stillwater. He withdrew his money from the Stillwater Farmers Bank, he groomed and brushed his horse, he cleaned his saddle, and he bought a new outfit of traveling clothes: hat, shirt, trousers, and boots. He also bought two boxes of cartridges for his Colt Peacemaker six-shooters and a box of shells for his Winchester .73 rifle. And finally, he bought a little jerky to eat on the way to Guthrie.

While he was taking care of these chores, his mind occasionally wandered to the pretty Clara Beaufort whom he had met at the Star Saloon. He remembered her beautiful face, her poise, and her shapely figure; and he felt irritated because she apparently belonged to this Kid Carver whom he suspected had been a part of the Kinney gang. He ducked a few times into one of the Stillwater saloons or eating places, or he wandered the street, hoping to get another glimpse of her. But, he never saw the girl. He, of course, did not know that she had gone off to Ingalls with Kid Carver.

On the third morning, Frank Lowery ate breakfast with his fellow cowpuncher Jesse Meade at the Broadway

Cafe. Meade had already packed his gear in preparation for returning to the QB Ranch after this meal. Frank Lowery himself had planned to finish up any business today and then leave for Guthrie the first thing the next morning.

"Do you want to come out to the QB and say good-bye to old man Barker and young Rosie?" Meade asked. "She's always had a thing for you, Frank."

"I don't know." Frank hesitated. "They haven't seen me for some time now, and there's no sense visiting them before I ride off again. Who knows when I'll be back, if I ever do come back."

"You've got all day," Meade said, "and I think they'd be mighty disappointed if you didn't see them. Young Billie Stevens would sure like to see you. He thinks the world of you, and surely you'd want to say good-bye to him. You've got your gear all packed and your horse cleaned and groomed. Why don't you come out there with me? You can be back by early afternoon and you'll have the rest o' the day to rest up."

"Maybe you're right," Frank nodded.

After breakfast, the two men led their horses from the stable at the McFadden Boardinghouse. Meade told Mrs. McFadden that he was leaving but that Lowery would be there until the next morning. Thus, they would not be there a full week and should not have to pay for a full week's stay. Mrs. McFadden grumbled, but she agreed to take four dollars for the room and only a dollar fifty for the stalls that had housed the horses of the cowpunchers. She felt better when the men paid her cash in hand.

Lowery and Meade left town and within a half-hour they had reached the wide expanse of grassland and they could see the splintered peaks of rising hills that lay

42

silhouetted against the still low morning sun. Somewhere in the hills a coyote howled, even at this late daylight hour. Frank Lowery and Jesse Meade squinted at the arroyos and gullies that snaked across some parts of the grasslands and stared at the patches of cracked earth that dotted other areas of the rolling plains. The bare spots would remain at least until the next spring, until the winter moisture revitalized the land again.

By midmorning, beyond the stretches of grass, the riders finally saw the huge spread of the QB Ranch. They first discerned the rambling hacienda-style ranchhouse, next the barns, and then the wooden bunkhouses for the twenty hands who worked on this spread. The QB, of course, was one of the largest ranches in Pawnee County, and Moses Barker needed plenty of help to keep the business going.

Finally, the pair saw the group of men working on one of the cracked patches of earth where they had probably been toiling since early this morning. The cowhands had huddled in a circle around a fire where they were branding struggling, bawling calves with a hot iron. A burly man, tall and muscular, sat erect atop his horse and directed the half-dozen hands, who had rounded up these animals. The burly man leaned from his saddle and peered at the two riders. Then a grin cracked the weatherbeaten face of Jed Stevens, the foreman of the QB Ranch.

"Goddamn," Stevens said to his hands. "Looks like Meade and Lowery are finally back." The ranch boss trotted out to meet them. "Hi, boys, good to see you." But then Stevens frowned. "Frank," he looked at Lowery, "I see Jessie's gear, but I don't see you carrying anything."

"I didn't come back to stay, Jed," Lowery answered the QB foreman. "I only came to say good-bye to Rosie, Mr. Barker, and maybe you and Billie."

"Good-bye?" Stevens hissed.

"I'm giving up cowpunching," Lowery said. "I'm going to Guthrie in the morning. Maybe I'll take a job in one of those saloons as a bouncer. I've had some offers. A man I met just before the drive wants me to work in his place. They pay a lot better and the work is nowhere near as hard."

"They want your gun, Frank, and you can get yourself in a lot of trouble with a job like that," Stevens said.

"You know I don't use firearms against other men," Frank answered. "Still, I've got this skill and if I can earn good wages because of it, you can hardly blame me, can you?"

"No, I suppose not," the ranch foreman said. "Well, Mr. Barker and his daughter are at the ranchhouse. My boy is groomin' down his horse in the barn next to the house. I'd guess that all three of them will be happy to see you, but mighty disappointed to hear that you're leaving, just as I am."

When Lowery did not answer, Stevens looked at Meade. "Jesse, you may as well get yourself settled in the bunkhouse and you can work with the others after noon chow."

"Sure thing, Jed," Jesse Meade answered.

Stevens then turned to Lowery with his hand extended. "Well, Frank, if I don't see you again, good luck." He pumped Lowery's hand. "Come back and see us whenever you get a chance."

"I'll do that," Frank answered.

The QB Ranch foreman remained immobile atop his

horse and watched the two men canter away. Then he shook his head. Frank Lowery had been one of the best: hard working, reliable, and no complaints. He would surely regret losing him. He would have given Lowery more pay, even made him a straw boss if he could, but the ranch foreman knew he could not do that. He could not ask Moses Barker to give Lowery such a promotion over men who had been there much longer.

And Stevens regretted Frank's decision for another reason: it was bad business taking a job as a bouncer in a Guthrie saloon. Lowery would face too many crass men: drunks, would-be gunmen, ornery cowhands, harsh gamblers, and a host of other seedy characters who might want to challenge the man. Lowery would end up in a gunfight sooner or later, and if he killed even one of these men, others would be after him to take him down so they could enhance their reputations. But Jeb Stevens could hardly tell Frank Lowery how to lead his life.

When Frank and Jesse loped into the big yard before the hacienda, they saw Moses Barker outside trimming some low hedges around a circular flower garden in front of the building. The ranch owner looked up and grinned when he saw the pair, and he waited for the men to dismount. Then, Barker came toward them and offered both of them a strong handshake.

"Good to see you back," Moses said.

However, neither man answered and Barker frowned. "What's the matter?"

"I'm not coming back, Mr. Barker," Frank Lowery said. "I'm going to Guthrie where I've got a job."

"A job? What kind?"

"I really have two or three offers down there," Frank said. "It doesn't matter which one I take. I can only say that I've decided to move on."

"Jesus, Frank, didn't I treat you well?"

"I couldn't have asked for a better employer," Frank said, "and I regret this decision. But I've given the matter considerable thought, and I just feel that I've got to do it. If things don't work out, why maybe I'll come back to work for you again—if you still have a place for me."

"There will always be a place for you here, Frank; you know that."

"I appreciate your concern." Lowery nodded. "I rode here this morning with Jesse to say good-bye to you, Rosie, and young Billie. I've already seen Jed out on the range."

"She'll be as disappointed as I am," Barker said. "And Billie rode off with that new horse. Only the good Lord knows when he'll be back. I'm afraid you've missed the boy." Then Barker looked at Meade. "Jesse, you might as well settle in and take care of your horse. You can go out on the range after noon chow."

"Jed already told me that," Meade said. He looked at Lowery. "Frank, good-bye and good luck." He shook his companion's hand. "If you ever need a friend, why just remember that I'll always be here."

"Thanks, Jesse."

Meade nodded, took the reins of his mount, and ambled away. Barker and Lowery watched until Meade had disappeared into the horse barn. Then the QB Ranch owner looked at Lowery. "Come inside, Frank. Rosie is in there and I'm sure she'll be pleased to see you."

In the parlor, young Rosie Barker was straightening some photographs on the mantelpiece when the two men entered the room. She turned at the sound of footsteps, saw Lowery, and smiled happily.

"Frank! It's sure good to see you again."

Frank Lowery studied the youthful, eighteen-year-old Rose Barker. She was surely as pretty as any young thing he had ever seen, a girl that any man would appreciate as a wife, especially since her father owned this big cattle spread. Her sparkling blue eyes radiated a vibrancy and a lust for life that would infect anyone who saw her. Rosie's trim, shapely body could arouse any man. Her light brown hair, clean and shiny, hung down in smooth strands.

"Hello, Rosie," Frank said.

But suddenly the girl's initial delight turned to curiosity. A frown erased the smile on her oval face and her eyes hardened. What was Frank doing here in the parlor? If he had just returned to resume work on the ranch, why hadn't he put his horse away, gone to the bunkhouse, and changed into work clothes?

"Frank, is something wrong?" the girl asked.

"He's not comin' back, Rosie," Moses Barker said. "He's goin' to Guthrie to take a job there. He only stopped in to say good-bye."

"Good-bye?" Rosie gasped.

"I'm sorry," Frank said.

"Frank," the girl took his wrist, "sit down." Lowery nodded and sat on the divan next to her, while Moses Barker remained standing. "I've got an idea why you're doing this," she said. "It's because of Sarah, ain't it?"

"Sarah?"

"It wasn't no secret," Rose Barker said. "Half the people in Pawnee County knew she run off on you while you was away on that cattle drive. I know how terrible you must feel, and I know how much this hurt you. But maybe it was for the best. Suppose she did somethin' like that after you married her? Then you'd have had some real trouble."

Frank did not answer.

"She wasn't any good, Frank," Rosie continued. "She went off with that Slim Timberlane, but I can tell you there were other men she took to besides Slim, and always behind your back. But we all knew how much you cared for her, so none of us had the heart to tell you about it. You wouldn't have believed us anyway, so it was best for you that things turned out as they did."

"You're just being kind, Rosie," Frank said.

"No, Frank, Rosie is tellin' the truth." Moses Barker now spoke. "You've got a lot of friends here on the ranch and more in Stillwater. You can always count on them. Why I'd guess that Jesse Meade would cut off one of his arms or legs for you; and me and Rosie would surely do whatever we could."

"That's right, Frank," the girl said.

Frank Lowery looked at the girl and he could not help but notice the hint of admiration and the tint of a plea in her eyes. He had suspected for some time that the girl liked him, perhaps even loved him. But he also realized that he could never be the right man for this sweet, innocent girl. She deserved more than he could ever give her. She deserved one of the affluent, well-mannered young men who came from other wealthy ranches in Pawnee County—the son of a prosperous rancher who could give her the kind of rich life she had been accustomed to, a man who moved in the same high, influential circles that she did. Frank would simply cheat her out of this kind of future.

Of course, Frank Lowery would have had no trouble with this beautiful girl as a wife. He could certainly have

48

learned to love her, and he could surely have appreciated her as a mate. But, he had too much pride, and too much respect for Rosie Barker, to encourage any kind of relationship with the young woman. Once he was gone, Rosie would not think about him anymore, and she could turn her thoughts to the kinds of suitors who would keep her in the upper-class social circles where she belonged.

"Rosie," Frank said, "I appreciate everything you told me, and I'm grateful to you and your father for wanting to help me. However, I've thought about this for some time. It's best that I leave Stillwater and move on to Guthrie. As I told your father, if things don't turn out, I'll come back and maybe work for him again—if he's still got a job open."

"And that's your last word, Frank?"

"I'm afraid it is," Frank answered the girl.

Rosie got up from the divan. "At least let me give you some coffee and sweet rolls. I just baked them this morning."

"I'd like that," Frank said.

He watched the girl move off into the kitchen before he then looked up at Moses Barker who had come over to him and begun to speak.

"Frank, you know that girl has a deep admiration for you. She never showed any kind of affection for any other hand like she's shown for you. But then, she ain't so dumb. She can see that you always keep yourself neat and clean, that you take care of yourself, that you quit carousin' and drinkin', and that you're modest and respectful. And most of all, you got some education. I can't say I'd disapprove if she wanted to marry you."

"Mr. Barker," Frank said, "there's no way I could give Rosie the kind of life she ought to have. There's a lot of

49

young men in the county who come from families with money and class, and Rosie shouldn't have to settle for anything less than one of those kind of men."

Moses Barker did not answer.

Rosie returned to the parlor and set down a tray with a silver coffee pot, sugar bowl, creamer, cups, silverware, and a plate of hot rolls. She poured three cups of coffee and then gestured. "Help yourself to the rolls, Frank."

Lowery nodded and took one of the rolls. Moses and Rosie followed.

Rosie looked at Frank again. "Do you want to stay for lunch? We can do a little ridin' for the rest o' the morning."

"I think I'd best go back to town," Frank answered. "There's a few more things I need to do. I'll be leaving for Guthrie at sunup."

The girl nodded, obviously disappointed. She took a sip of coffee and then spoke again. "Frank, will you write? Let us know where you are and what you'll be doin'?"

"I sure will," Frank grinned.

Fifteen minutes later, Frank Lowery was again atop his horse in the yard in front of the hacienda. He reached down, first shook the hand of Moses Barker and then delicately took Rosie's hand. The girl, however, gave him a firm grip and looked hard at Lowery. Frank pursed his lips, but he made no attempt to loosen the girl's hold until she finally let go.

"God go with you, Frank," Rosie Barker said with a remorseful crack in her voice.

Moses and Rose Barker stepped back and watched Frank Lowery veer his horse before he trotted out of the big front yard. He turned once to wave good-bye and he then spurred his horse into a mild gallop. The duo in the yard stood motionless, staring to the south until Frank Lowery had faded from view. Neither said anything. The girl simply turned and went back to the ranchhouse, while Moses picked up his shears and returned to trimming the small hedge around his flower garden.

Frank Lowery arrived back in Stillwater shortly after noontime, but he felt tired and dirty after the ride out and back from the QB Ranch. He simply stabled his horse in the animal stable behind the boardinghouse and then went up to his room. He unbuckled his gunbelt, took off his boots, and then flopped full on the bed. He was not very hungry because he had eaten a solid breakfast and then had the snack at the ranch. But he was tired, and within minutes he had fallen asleep.

Lowery awoke about four o'clock, surprised that he had slept over two hours. He undressed, washed up with water in the basin, and then shaved. He cleaned his boots and then put on a clean shirt, trousers, and his footwear. He had just buckled on his gunbelt when someone knocked on his door. Lowery frowned. Who would be calling on him at the McFadden Boardinghouse? Frank opened the door a crack, while he kept his hand on his holstered gun. He stared in astonishment when he saw a smiling Clara Beaufort standing there.

"Can I come in, Mr. Lowery?"

Frank opened the door and ushered the visitor inside. Clara Beaufort was clad in a neat blue dress that fit her perfectly and accented her shapely figure. A friendly warmth radiated from her dark eyes. Still, Frank was both stunned and curious. What was this girl doing here?

51

"Mind if I sit down?"

"How did you know where to find me? And why do you want to see me?"

The girl flopped into a chair and then gestured. "I've been alookin' for you all day. I finally learned that you was stayin' here in this boardin' house. I took a chance and I found you in." She leaned forward and smiled again. "I must tell you that I've taken a shine to you."

Frank Lowery did not answer.

"Would you like to go to the Broadway Cafe?" Clara Beaufort continued. "The two of us could have dinner together. It's my treat. Is that all right?"

"I guess so," Lowery grinned, but he was still full of curiosity.

"I see you're quite cleaned up and neat, like the last time I saw you. Where did you intend to go this time?"

"Just to supper," Frank said.

"Well then, now you'll get your dinner free; anything you want," the girl said. "My treat, like I told you."

Lowery looked warily at the visitor. "Why would you buy me a meal? You don't even know me."

"Let's say that I like you and that I want to talk to you. Now, when I want somethin', I usually do what I can to please myself." She rose from the chair. "You ready to go?"

"Sure."

The pair left the boardinghouse, walked east to Broadway, and then ambled along the boardwalk. The pedestrian crowd had thinned by this time of day because the hour was still early for the night life. Within a few minutes they had reached the cafe, and the pretty Clara Beaufort stopped next to the entrance.

"Mr. Lowery, I hope you don't think I'm forward in

wantin' to see you again, or in buyin' you supper. Some people might not think it proper for a woman to act that way. You don't mind, do you?"

Frank Lowery looked hard at the girl. This whole business seemed unnatural. He had understood that this girl belonged to Kid Carver, and as Frank recalled, Carver had been somewhat piqued when he had seen her sitting with Frank that morning in the saloon. How, this pretty woman had said she was eager to see him again, somebody she had only talked to for a short period at a table a few days ago. What was her motive for this strange behavior?

"I'm treating you, Mr. Lowery," Clara Beaufort said still again. She hooked her arm around Frank's left elbow. "Let's go."

Inside the restaurant they sat down at a table and a waitress brought them menus. Clara Beaufort gestured to Lowery, reminding him that he could order anything he wanted. When Lowery said he'd like a T-bone, somewhat expensive, Clara did not protest. She herself ordered a ham dinner. For the next hour they said little to each other as Frank devoured his meal and the girl ate daintily. They topped off the delicious repasts with hot apple pie and cheese, and when they finished, Frank leaned back in his chair, patted his stomach, and sighed in contentment.

"You had enough, Mr. Lowery?" the girl asked.

"Never ate so much," Frank answered. He then leaned over the table and looked hard at the girl before he grinned. "Miss Beaufort, I'm smart enough to know that a near total stranger, especially a woman, isn't buying somebody an expensive dinner like this for no reason. Now, what is it you want from me?"

The girl reached over and held Frank's hand. He felt an exhilarating shock race through his body from the soft, warm touch. "I want you to be rich, Frank. You don't mind if I call you Frank, do you? I don't mind if you call me Clara."

Frank Lowery only frowned.

"You wouldn't mind a few thousand dollars in your pocket, would you, Frank?"

"I don't understand."

"Bronco Kinney wants to see you," the girl said. "He'd like to have you join him in a little caper that could be worth an awful lotta money. He wants your gun, and he's willin' to pay for it."

Frank Lowery shook his head and then grinned. "He sent you after me? Why didn't he come himself or send that friend of yours, that Kid Carver?"

"To tell the truth," the girl said, "I'll earn considerable money for myself if I can persuade you to join up with Kinney. And I must say, I like money, and I like those who have money." She leaned forward and smiled again at Frank. "Don't you think you could have a good time with me?"

Frank Lowery gulped and then felt a tremor race through his body once more. She was obviously desirable, no question about that. Yes, he could certainly enjoy her company. He rolled his tongue around his lips as his heartbeat quickened.

"Well, Frank?"

"What about this Kid Carver? I was led to understand that you were his woman."

Clara Beaufort shrugged. "He don't mean that much to me. He may think he's got a claim on me, but he don't own me. Nobody owns me. I do as I please."

"This Carver works for Kinney, too, doesn't he?"

"Yes."

"Well, he wouldn't like to see you warming up to me, would he?"

"Like I said, he don't own me." The girl squeezed Lowery's hand. "What do you say, Frank? Just a couple of hours' work and you can have a lot of cash—and so could I. Then we could enjoy each other's company and have plenty o' money besides."

Frank Lowery felt his heart beat again, but once more he hesitated. He remembered Marshal Fred Egan and that posse he had met on the trail. They were probably even now hunting for Bronco Kinney and some of the others. Frank also remembered that Egan had not needed much time to learn the identity of two of those Wells Fargo bandits, and Lowery was sure that sooner or later Egan would catch up to them. The marshal was smart, tenacious, and determined. Few outlaws in the territory escaped him for very long. No, not even this inviting Clara Beaufort could persuade him to become an outlaw. He would spend most of his time on the run, always wondering when they would catch him. He could never enjoy any kind of fun or relationship with Clara Beaufort with a continual fear hanging over him. Still, Frank Lowery was disinclined to give the girl a straight no answer.

"What you say is tempting," Frank Lowery said, "but the truth is I'm going to Guthrie in the morning. I've got a commitment there that I've got to keep," he lied. "But, I'd sure like to see you again. You'll probably be able to find me somewhere in Guthrie if you have a mind to look for me. I'm afraid you'll have to tell Bronco Kinney that I can't join him right now."

"Too bad," the girl said. "You might be missing the best opportunity o' your life." She smiled again and

55

squeezed his hand again. "We could go back to your room; maybe I could change your mind."

"Nothing would please me more," Lowery grinned. "But, like I said, I can't join Bronco right now. I sure appreciate your company and seeing as how you couldn't persuade me, maybe I should pay for these dinners."

"No, no," the girl said. "I said it was my treat, and I won't welch."

"If that's what you want," Frank said.

Clara Beaufort paid for the check, a bill of nearly five dollars, and they walked out of the Broadway Cafe. They moved slowly up the boardwalk, the girl again hooking her arm around Lowery's elbow. She occasionally looked at Frank and smiled. They had walked about a block when the girl stopped.

"This is as far as I go."

"I was hoping we could spend the evening together," Frank said.

"I'm afraid not," Clara answered. There was now a tinge of coolness in her voice. "You'd best go on. I'm waiting to meet somebody here."

Frank Lowery could take the hint. "Like I said, I'll be in Guthrie." Then he abruptly left her and walked alone up the boardwalk. When he turned to cross Broadway and head to his boardinghouse, he caught a faraway glimpse of Clara Beaufort. She was now standing next to the lean Kid Carver, and the two of them were obviously arguing as they gestured emphatically to each other.

Frank Lowery scowled. He should have known. They had used this alluring girl to bait him into joining a band of outlaws. Frank was glad he had not succumbed.

Chapter Four

Early the next morning, Frank Lowery loaded his gear on his horse, stopped at the Broadway Cafe for a good breakfast, and then started south toward Guthrie. The day had broken with a clear sky and the prospect of warmth. After Frank rode leisurely out of Stillwater and reached the open highway, he craned his neck to look behind him, regretting for the moment his decision to pull out of a place he had known for a long time. Most people in and around Stillwater knew him and liked him, and Moses Barker and his daughter Rosie had always treated him well. Frank had almost felt like a member of the family at the QB Ranch. Yet he was sure he had made the correct decision: a new town, new people, and a new environment would enable him to forget Sarah Langdon.

But Frank Lowery also thought of the shapely Clara Beaufort, a girl he certainly appreciated. He felt cheated, however, because she had deceived him, even though he hardly knew her and he had no reason to expect honesty from her. Lowery had not even minded her motive of trying to lure him to join Bronco Kinney so she could make some money for herself, but he abhorred the fact that she had apparently plotted it all with Kid Carver, whom he decided he disliked. Frank was glad that Carver had failed in his mission.

Lowery loped southward for about two hours, with the sun rising ever higher in the sky and now radiating heat that drew perspiration from his tall, muscular body. Occasionally, Frank wiped the sweat from his neck and face, or he tilted his hat to allow air to soothe his moist crop of sandy hair. Finally, Lowery spotted a small ranch and he steered his horse off the highway before he cantered up the pathway to a yard in front of a low-slung log-constructed house.

A young lad of about ten stood in the yard. He stiffened when he saw the rider come toward him. Then the youth darted away and bounded into the house, yelling as he ran.

"Maw! Maw!"

By the time Frank reached the house, a woman with an apron around her waist and a bandana around her head came out the front door, with the boy trailing behind her. She carried a rifle balanced on the crook of her elbow as she looked up at Frank. "What do you want, mister?"

Frank looked down at the woman and felt an immediate sympathy for her. Her dark hair hung in disheveled strands from under the bandana, her face looked tough and wrinkled from too many years of hard scrubbing on this farm. Her bare arms had pot marks, old scars from the endless chores of hauling or carrying or chopping, or doing a multitude of other hard tasks. Bags had already emerged under her dark eyes, even though Frank judged the woman to be no older than her early thirties. He almost grinned, remembering the daintiness of Clara Beaufort, Sarah Langdon, or Rosie Barker, with their smooth skin and neat grooming. Yes, life was unfair. This woman had suffered all the difficulties of a hard life, while those other women had lived in relative comfort.

"Sorry, ma'am." Frank Lowery doffed his hat. "I didn't mean to intrude. I've been on the trail for over two hours, on my way to Guthrie from Stillwater. I wonder if I could ask to water my horse and maybe get a drink myself."

"The trough is over there." The woman cocked her head sharply.

"Thank you," Frank said before he loped across the yard.

The woman and the boy stared at Frank with a mixture of admiration and curiosity. The man was well dressed and neatly shaven. His horse was well groomed, still clean after all this time on the trail. These sodbusters were not accustomed to anyone like him.

Frank Lowery satisfied the thirst of both himself and his mount, while the woman and her son watched warily, wondering if Lowery had only stopped for water or whether he had some evil motive. However, they lost their tenseness when Frank remounted his horse and loped across the yard. He stopped only for a few seconds to doff his hat again.

"I'm obliged to you, ma'am."

The woman nodded and watched the stranger trot off to the main road, veer onto the highway, and then continue his ride south. When he had almost disappeared from sight, the woman shrugged and walked back into the house, while the boy, trailing after her, still craned his neck for one last glimpse of the recent visitor.

Frank loped on for about another hour before he saw two men coming up the highway from the south. He did not recognize them, but he instinctively put his right hand on the butt of his holstered six-shooter, showing the same wariness as had the woman and her son at the small ranch behind him. Frank moved slowly up the road until the two men came abreast of him and reared their horses to a stop."

"Hello, mister," one of them grinned. "Can you tell us how much further it is to Stillwater?"

"About nine or ten miles."

"Goddamn," the other man cursed, "that means we ain't likely to get there before noon."

"I wouldn't think so," Frand said.

"Do you know if a man can find work up there?" the first rider asked.

Frank Lowery shrugged as he studied the pair: rather coarse in appearance, their clothes of cheap cotton and quite caked with dust and dirt, their faces bearded and grimy, and their mounts quite soiled from apparent hard riding and lack of care. Lowery judged the duo to be drifters, two men apparently looking for only enough work to earn a little money so they could continue their nomadic life.

"There are a few ranches around Stillwater," Frank said. "If you know anything about cowpunching, I suspect you can probably get a job at one of them. Stop in at the hotel in town. George Cummings is pretty well up on who needs help thereabouts, and maybe he can steer you somewhere." But then Frank frowned. "There's a lot more ranches around Guthrie. How come you fellows didn't look for a job there?"

The two men only exchanged glances, and Frank suspected that they had probably worked at a ranch in the Guthrie area, but only long enough to collect a pay before moving on.

"To tell the truth," one of the riders finally answered Frank, "we didn't want to stay around Guthrie. We found the marshal and his deputies down there mighty harsh, and a man can't have too much fun in that town."

Frank grinned. "Yes, Marshal Fred Egan doesn't like too much wildness around Guthrie, especially rampant shooting of firearms."

"We came all the way from Texas." The second man now spoke again. "Been on the trail for more'n two weeks."

Lowery looked at the men in surprise. "My God! Texas? I heard the pay for cowhands down there is quite a lot higher than it is up this way: fifty a month and board, instead of the thirty a month and board they pay around here."

The first man leaned from his saddle and grinned. "You heard wrong, mister, dead wrong. No ranch owner in Texas is payin' that kinda money, and in fact, some o' them don't even want any help. That's why we left."

"Jesus, it's hot." The second man suddenly spoke again. "Do you know where we can get a drink 'a water around here?"

"No," Frank said. "You'll probably need to wait until you reach Stillwater. There is a ranchhouse about two miles up the road, but I wouldn't go there. I tried to stop at the place to water my horse, but the man and his wife were quite unfriendly. They ran me off the place with buckshot," he lied.

"Then we'll stay clear o' that place," the man said.

Frank Lowery did not trust these drifters. He knew that such men had little conscience, the type of itinerants who would not hesitate to rob a woman alone with a small

61

son; the type who might even ravage such a woman and then perhaps beat her up or even kill her. He was glad he had convinced this pair to avoid the small ranch.

But now, one of the two men began to circle slightly behind Frank while the other stood facing Lowery with a wide grin on his face. However, Frank could also see the hint of malice in the man's eyes, and he suddenly became suspicious. These drifters now had another sure purpose in mind—to rob him, take everything he had, including his horse, and leave him perhaps injured or even dead on the trail. Frank looked at the vast expanse of emptiness around him: no one in sight. Yes, this would be a good place to do him in. Frank's suspicions grew when the man facing him leaned from the saddle and grinned again, but did not speak.

Frank turned to glance at the man who was now behind him and who was also grinning, with an obvious hint of sadism. When Lowery turned to face the first man again, the drifter once more eyed Frank with a cat-and-mouse stare. "You look quite prosperous, mister, and surely you wouldn't mind sharing some o' what you got with a couple o' down and outers, would you?"

"Like I said," Frank answered soberly, "when you reach the hotel in Stillwater, talk to George Cummings. If there's jobs around he can tell you about them."

"I suggest mister," the man behind Lowery now said, "that you'd best get down from that horse." When Frank turned, he saw the man pointing a gun at him. Lowery turned to the first man, who only grinned again.

Frank slowly dismounted and when he reached the ground he shuttled his glance between the man aiming the gun at him and the first man with the simmering grin on his face. Lowery knew he had trouble, but he also knew his own ability for a quick draw. He had never fired at a man before, but he suspected that the aimed six-shooter barrel was no different from a rattler's pointed fang or a cat's sinister eyes before the creature struck. And, as poisonous snakes and wild animals often posed a threat, so too did these two men. Frank's instinct for self-preservation now superseded all other considerations.

"Drop the gunbelt, mister," the man holding the gun said.

However, in a fleeting second, Frank drew his Colt Peacemaker and fired a quick shot that blew the weapon out of the second drifter's hand, them Frank fired a quick, accurate second shot that cut away the gun and its holster. This other would-be bandit gaped, petrified.

And suddenly, Frank no longer felt qualms or guilt for having shot a man. Such an act was not so hard, after all. He had often wondered if he could shoot at a fellow human being, and he had now discovered that he could. He had also learned that he was perfectly capable of defending himself. And best of all, he saw that he could disarm someone with accurate shooting, eliminating the necessity to kill.

Frank now ordered the two men off their horses, disarmed them, and took the reins of their horses. "Now you two can start walking to wherever it is you want to go."

"Jesus, mister, you gonna leave us out here in this wilderness without guns or horses?" the first drifter complained. "We could die out here."

"I doubt that; there's usually a lot of traffic on this road. It's obvious that you men are too dangerous to be carrying guns. As for the horses, why you can walk back to Guthrie and ask the marshal for them, while you explain why I took them." Then, in a fit of anger, Frank pistol whipped one of the men, drawing blood from his forehead. "I ought to kill both of you right here. Now start walking before I change my mind."

The two drifters, quite terrified, broke into a quick trot, and even ran faster when Lowery fired a shot into the air.

Lowery waited until the two would-be waylayers were almost out of sight before he remounted his horse, took the reins of the other horses, and then continued southward. He moved on for almost two more hours, with the sun now high overhead, and once more the heat drew beads of sweat on his neck and face. Finally, he saw Guthrie ahead of him, and he loped a little faster. He was hungry again, and quite thirsty, and he began to itch from the hot, six-hour ride.

When Frank reached the main thoroughfare, 2nd Avenue, he found the street much busier than the main street of Stillwater. Men on horses or atop wagons crowded the wide avenue as they moved, shopkeepers appeared busy loading buckboards with all kinds of supplies. Pedestrians jammed the boardwalks, going in and out of the two banks in town, the restaurants, and the array of shops. He could hear the fast notes of piano music echoing from two of the several saloons in town, drinking places that had already opened for business.

Frank's first instinct was to stop somewhere for food and drink. He felt dirty and tired. However, he loped up the street until he had found the jailhouse, where the marshal maintained his office. He dismounted, tethered the horses, and went inside where he found a single deputy.

"Pardon me," Frank said, "but is the marshal around?

Or Jack Stone?"

"They're around town somewhere," the deputy said. "Can I help you?"

"My name is Frank Lowery, and I just came from Stillwater. I got a couple of horses outside that belonged to a pair of drifters who tried to hold me up. I managed to disarm them and then sent them on their way. I'd like to turn these horses over to the marshal."

The deputy looked at Lowery in surprise and then walked outside with him. He looked at the rather haggard mounts and then grinned at Frank. "Everything they say about you must be true. And you're an honest man as well. You could have just sold those animals and saddles."

"They aren't mine, and I don't want them."

The deputy nodded. "Just leave the horses tethered there. When the marshal comes back, I'll tell him what happened."

"Fine," Frank said. Then: "Oh, one other thing. Can you tell me where I can find a boardinghouse in town, one that can also stable my horse?"

"Try Howard's Boardinghouse," the deputy gestured. "It's on the street two blocks over, 4th Street. He keeps a nice place because he's got a scrub woman, and his prices are reasonable. He's also got a tub, so you can take a bath there if you have a mind to do so."

"Thank you," Frank said. He then remounted his horse and rode up the main thoroughfare, weaving around the traffic until he reached the intersection. Then he swung right, loped for two blocks, and soon saw a big two-story house with a neat sign over the front porch: Howard's Boardinghouse. Frank dismounted, tethered the horse, and walked across the porch. He yanked the bell rod and heard the dinging echo from within. A moment later he heard footsteps, and then a rather obese, middle-aged man opened the front door and studied the visitor.

"Yes?"

"I'd like a room and stable if they're available," Frank said.

"You look decent enough," the man answered, "but appearances don't always tell the truth about people. I've got accommodations, but I'll have to ask for a week's rent in advance, four for the room and one for the stable. I do furnish hay, but you'll have to keep the animal groomed yourself."

"I understand," Frank nodded. He pulled a five dollar bill from a roll and the man stared. "I understand that I can also take a bath here," Lowery said as he handed the man the money.

"Yes, sir," the landlord grinned. "I'll give you a room on the second floor, nice and cheery, with a big window facin' the street. The bathhouse is out back, right down the rear flight o' stairs. Would you like me to draw some hot water and soap for you? I can heat the water in no time."

"I'd appreciate that. I just had a hot ride from Stillwater."

"The bath will be ready in about fifteen minutes," the obese man said. "Meanwhile, you can take your horse out back and stable him, then come up to the second floor on the same back stairs to your quarters. Room twenty-one."

"Thank you," Frank said.

Lowery left the porch, untethered his horse, and led the animal through a narrow gangway to the rear of the house. In the back he saw the long stable and led his horse inside. He found ten stalls here, with only two of them occupied, so Howard Trembley apparently did not have many roomers at the moment. Frank directed his mount into one of the stalls before he untied his gear and laid it on the floor outside the stall. He then unbuckled the saddle and reins and hung them on a railing. He found a brush on the wall and quickly brushed down the animal to wipe away some of the sweat and itch.

Lowery patted his horse's nose and left the stable, hauling his bundled gear with him. He came up the back stairs, walked through a hallway, and stopped before a door marked Room 21. When he got inside, he blinked from the brightness pouring through an almost floor-length window. The room was immaculately clean, and the bed comfortable when he sat on it. Yes, this room would do nicely, but he could ill afford five dollars a week for very long without a job.

Frank unpacked, putting his clothing neatly inside the drawers of a dresser. Then he took out his razor, brush, and soap mug and shaved and washed his face with water in a basin on the stand. He took a clean shirt and trousers and flung them over his shoulder along with a room towel and headed for the bathhouse downstairs. He felt invigorated inside the warm tub as he cleaned his itchy body quite thoroughly. By the time he finished, dried off, and dressed, the obese Howard Trembley had come into the room.

"I put a fresh towel in your room," the man said, "and also changed the basin water that you washed and shaved with." When Trembley saw the heap of dirty clothes on the floor, he looked at Frank again. "I do have a laundry boy who comes in twice a day. If you'd like those clothes cleaned, why I can have it done for you for ten cents."

"That'd be fine," Frank said.

Trembley nodded, picked up the clothes, and dumped them into a basket. He took a tab, wrote Room 21 on it, and then looked at his guest. "By the way, what's your name? I like to write it on the tag, so's there won't be any mistakes. Anyway, I like to know who my tenants are."

"Lowery; Frank Lowery."

Trembley nodded again and wrote the name on the tag. "You'll have these clothes fresh and clean by tonight."

By now, Frank was combing his hair. He looked at Trembley. "Is there a good place to eat hereabouts?"

"Try the Guthrie Restaurant. It ain't but two blocks from here."

"And do you know a Mr. Carl Markham? He runs the Silver Nugget in town. Can you tell me where I can find him?"

Trembley rubbed his chin and then looked curiously at Frank. "That's a kinda rough place, and Markham has a bad reputation. Most people in town have nothin' to do with that man. Marshal Egan has had some trouble in the Nugget and even more with Markham. But I suppose it ain't any o' my business. Markham's place is about a block up from the Guthrie Restaurant."

"Thank you," Frank said.

Within a half hour, now neatly dressed in shirt, trousers, hat, boots, and gunbelt, Frank Lowery walked along the boardwalk of 2nd Avenue. He was hungry, but he decided to stop first at the Silver Nugget, to look into Markham's job offer as a bouncer with good pay. Lowery didn't really know if he'd like the job, but he realized he needed work. Besides, such a job would be relatively easy and the wages were supposedly quite high.

When Lowery entered the saloon, he saw only a few men there. A foursome played poker at one of the tables, while two men stood and drank at the bar. Two women in their thirties, and not able to hide the wrinkles on their faces with heavy mascara, loafed near one of the empty dice tables. The two prostitutes straightened when they saw the handsome, neatly dressed Lowery. They watched him as he walked up to the bar and spoke to the bartender.

"Pardon me, but I'm looking for Carl Markham."

The bartender studied the visitor and especially the low-slung holster. "He ain't here right now; won't be in until later this afternoon."

"I'll come back."

"Can I tell Mr. Markham who called?"

"Lowery; Frank Lowery. I met him in Stillwater several weeks ago and he said he'd give me a job if I ever came to Guthrie. I'm staying a couple of blocks away at the Howard Boardinghouse."

"I heard o' you, Mr. Lowery," the bartender said, "and I think Mr. Markham will be glad to see you. As I said, he should be here later this afternoon. If you want to come back about four, you'll be sure to catch him."

"Thank you," Lowery said.

The bartender, the two men at the bar, and the two prostitutes watched Lowery leave the saloon, but none of them spoke. Frank ambled up the boardwalk again until he reached the Guthrie Restaurant. This place was also sparsely occupied at this time of day, and within a few minutes a waitress took his order: a bowl of vegetable soup, the ham dinner special, and coffee. Lowery sat facing the window as he ate his meal. He was about halfway through when someone peered at him through the window, came inside, and strode briskly up to his table. It was Fred Egan.

"Goddamn, Frank," the marshal said, "what the hell are you doin' here in Guthrie? Did you come to take me up on my offer?"

"Hello, Marshal."

"My deputy told me what happened," Egan grinned, "you doin' in a couple 'a drifters who tried to rob you. You handled it real well; just takin' their mounts and guns and sendin' them on their way. I've been lookin' all over town for you. Well, did you come to see me?"

"At the moment, I'm just enjoying this meal. I've been on the road since sunup, checked into Howard's Boardinghouse, took a bath, cleaned up, and then came here to eat. I'm mighty hungry and thirsty."

"How come you left Stillwater? Did you quit the QB Ranch?"

"Yes, I've got other plans," Frank said. "I came here to see a Carl Markham. He promised me a job at good wages when he was up in Stillwater a few weeks ago."

Egan looked irritated, then flopped into the chair opposite the diner. "Frank, you don't want to work for Markham. He's in all kindsa shady deals, and he'll drag you down with 'im. He only wants your gun and to get more involved in illegal enterprises."

"But running a saloon isn't illegal, is it? He wants to hire me as a bouncer."

"No, but that saloon is only a front," Egan said. "We suspect him o' dealin' in white slavery, with a lotta unsuspectin' young women taken in. Then he's suspected o' rustlin' cattle and selling contraband. In the saloon itself, we've heard that his people have been rollin' drunks and cheatin' at the gaming tables. He's got three or four rough boys now, but he'd have a real winner with you and your gun."

"But you're only talking suspicions. Do you have any proof?"

"No," Egan said, grimacing, "that's why I haven't been able to arrest him. But I'll get the goods on him one of these days."

Lowery shook his head. "I've got to have a job. My savings can't last more than a couple of months.

"You know I'd like you to work for me as a deputy, Frank. You're very intelligent and honest, and you can handle yourself well. If you'll join us, I promise I'll get you fifty a month."

"Fifty a month?"

"I know it ain't much compared to what you might get from Markham," Egan said, "but at least it'll be honest money." The marshal gestured. "This Oklahoma Territory is growin' more populated every day. Hundreds o' new settlers are comin' here all the time to go into ranchin' and farmin' and businesses. We've got to rid the territory o' scum, killers, and connivers like Markham. We need men like you who can help us to do that."

"I wasn't complaining about the fifty a month," Frank grinned. "I'm surprised that the pay for a deputy was so high."

"Ordinarily it ain't," Egan said, "but I can convince Washington that you'd be worth it, especially since you know the territory so well. And like I said, Oklahoma's growin' bigger every day. It won't be long before they'll have to split more o' the territory; put a marshal in Stillwater, Tulsa, and maybe some other places. Why you'd be sure to get one o' them jobs."

"To be honest, Marshal, I never gave much thought to

being a lawman, even though you've been trying to convince me for some time."

"It's honest work and it's important work," Egan pointed out. "Somebody's got to protect people on the ranches and farms and in the towns. They can't be livin' in fear when they're tryin' to make a life for themselves. I see the day not far off when they'll even bring Oklahoma into the Union as a state. Wouldn't you want to be a part o' that kinda future?"

"I suppose it would give a man a good feeling."

"And you've got an education," Egan pointed. "Why you could rise high in the federal service, far above even a marshal. You could be a district supervisor some day or even end up in Washington if you had a mind to go there. You're still young, Frank, and you got plenty o' time to do well in law enforcement. They got these new civil servant examinations now, and those that score high on the tests can get good promotions. With your school learning and common sense, after you get some experience, why I'm sure you'll do all right."

"I'd guess I couldn't get any better experience than working under you."

"I appreciate that kinda faith in me," the marshal said, "but I was thinkin' o' your own future, Frank. I suspect you left the QB Ranch because you had an awful hard life with little pay, and even less future. It certainly was not the kinda life for a man like you. But, there are real opportunities in law enforcement. As more people come West, the government needs to get more good men. You'll learn very fast and you could be a real asset with your fast gun. You won't have to use it very much. Believe me, most outlaws are cowards and they give up real quick when they've been cornered or run down; and they usually stay clear o' lawmen if they can."

Lowery only listened.

"Now you take those two drifters on the trail," Egan pointed. "If you had been wearin' a badge, they wouldn't have tried to rob you. No," he shook his head, "you'd be more safe on a trail with a badge than without one."

Frank Lowery pointed his fork at the marshal. "What about Bronco Kinney? He seems to be running loose with impunity."

"My guess is that he'll go into Ingalls after he's hid out a while in those Cimarron badlands," Egan said. "There's also a lot of other wanted men in that robber's roost. I'm going in there some day with a small army to clean up Ingalls once and for all. You might even like to be in on that."

"I've got to admit, you make a lot of sense, Marshal," Frank Lowery said, "and I'm certainly not opposed to being on the side of the law. Why don't you let me think about your offer."

Fred Egan grinned, rose from his chair, and patted Frank's free hand with his own free hand. "I can't ask for more'n that. You think about my offer for the rest o' the day, even tonight, and I hope you'll come into my office to see me in the morning."

"Maybe I will."

"Enjoy your meal. They've got a good chef in this place."

Frank Lowery nodded and watched the marshal leave the restaurant. But, when he returned to his meal, the food did not go down as fast nor taste as savory as it had earlier. Frank Lowery now faced an agonizing decision: working as a bouncer with good pay and easy labor, or working as a deputy with less pay and perhaps longer hours. The choice should have been easy, but not for Lowery.

There was no doubt that both Markham and Egan wanted him for his gun and his intelligence. However, did he dare use his talents for someone like Markham, whose activities were suspect? Frank scowled, suddenly sorry that he had met Fred Egan today. He had expected to work for Markham if the man still wanted him, but now, after listening to the marshal, he felt serious doubts. He especially remembered that even his new landlord, Howard Trembley, had downgraded Carl Markham.

Frank Lowery barely enjoyed the rest of the meal. Still, he cleaned his plate because he had one excellent consolation: he was at least sure of a job in Guthrie.

Chapter Five

After Frank finished his meal at the Guthrie Restaurant, he walked up the street to the Guthrie Merchants Bank. Inside he saw the chief cashier sitting behind the desk in an area cut off with a railing, while two tellers behind the cages served three customers. Frank walked to the railing and leaned over.

"Pardon me, sir."

The chief cashier looked up. "Can I help you?"

"I'd like to open an account here."

"Of course," the man answered, rising from his chair and opening the gate. "Come in and sit down." When Frank seated himself, the banker pulled out a sheet of paper and laid it flat on his desk.

"Now, how much would you want to put away?"

"About a hundred dollars."

"That's a fine start," the man nodded. Then he asked for his name: Frank Lowery; residence: Howard's Boardinghouse; occupation: none at present, but expected to be employed by the end of the week. No, Frank didn't know where, but he was considering two or three jobs. The banker eyed Frank Lowery with a hint of suspicion, wondering how someone could be considering two or three jobs, when many men could not even find work. However, he did not comment as he filled out the application.

When the banker finished, he turned the sheet around and handed Frank the pen. He was about to ask the applicant to make his mark, since most people with small accounts were generally of the lower classes and quite illiterate. However, before the man spoke, Frank quickly wrote his signature with a neat flair. The banker looked at the name and grinned.

"You write well."

Frank did not answer, but peeled off a hundred dollars from his wad of bills and handed the money to the banker. Frank was not about to carry around this kind of cash, which he could lose to some waylayer or burglar, a confidence man if he drank too much, or perhaps at a gaming table. He still had thirty dollars left, enough to keep him in food and lodgings for the next two or three weeks, by which time he would surely be fully employed.

The banker took the money, counted it, and then filled in the date and the amount in a small passbook, making out the book to Lowery and telling him to guard it well. He informed Frank that if he came into the bank to withdraw any money, they would require him to write his name and they would then check the signature with the signature on the application.

His business finished, Frank rose from the chair, and the banker shook his hand with a grin. "You won't be sorry you left your money with us, Mr. Lowery. Our bank is as safe or safer than any bank in the territory. We keep a full-time guard and we have an alarm pedal behind our counters that sends a direct telegraph alert to the marshal's office. And we have one of those new safes that can't be opened with explosives."

"I'm sure my money will be all right here."

"When you start working," the banker pointed out, "you should try to save some of your wages every payday. Before you know it, you'll have quite a sum; and we'll pay you two percent interest on your savings. Then, in time, maybe you'll have enough put away to start a business or a farm or a ranch. I can tell you, we're always willing to lend money to someone who shows a desire to work steady and a desire to save money."

"Yes, sir," Frank said. He took the passbook and left the bank, with the chief teller staring after him, wondering who the man was and what kind of job he would have in Guthrie. Of course, it didn't really matter to the banker. Frank was depositing money, not trying to borrow money.

Frank Lowery meandered around town for the next two hours, not doing much of anything except to look in some of the shop windows, at the stables, and at the hotel. Or he studied some of the people who paraded up the boardwalk or who rode wagons or horses on the street. No one spoke to Lowery; nor did he speak to anyone. But then, Frank didn't know anyone in Guthrie. At about midafternoon, he walked back to his boardinghouse and into his room. He took off his gunbelt and then flopped on the bed. Within minutes he had fallen asleep.

A few hours later, he jerked awake as hard knocks rattled his door. Frank rose to a sitting position, sat on his bed, and stared at the entrance. "Who's out there?"

"Open the door, Lowery!" a voice echoed from the outside.

Frank frowned. He didn't know anyone in town and the voice certainly didn't belong to Marshal Fred Egan or his landlord, Trembley. Lowery shuffled to the door and opened it. A rather small, thin man lurched into the room and pointed sharply. "Mr. Markham wants to see you."

Frank studied the intruder: a hard, haughty face, beady dark eyes that reflected an aura of arrogance, and a gunbelt that lay low on his thigh. The man's voice had been harsh and demanding and Frank felt irritated.

"Do you always act like this? Barge into somebody's room like you have the right to make them do whatever you want?"

"You came to the Nugget, Lowery," the man pointed. "You wanted to see Mr. Markham. You told the barkeep where you were stayin' and that you'd be back later; four o'clock, I think you told him. Well, it's almost dusk, and Mr. Markham is still waitin' for you."

"I'm sorry; I fell asleep."

"You're awake now. Let's go."

"I got to wash up."

"Forget it. Come right now. Mr. Markham don't like to have nobody keepin' 'im waitin'."

"And I don't like to be rushed," Lowery answered. "You'll have to wait until I clean myself up."

"No, you come right now," the man cried haughtily, reaching for his gun.

Frank Lowery grabbed the man's wrist in a faster-than-the-eye grip, twisted his arm and jammed it behind the visitor's back until the man winced in pain, helpless in the hammer lock. With his other hand, Frank extracted the man's gun from his holster and tossed it on the bed. Then he led his victim to the door and shoved him outside so hard that the visitor sprawled to the floor of the hallway.

"Now, you listen, mister." Frank pointed at the downed

78

man with a threatening gesture. "Nobody rushes me or intimidates me. You go back and tell Mr. Markham that I'll be out to the Silver Nugget as soon as I clean up. Now get out of here."

The man rose slowly to his feet. "I ain't supposed to leave here without you comin' with me."

Lowery gripped the man again and once more wrested his arms in a hammer lock. He forced the man to the end of the hall, where he gave him a shove. The visitor reeled down the stairs and only by gripping the railing did he save himself from tumbling to the first floor. He looked up at Frank and spoke in a rather weak tone.

"What about my gun?"

"You'll get it in good time. Now get out of here."

As the man staggered out of the front door of the boardinghouse, the landlord, Trembley, stood in the downstairs hallway and watched. Then, the obese man came up the stairs and into the second-floor landing. "I'm real sorry, Mr. Lowery. I know I had no business giving that man your room number, but he pulled a gun on me and made me stay downstairs. I didn't know what else to do."

"That's all right, Mr. Trembley. Don't worry about it."

Then the landlord grinned. "You handled 'im, though."

Frank Lowery nodded, dismissed Trembley, and walked into his room, closing the door after him. He washed his face and hands, combed his sandy hair, and brushed his boots with the room towel. He put on his gunbelt and slipped the visitor's gun into his waist. He set his hat on his head neatly before leaving the room. By the time he got outside, the sky had darkened to enveloping dusk. Frank found the town crowded now and lights sending bright glows into the street. He soon reached the Silver Nugget, the biggest and busiest saloon on 2nd Avenue.

Lowery wove through the crowd and up to the bar, where the bartender he had seen earlier now worked feverishly with a second barkeep. Hordes of men were in the saloon now, many at the bar, and waiters moved about swiftly, taking orders. Frank could not even get near the barkeep, but he saw the small man standing near a door and he walked up to him.

"Tell Mr. Markham I'm here."

"I don't know if he wants to see you now," the man answered disdainfully.

"Is he in there?" Frank cocked his head at the door behind the small man.

"Yes, but like I said, he might be too busy to see you now."

Frank Lowery handed the small man his gun and then shrugged. "It doesn't matter to me; I've got some other offers. And don't try to use that gun," he pointed. "I've unloaded it."

As Frank started to move off, the small man gripped his arm. "Wait, I'll tell Mr. Markham that you're here." Frank saw the near panic in the dark eyes and he suspected that the man had orders to bring Frank Lowery in as soon as he got there. If Markham knew that his employee had turned Lowery away, the small man would certainly have been chastised, at the very least.

"You just wait, Mr. Lowery. I'll talk to Mr. Markham." Now it was mister. Yes, the Silver Nugget henchman was rattled. A moment later, the man came out of the door and gestured. "Mr. Markham says to go right in."

Inside the office, the short, squat Carl Markham grinned eagerly at the visitor. "Goddamn, Lowery, I'm glad you came to see me. I can tell you, if you decide to work for me, that would be one of the best decisions you ever made. You'll find that I pay well and treat my people well. You'll be a real asset, because you're big and strong. A fast gun and plenty of strength makes a man, and you'll impress the kind of people I need to deal with."

"It was my understanding that you wanted me to work as a bouncer; keep order in the saloon, so to speak."

Carl Markham smirked. "Well, since I talked to you in Stillwater, things have changed somewhat. I don't really need you to work here. I need you more to ride shotgun for me."

"Shotgun?" Lowery asked.

"I often have a wagon or two loaded with important merchandise that I need to move," the Silver Nugget owner said, "and I need somebody to protect these wagons on the trail."

"What kind of merchandise?"

"That really don't matter to you," Markham said. "All you have to do is to ride shotgun and to keep your mouth shut."

Frank Lowery leaned over the desk and glared at Markham. "Could that gossip be true? Would you be carrying contraband and stolen goods? And even women to put into prostitution?"

"You've been listening to the wrong people," Markham said, obviously annoyed. "There's a lotta folks who envy my successful enterprises and they say bad things about me."

"I'm afraid you've made me suspicious, Mr. Markham," Lowery said ."You don't want me to ride shotgun to protect you from highwaymen, but from the law, isn't that right? Do you actually expect me to shoot at lawmen who might want to stop one of your wagons to check its contents for contraband?"

Markham made a face. "That marshal don't understand. He's just out to get me."

Frank Lowery rose from his chair. "I'm sorry, but I don't think I want any part of your so-called enterprises. I might be a lot of things, but I don't intend to get mixed up in anything illegal, or even anything that's a little shady."

"What are you, some kinda puritan missionary?" Markham barked. "You got a fast gun, you're big and strong, and you got plenty of smarts. If you're unwillin' to make some good money from those talents, you ain't got much common sense. I can tell you, the law don't have a thing on me; they never proved that I did anything wrong, and they ain't likely to do so. I'm offering you a good opportunity, Mr. Lowery, a chance to go far."

"You know, Mr. Markham," Lowery grinned, "that's the same thing Marshal Egan told me, only he says I can go far in law enforcement."

"Law enforcement?" Markham gestured. "You can't be seriously considering anything like that, can you?"

"I don't know what I'm going to do. I'll think over your offer, just as I'll think over the marshal's offer. I'll give you my decision in a day or two."

"All right, I'll give you a couple of days, but no more," Markham said. "You know I can get a lotta fast guns to work for me, but I like you. That's why I'm offering you the job."

"I'll see you, Mr. Markham."

When Frank Lowery left the Silver Nugget, he felt

somewhat relieved. The street felt almost clean compared to the immoral stench inside Markham's office. He decided he did not like Carl Markham, nor the small henchman who worked for him, and he suspected he would not likely approve of others who worked for the owner of the Silver Nugget Saloon. Lowery sighed. For the moment, he would go to the Guthrie Restaurant for supper and return to the boardinghouse for the night. He would wait until morning to make a decision.

In Robbers Roost, Ingalls, Oklahoma, big Bronco Kinney was quite disappointed when he learned that Clara Beaufort and Kid Carver had failed to convince Frank Lowery to join his gang. He derided the girl, claiming she had not turned on enough charm to lure the man to Ingalls. However, as Kinney berated her, Clara Beaufort mustered the courage to respond.

"He ain't the kinda man you think he is," she gestured angrily. "He's got a conscience and principles, and he cares for people. He ain't easily taken in. I all but offered to go to bed with him, but I still couldn't change his mind. I must tell you, money don't mean a damn thing to Frank Lowery. He seems to be the type of man who wants to keep good moral habits and a respect for the law."

"Maybe I should have sent somebody else to convince him," Kinney growled.

"You ain't goin' to convince him no matter who goes after him," Clara said. "He's simply a fine man with good character; the kinda man that people can hold in high respect."

"You got a hankering for him or something?" Kinney grinned.

"I'm only tellin' you what he is," the girl said. "Besides, he said he was goin' to Guthrie because he had somethin' to do down there, so he probably ain't even in Stillwater now."

"Forget about Lowery, Bronco." Kid Carver suddenly spoke up. "I got a suspicion the man ain't nothin' but a coward, anyway, and his fast gun is only reputation and not fact. I'd guess the reason he didn't want to join us was because he's scared we'd find out that he ain't really nothin' but a stumblebum cowhand."

"I don't know," Bronco said. "An awful lotta reliable people have seen Lowery's fast draw and accurate aim."

"Sure, maybe against rattlers and liquor bottles on a fence post," the Kid grinned, "but how would he do if he was facin' somebody who might shoot back? Why he'd probably freeze like a slab of ice and just stand there to get killed."

"I don't believe that's so," Clara Beaufort said, suddenly defending Lowery.

Kid Carver glared at the girl. He felt piqued because she had expressed an admiration for Frank Lowery, and he liked to think that Clara Beaufort was his girl and held him on a pedestal. He considered the girl his woman and he resented anyone else sharing her empathy or respect. In retrospect, he remembered that Clara had been a little too friendly at the saloon in Stillwater that morning, and perhaps even more friendly to Frank Lowery on her next meeting with the man in Stillwater. However, he did not scold Clara, for such a rebuke could only drive a wedge between them. He settled for the glare and then turned to Bronco Kinney.

"Forget Lowery. We don't need him, and that will be one less that we have to share with."

"Maybe you're right," Kinney nodded.

Bronco Kinney had certainly planned well for this big job, the robbery of the Abajo Springs Mining Company. He had won the cooperation of the clerk in the firm's office. The insider had told the outlaw leader the best time to show up—early afternoon, when everybody was in the mine after noon chow, and when the safe would be loaded with gold and money before shipment of the precious metal to Stillwater and the cash payment of wages to the miners. The clerk had also explained that only two guards would be on duty, and if they silenced them, there would be no trouble. The less-than-honest insider had readily agreed to also get hit over the head and tied up for his share of the booty.

By seven o'clock on the morning of the planned robbery, the band of outlaws had saddled up and trotted out of Ingalls: Bronco Kinney, Kid Carver, Colorado McGuire, Rowdy Joe Wheeler, Jim Clayborn, and Clara Beaufort. The girl would not participate in the robbery, but she would act as lookout and prepare meals for the gang on the trail.

Kinney planned to deal with the two guards, who protected the mining company office, in a simple manner. He and Clayborn would masquerade as independent prospectors who had been working in the hills. They even carried picks and shovels on their horses. Bronco and Clayborn would approach the guards as the others in the band advanced stealthily from hiding. Then, when Bronco and Clayborn held the guards' attention, McGuire, Wheeler, and Carver would jump the sentinels and subdue them.

The sextet rode for most of the morning and by noon they had stopped in a brake of trees for a midday meal.

85

Two of the men built a fire while Clara Beaufort fried some bacon and rolls in a pan and she brewed coffee in a pot. She ignored Kid Carver and the man grew somewhat sullen, convinced that her thoughts were on that despicable Frank Lowery. However, he said nothing to her as she went about her business of preparing the meal for the six of them. Still, he felt an increasing anger toward this cowpuncher whom he had seen only once in his life.

After the gang finished their meal, Bronco Kinney gave final instructions before they rode to the Abajo Springs Mining Company. "Now remember, you three," he pointed to Wheeler, McGuire, and Carver, "stay outa sight. We don't want them guards to know that anybody's comin' near that office but me and Clayborn. But you'll need to come real close so you can take 'em in a hurry. And I got to remind you again: no shootin' unless it's absolutely necessary. The clerk will be waitin' for us inside with the safe open, so we'll only need to use enough dynamite to make it look like we blew the safe. If everybody's in the mine, like the clerk says, why we can get outa there without anybody even knowin' we robbed the place."

"What about me?" Clara Beaufort asked.

"You're to keep watch, like I told you," Kinney answered. "You just loll nearby. If it looks like somebody's comin' toward the office, you fire your rifle twice, understand?"

The girl nodded.

"We don't expect to see nobody show up, however," the gang leader said, "so you may only be comin' along for the ride, Clara."

The girl did not answer.

The seven riders soon continued on and the mining company grounds eventually loomed into view ahead of them. They could distinguish the rows of clapboard shacks that housed the company employees, the big stables and wagon barns, and the big chow hall. They also noted the mining company office at the far end of the cluster of structures. And, as Kinney had been told by the office clerk, the camp was deserted because everybody was indeed back in the mine by this early-afternoon hour. If the clerk had been accurate as to this point, he was probably correct on the second and more important point: gold from the mine was ready for shipment to Stillwater, and cash from the bank was ready to pay the wages of the miners on this Saturday afternoon.

As the gang approached the complex of buildings, Kinney gestured for McGuire, Wheeler, and Carver to move off to come in stealthily from the flanks toward the mining company office. Clara Beaufort stopped and remained on her horse about two hundred yards from the office, behind one of the housing shacks where she would be obscured, but from where she could see anybody who might be heading for the office.

Meanwhile, Bronco Kinney and Jim Clayborn loped leisurely toward the office. In their prospector gear, and with the picks and shovels dangling from their mounts, they looked above suspicion. The two guards in front of the building merely raised their rifles but made no move to stop the pair of oncoming riders. They watched Clayborn and Kinney dismount with two bags in their hands and they waited until the duo approached them.

"All right boys, hold it right there," one of the guards said.

"We got a good find," Kinney said, "and we'd like to cash in these nuggets."

"Let me see," the other guard said.

"Sure," Bronco answered as he and Clayborn opened their small pouches and revealed a few gold nuggets sparkling inside.

"That ain't much of a catch," the first guard grinned, "but you can go inside. The clerk will weigh them stones for you and then pay you. But you'll need to leave those rifles out here with us."

"Sure," Bronco Kinney said.

Kinney and Clayborn had done their job well in holding the attention of the guards long enough for the other three outlaws to pounce on them. Suddenly and without warning, the trio whacked the two men on their heads with billy jacks and knocked them unconscious. Then Bronco left Wheeler outside to watch the stunned men, while he and the others went into the office. The clerk smiled eagerly when he saw the men, for he recognized Bronco Kinney with whom he had conspired.

"You can set the small charge now," the clerk said. "You won't need to use much, because I have the door open."

Wheeler and Carver nodded before they set a single stick of dynamite along the door edge and lit the fuse. All inside then sheltered themselves from the explosion, which only blew open the door that was already ajar. Then, swiftly, the bandits hauled out bags of gold and stacks of wrapped bills and stuffed them into the bags they had brought with them. Within a few minutes, the four men had cleaned out the safe.

"Okay, let's go," Kinney said.

"What about my share?" the clerk asked.

"Yes, your share," Kinney said. He then grinned at Kid Carver. "Give the man his share."

"Then you'll have to hit me on the head, but not too bad," the clerk said. "And then you'll need to tie me up."

"We'll do better than that," Carver said. The Kid then raised his rifle and without an inkling of warning fired two shots point blank at the clerk. The slugs opened the man's chest, erupting geysers of blood while sending the clerk bouncing hard against the safe. He was already dead when his bloody body collapsed to the floor.

"No sense in takin' any chances," Carver said. "They'd suspect him right off and they'd most likely make 'im talk."

Bronco Kinney nodded.

The quintet then cautiously left the office. They saw no one about except for the unconscious guards. But, as the clerk had told them, everybody would be in the mine at this hour of the day, and probably no one had heard either the explosion or the shots. The outlaws hurried out of the camp, remounted their horses, and loped slowly, with Clara Beaufort joining them after they had gotten a mile away from the place.

"I heard some shots," Clara said, "and it was my understandin' that there wouldn't be no shootin'."

"We had to take care of the clerk," Carver said.

"You shot him?" Clara gasped.

"Shot him dead," Carver grinned. "We wasn't leavin' him behind to talk to the law if they pressed him."

"But you said he was a part of this," the girl said.

"Forget it," Bronco Kinney gestured. "The Kid did what he had to do."

"Not for me," the girl protested, "you're animals, killin' a man who helped you to pull off this robbery as easy as you did. I don't want no part o' killings like that. You can go your way, and I'll go mine."

"Stop talkin' like a fool, Clara," Carver barked. "You were in on this like the rest of us."

"Not if there was any killin' involved," she said. "I didn't agree to no cold-blooded murder. I'm not goin' back to Ingalls with you. I'm goin' to Stillwater."

"You're comin' with me," Carver said angrily.

"You'll have to kill me," the girl answered. "That's the only way I'll go along with you and the rest of these assassins."

"I know what you want," Carver scoffed. "You want to go all the way to Guthrie so's you can be with that coward Lowery."

"It's none o' your damn business what I want to do. It's enough to know that I don't want nothin' more to do with you, Walt, not with somebody who'd kill a man in cold blood without reason. And I don't want nothin' to do with the rest o' you who'd let Walt do this." She glared at the others.

"You'll come with us or else," Kid Carver threatened.

"Forget her, Kid," Bronco gestured. He reached into his saddle bag and took out a packet of bills and offered it to the girl. "You can leave without a dime or you can leave with this stack 'a money, about a thousand dollars. The cash will let you live pretty high for quite a while."

The girl hesitated but then took the money.

Bronco Kinney grinned. "Now that makes you a full partner in this. Remember Clara, if you ever say anything about this or you tell the law about our whereabouts, you'll hang with the rest of us."

"I won't talk," the girl said. "I just don't want nothin'

more to do with any of you."

Clara Beaufort remained erect on her horse and watched the quintet move off. She sat immobile, staring, until the outlaws were out of sight. Then, she dropped the wrapped stack of bills into her saddlebag, veered her horse, and loped southward toward Stillwater.

Chapter Six

Frank Lowery awoke when a flood of daylight poured through the nearly full-length window of his room at Howard's Boardinghouse. He yawned, rose out of bed, and peered into the street, blinking from the brightness. He saw no one about, so he guessed the hour was still early. Frank ambled to the dresser and looked at his pocket watch: six-thirty. He then went to the water basin and washed up before he shaved and dressed. By seven he left the boardinghouse by the back stairs and entered the stable where he gave his horse a portion of hay. Then Frank walked to 2nd Avenue. Here, on Guthrie's main street, he jostled through the crowds.

When Lowery entered the Guthrie Restaurant, he found the place jammed with patrons and the waitress offered him a choice of sitting with someone else at a table or of waiting for a table to become available. Frank shrugged; he didn't mind if the customer there didn't mind. So, the waitress led Frank to a table.

"Jack," she said to the man sitting there, "do you mind if this customer sits in the empty chair opposite you?"

The man at the table, Deputy Marshal Jack Stone, merely shrugged. He was a medium-built man, with a clean, oval face, dressed in a neat suit. He looked up, saw Frank, and then smiled.

"Lowery! Goddamn! Sit down."

When Frank sat in the chair, he ordered toast, eggs, sausages, and coffee. The waitress scribbled on a pad and walked away. Meanwhile, Stone studied this unexpected breakfast companion with his blue-gray eyes and grinned again.

"It might be a while before you're served. This place is always crowded at this time of mornin'. I keep tellin' myself to come in here earlier, but I still show up at the height o' the busy hour."

Lowery nodded.

The well-dressed Stone took a sip of his coffee and then looked at Frank again. "I heard you were in town, and I heard about that incident you had with those drifters yesterday. I guess you're everything they say you are. But what are you doing in Guthrie? Why aren't you cowpunching at the QB Ranch?"

"I had enough of that kind of work," Lowery said. "I have a couple of job offers here in Guthrie, and I waited until this morning to make up my mind on which one to take."

"You're lucky," the deputy gestured. "Most people who drift into Guthrie find it hard to get a job. Employment has been tight lately. The harsh, dry summer, I suppose. It cut down on crops and livestock, and most farmers and ranchers don't need as many hands as usual. And, of course, with the agriculture and cattle business down, it means the local merchants don't need much help, either."

"This town looks busy enough," Frank said.

"Oh, I'm not sayin' there isn't plenty of people

working," Stone said, "but it could be more active." He leaned forward and looked hard at Lowery. "What kind of job are you looking into here? I know that old man Barker at the QB Ranch is one of the best employers in the territory. If you intend to work on one of the ranches hereabouts, you won't find anybody as good as Barker."

"Like I said, I don't intend to do any more cowpunching."

Stone studied the neatly dressed, cleanly groomed Lowery and grinned again. "You never struck me as the cowpuncher type, anyway." He glanced at Frank's holster, slung low, and he pointed at the gun. "Do you intend to get a job where you can use that weapon? We all heard how good you are with it."

"I'm not a gunman," Frank said.

Stone nodded. "Am I prying asking you what kind of job you intend to take in Guthrie?"

"Maybe join you," Lowery grinned. "As you know, Marshal Fred Egan has been trying to get me to work for him as a deputy, and I considered his offer. I also had an offer from Carl Markham of the Silver Nugget to ride shotgun for him."

Stone shook his head. "Those two jobs are as far apart as day and night. You've got quite a decision to make: an honest law enforcement job with low pay or a shady, maybe illegal job for a crook at pretty good wages."

"So it seems," Lowery said.

"Goddamn, Lowery, I wish you'd work for Egan. It sure would be nice to have you with us. We heard from people in Stillwater that there's no man up there who can draw faster and shoot straighter than you can. Yet, we also heard that you never drew your gun on a man. Is that true?"

"It was until yesterday" Frank said. "When those two drifters tried to rob me on the trail, I didn't have any choice but to disarm them. I was lucky with my fast draw so I didn't have to kill them. I was able to just send them on afoot."

"That's just the kind of men we need in the federal enforcement service," Stone said, "men who only want to uphold the law and bring in suspects when they can, instead of shooting down such wanted men with vigilante tactics. I can see why the marshal would like you to work for him," the deputy pointed. He took another sip of his coffee and then gestured again. "Would I be too nosy if I asked you which of these jobs you intend to take?"

"Like I said," Frank answered, "I've been giving this plenty of thought since yesterday, and by the time I left the boardinghouse this morning, I made up my mind quite surely."

"Well?"

"I'm going to work for Marshal Egan, if he still wants me," Frank grinned.

"That's a real good choice," Stone said. He reached over and pumped Lowery's hand. "Maybe you won't make the kind of money you could with that conniving Carl Markham, but you'll have a clear conscience and real pride in helping to rid this territory of some of the riffraff that roams about—like those would-be waylayers you took care of yesterday."

Then the waitress suddenly appeared and laid Frank's breakfast on the table, leaving the bill with the plate, butter dish, and cup of coffee. "You can pay on the way out," she said to Frank.

"Thank you, ma'am."

"Looks like you'll have yourself a hearty meal," Stone

said, rising from his chair. "I must say, it was a real pleasure seeing you again, Lowery, and now, after talking to you, I can see that you're also a real gentlemen. If I can be of any help to you around Guthrie, why you be sure to call on me. We'll be working together, and I hope we can be real close."

"I'll remember that," Frank said, "and thanks."

Lowery watched Jack Stone leave the restaurant and he then dug into his breakfast. He ate ravenously, for he was hungry. Within ten minutes he had cleaned his plate and drunk two cups of coffee. He rose from his chair, dropped a ten-cent-piece tip on the table, and paid his bill. Outside again, he wove his way through the crowds on the boardwalk and soon reached the marshal's office, where he walked inside and found Egan talking to Deputy Jack Stone.

"I want to make sure that stage robber don't get loose," Egan was telling Stone. "I want you to go to the telegraph office and wire Sheriff McLoughlin in Wichita. Tell him to hold the man until we can get him extradicted back here. They're not to allow the man bail, or we'll never see him again."

"I'll point that out in the telegram," Stone nodded.

The marshal turned at the sound of Frank's footsteps and grinned when he saw the visitor. "Frank, Jack told me the good news as soon as he came in from breakfast. You came here to accept my offer, I hope."

"If it's still open," Lowery said.

"Of course, it's open," Egan answered.

"Then I'd like to try this job."

"That's good, Frank, real good," Egan said. "I'll take you to Judge Kirkland and swear you in right away. Then I'll telegraph Washington and tell them you're on the payroll at preferred wages, fifty a month. I want to put you right to work. There's some papers you need to fill out that we'll need to send to Washington. All the documents should be back here in about a week or ten days and we can make the job permanent, retroactive to this date."

"That'll be fine, Marshal."

Jack Stone extended a hand to Frank. "Like I said, Lowery, it'll be nice to have you with us. God knows, we can use a man like you."

"I hope we'll get on well," Frank answered the deputy.

"There won't be any trouble," Stone said. He then looked at Egan. "I'll go to the telegraph office now." When Egan nodded, the deputy marshal grinned again at Frank and then left the office.

Marshal Fred Egan gestured Frank Lowery into a chair. "I don't expect any problems. Washington almost always approves of a new deputy that's been recommended by a district territorial marshal, unless the man had a criminal record. You don't have any, do you?" Egan asked.

"Not that I know of," Frank said.

For the next hour, Frank Lowery filled out the personal application sheet, giving his background and work experience, reasons why he wanted to join the law enforcement service, and outlining his expectations. He also included his height, weight, eye color, hair color, and build. And finally, he signed the section that asked him to swear that he had no criminal record. Egan then filled out his part of the application, signed it, slipped it into an envelope, and sealed it.

"This'll be on the next stage out of Guthrie."

Only an hour after Frank had come into the marshal's

office that morning, he was standing before Judge Kirkland to swear allegiance as a deputy U.S. marshal. The ceremony, before two witnesses, took only several minutes, and when it ended the judge shook Lowery's hand before Egan took out a silver badge with the inscription U.S. Deputy Marshal and pinned it on Lowery's chest.

"Now we're goin' back to the office," Egan told Lowery. "There's a handbook I'd like you to read over quite thoroughly and understand well. It gives you all the information about how to deal with suspects and wanted men, the nature of your job, and what will be expected of you. The book also has a lot of rules and regulations you'll need to follow as a federal law enforcement officer."

"Suppose I couldn't read?"

"We don't hire anybody in the federal law service who can't read," Egan said.

Back in the marshal's office, Egan gave Lowery the handbook and told him to read it carefully, study its contents, and familiarize himself with all requirements and suggestions. Egan advised Lowery to go back to his boardinghouse room and spend the remainder of the day reading and absorbing the contents of the manual. Then he was to report for work the first thing in the morning, about seven o'clock, at which time Egan would have his first task.

Frank Lowery spent the bulk of the day digesting the information in the handbook. He read the contents twice and some of the material three times to thoroughly acquaint himself with the information. He studied how to obtain search warrants, how to handle suspects, how to make out arrest reports, how to question witnesses and wanted men, how to handle prisoners, and how to deal with a host of other things. He did not leave his room until after dark, when he ambled up 2nd Avenue to get himself an evening meal. On his way he stopped at the Silver Nugget and asked to see Carl Markham. The bartender gaped at the sparkling badge on his shirt and then nodded toward the private door.

"He's in there, but I don't think Mr. Markham will be happy to see you."

Lowery did not answer. He moved away from the bar and rapped on the door. When a bellowing voice responded, "Come in," Lowery walked inside. At first, Carl Markham grinned, but when he saw the star on Lowery's chest, he gaped.

"I just came to tell you I won't be working for you," Frank said.

The Silver Nugget owner rose from his chair and shuttled his glance between the badge and Lowery's gray eyes. "You're the worst damn fool I've ever met, Lowery. A man with your talent and brains and you sign up as a cheap pay deputy? You must have lost your senses."

"I suppose some people would say that," Lowery answered, "but a man has to do what he thinks is right."

"Right!" Markham barked. "Why you could've had more with me in a month than you'll make for a whole year workin' for Egan. And now," he added, "you'll need to make a lotta people unhappy, and they won't like it. You'll soon have plenty o' men looking for you. This territory is what you might call an open society, where everybody does as he damn pleases, and where they don't like any interferrin' from lawmen."

"You mean like robbery and cheating and extortion?" Lowery asked. "I'm sorry, Mr. Markham, but the marshal convinced me that he was right to have me work for him instead of you. To be honest, I like to think that maybe I can have something to do with making this territory a safe place for honest people. I like the idea of doing what I can."

"You're a fool," Markham said again.

"Maybe so," Lowery answered, "but I only stopped by to tell you my decision. Since you were kind enough to offer me a job if I ever got to Guthrie, I felt I owed you that much."

"You're makin' a big mistake, Lowery."

"If I am, I can always quit."

Frank Lowery was glad to leave the Nugget. As on the previous day, he again felt clean once he got outside. He continued on to the Guthrie Restaurant, where he ate a hearty meal. He then went into one of the local saloons where he drank only a single glass of beer and studied the array of men at the gambling tables and gaming machines. Occasionally, he watched one of the prostitutes go upstairs with a patron. Drinking, gambling, and prostitution were quite legal in the Oklahoma Territory.

When Frank returned to the boardinghouse, he studied the manual yet again, poring over the material for three more hours under the light of a lamp.

At seven the next morning, Frank Lowery arrived at the marshal's office. Egan and Deputy Stone greeted him quite warmly, and the marshal asked, "Frank, would you mind going up to Stillwater? I got a prisoner here who has to be confined to the town jail there because his crime was in their jurisdiction and they want to try him there. You can leave the man in the custody of the town constable, Isa Hutchinson."

"Whatever you want, Marshal," Lowery said.

"You don't even have to come back today," Egan said. "We have an agreement with Mae's Boardinghouse and the Broadway Cafe in Stillwater to lodge and to feed any of our deputies who are up there on business. I'll give you an authorization card and you can show it and sign for any expense."

"I could probably make it back by some time tonight."

"Stay overnight," the marshal said. "Maybe you'd like to visit with some old friends up there."

Frank Lowery did not answer.

Egan led Lowery to one of the cells. A rather coarse-looking man sat on the cot inside. The man was thin, somewhat below average height, and about five feet, five inches tall. He had a prominent, fleshy nose, a thick mustache, dark brown hair, and fierce black eyes. A growth of beard covered his narrow face. He glared at the two men like an angry, caged animal.

"This is Harvey Green," Egan gestured, "as savage a man as you'd ever want to meet. He's a thief, a mugger, a woman molester, and a rustler. His latest caper was at a farm just east o' Stillwater, where he ravaged and beat up a poor farm wife and then stole every penny he could find in the place. He left her bleeding and half naked. We caught up to him a couple of days ago and they want him back in Stillwater to try him in that township. Do you think you'd have trouble gettin' him up there?"

"I don't think so."

The man in the cell grinned and pointed at Lowery. "This dude is gonna take me there? Well, I got news for you, Marshal. He ain't never gonna get me to Stillwater, not him alone. You'd best call in a troop 'a cavalry to escort me, 'cause them's the only kind of escort that'll get me to a hangman's noose."

"We'll see," Egan said.

Of course, law enforcement officers in the Oklahoma Territory were hardly plentiful, and Egan could not afford to send more than one deputy out with this prisoner. As for the army, the post at Bryan Gully had enough trouble protecting wagon trains and running down renegade Indians, and they could not spare any soldiers to escort civilian prisoners, especially those who had not violated any federal laws, but only local territorial or state laws.

By eight o'clock, Green had been hoisted atop a horse, with his hands tied to the saddle horn and his legs firmly tied to the stirrups. Even if for some reason he could break away from his guard, he could not get far. In a hard gallop, if the horse struck even one depression or knoll with its hooves, the bounce would likely throw the rider askew from the saddle, and he might even topple from the horse to be dragged to death by the animal.

The sun was quite high by the time Lowery found himself and his prisoner on the open, desolate highway north of Guthrie. Lowery paced the mounts quite well, alternating between a walk and an easy trot. All during the ride, the prisoner said very little, but he often grinned smugly at his guard, as though he had full confidence that Lowery would never deliver him to the Stillwater jailhouse.

Frank, of course, remained alert, continually peering into the low hills or into the thick brakes abutting the road. He never spoke to the prisoner, but he realized that Green might have had some accomplices who might be hiding somewhere on the trail, waiting to ambush him.

"Hey, deputy," Green finally said, "can't we stop somewhere to rest? Maybe get some water? I'm getting

103

awful hot and I'm damn thirsty."

"So am I," Frank said, "but we aren't stopping anywhere. You can cool off and drink when we get to Stillwater."

"But that won't be for another two or three hours."

"Too bad," Lowery said. "I'm not stopping until we get there."

"You're a no good bastard," the prisoner cursed.

Frank Lowery did not answer. He yanked on the rein from the prisoner's horse and spurred the two mounts into a soft trot. However, the animals had only moved for a few hundred yards when Frank felt a restraint on the rein. He turned to see Green straining to slow down his mount.

"What are you trying to do?"

"I gotta rest," Green insisted. "Can't we rest for a few minutes?"

Lowery scanned the surrounding countryside, the plains to his left and the dense brakes to his right. He saw nothing and Frank was tempted to dismount and rest under the trees for a while. But then, he suddenly caught a flash of light from the trees up ahead. He guessed at once that the blink had come from a weapon. Could somebody be waiting for him up the road? He looked at his prisoner, who only grinned again.

Frank said nothng. He took his rifle from its scabbard, cocked it, and held it in his right hand, while he held the reins of the two horses in his left hand and slowed down, walking the two horses slowly up the road. As he moved on, Frank peered hard and soon detected what appeared to be human shapes in the brake up ahead, perhaps two hundred yards away. But he would be ready. He used his forearm to wipe away sweat from his face, still holding his cocked rifle on the ready.

Then two men suddenly stepped out onto the road with aimed six-shooters, and one of them cried out: "Hold it right there, deputy."

Frank Lowery knew he now faced a crisis. He had hoped he could use his skill of speed and accuracy with a gun merely to disarm these men and take them prisoner. However, both men held guns on him. He could not disable them, for if he quickly stopped one, the other might shoot him before he could take care of the second culprit. A tinge of dread struck him and he felt a tingle radiate through his body. He would need to kill both of them instantly, for he had to protect his own life. This thought raced through his mind, and within a mere one or two seconds he acted.

Within a fleeting second, Lowery swerved his rifle and fired twice in rapid succession. Both bullets struck home, hitting the two men squarely through their hearts. The pair flew backwards and fell flat on their backs. They were dead before they hit the ground. The ambushers had lost their lives before they even knew what happened.

Harvey Green, aboard his horse, gawked at the two men lying on the trail. He stared so fiercely that he did not even notice Lowery dismount and lead the two animals to separate trees, where he tethered them. When Frank looked at his two victims, he felt a slight nausea in his stomach, too aware of what he had done—killed for the first time in his life. Yet, strangely, the ill feeling inside of him was not nearly as bad as he had thought it might be, especially since he had acted to preserve his own life.

Lowery turned away from the two bodies and looked at his prisoner. "Were they friends of yours?"

But Harvey Green did not answer. He was too stunned by the quickness and accuracy of his captor. He continued to gape at the two men lying sprawled in the road.

"That wasn't very smart of them." Lowery spoke again. "They should have shot first, because I knew they were there."

Still Harvey Green said nothing and Lowery now hunted within the clump of trees until he found the two horses that obviously belonged to the ambushers. The prisoner watched silently while Lowery hoisted the two corpses atop the animals and tied them securely. Then he tied the reins of the mounts behind the saddle of the horse occupied by Green. When he finished these chores, Frank remounted his own horse and led the three burdens up the road: his prisoner and the two dead men.

Occasionally, Green turned to look at his slain companions draped over their saddles. Green's narrow face was now depressingly sober, a sharp contrast to the confident grin he had worn earlier. The prisoner glanced intermittently at the deputy, for Green was still awed, still shocked. He could not believe that anybody facing two men holding guns could raise and shoot his own weapon so fast and perfectly—and with one hand on the rifle, since the deputy had been holding the reins with his left hand.

The prisoner was now utterly disheartened. He had not doubted for a moment that his hiding cohorts on the trail would rescue him from this single deputy who was taking him to Stillwater.

However, after an hour on the trail, Harvey Green finally calmed down enough to speak to Lowery. "I must say, deputy, I ain't never in my life seen a man handle a

106

gun the way you did back there."

"It's my job."

"You must be out 'a your mind, working as a deputy marshal, I mean," Green said. "Do you know the kinda money you could earn with a fast gun like that? Why, I know people who'd pay you a small fortune." He leaned from his saddle with the grin again pasted on his face. "You turn me loose, deputy, and you won't ever be sorry. I'll recommend you to somebody who'll pay you at least four or five hundred a month for your gun. Now you can't make that kind 'a money in a year as a deputy marshal."

"But I'll have the satisfaction of knowing that an animal like you will get the punishment he deserves. What kind of a beast are you, anyway, to ravage a poor, helpless woman and then beat her to a pulp? All you had to do was to go to any saloon and for two dollars you could have had any whore you wanted."

Green shrugged. "It was impulse."

"Impulse, hell," Frank growled. "You're nothing but a damn sadist. You wanted to hurt that woman. You wanted to make her suffer; you wanted to torment her. You wanted to do everything you knew would cause her grief—ravaging her, beating her, terrorizing her. Well, those two back there," he cocked his head at the corpses, "won't hurt anybody again, and I suspect that you won't either, because there's a rope waiting for you in Stillwater."

The prisoner did not answer, as soberness again erased the grin from his narrow face.

About one o'clock in the afternoon, Frank Lowery finally loped up Broadway in Stillwater. People on the street, as well as shopkeepers in front of their businesses, stood rigid and watched the strange caravan: a lawman in the lead, a tied prisoner behind him, and two trailing horses carrying a pair of dead men. The spectators stared with even deeper curiosity when they recognized the lawman. Somebody on the boardwalk turned to a companion.

"Goddamn, that's Frank Lowery."

"Yeah, Lowery." The other man gaped. "What the hell is he doin' wearing a deputy marshal's badge?"

Spectators continued to babble, conjecturing, as Lowery came up the street and finally stopped at the small jailhouse, where the elderly constable, Isa Hutchinson, stood out front and gaped at the visitor and his encumbrances.

"My God!" the constable gasped. "Frank Lowery! Are you workin' for Marshal Egan now?"

Frank dismounted, tethered the horses, and pulled a sheet of paper from his pocket. "I'm delivering a prisoner, Harvey Green. He's wanted for assault, rape, and robbery in the Stillwater Township jurisdiction."

"What about them?" the constable cocked his head at the two dead men.

"A couple of Green's friends. They tried to bushwhack me on the trail to set the prisoner free. I was forced to kill them."

Isa Hutchinson did not answer as Lowery untied his prisoner, dismounted him, and led him into the jail. The constable followed the duo, then hurried ahead of them, fumbling for his keys and opening the cell door. After Lowery placed Green inside, Hutchinson locked the door.

"Don't get near him," Lowery warned the constable, remembering the details of the law enforcement manual he had read. "Keep yourself at a safe distance from the cell at all times, and be sure to get out your gun and aim the weapon at the prisoner whenever you open the door to bring him his meals or to bring him something else. That means you need to have someone in here with you whenever you open the door."

The constable nodded vigorously.

"You'd better get those two bodies over to the mortician. You can search them to find out who they are." Again the constable nodded and he then hurried out of the jailhouse. When he was gone, Frank Lowery turned and looked at the confined Harvey Green. "I hope that poor woman you attacked is well enough to see you hang."

The outlaw in the cell did not answer.

Frank Lowery sat at the small desk in the jailhouse, thumbing through some papers to kill time, looking at wanted posters and reading the brochures that often came to local constables from law enforcement organizations. Finally, Constable Hutchinson returned to the jailhouse and looked at Frank. "Everything is taken care of, Mr. Lowery. The mortician will handle those dead bushwhackers. But I went through all their possessions and I didn't find no identification on them, so we don't know who they are."

Lowery looked at Harvey Green. "Do you know?"

The outlaw shrugged.

"You can at least do one good thing in your life," Lowery said. "If those two were friends of yours, you ought to at least tell us who they are so's we can notify their families, if they have any."

Harvey Green sighed. "All right. Wilfred McCormick is one o' them and Hank Bent is the other. I've known 'em for quite some time. They're both from Witchita, Kansas and they did once tell me they had families back there. I guess the sheriff in Wichita can probably find their kinfolk."

"Thank you," Lowery said. Then he looked at Hutchinson. "I might suggest, constable, that you go over to the telegraph office and get off a wire to Wichita as soon as you can."

"I will, I will," the constable said.

Once more, while the constable was gone, Lowery lolled about the small jailhouse office. He again thumbed through printed matter on the desk, reading until the constable returned.

"We should hear from Wichita by the end of the day," Hutchinson said, "and if the families of them outlaws want their bodies shipped home, why we'll send them; otherwise, we'll just plant 'em in the paupers' section o' the Stillwater cemetery."

"Good," Frank said. He rose from the chair. "I'll leave you now, constable. Remember what I told you: don't open the cell door unless there's somebody else in here with you to hold a gun on the prisoner. That outlaw in there won't hesitate for a minute to try to escape, and he couldn't care how many people he had to kill to do it. There isn't any question that he knows what's in store for him, and he's desperate."

"I'll be careful," Isa Hutchinson promised.

When Frank Lowery left the jailhouse, a crowd of people was loitering outside. They tried to bombard him with questions, but he ignored them and walked up the street. When he reached the Broadway Cafe, he stopped, remembering that he had not eaten anything since early that morning. Frank was about to step into the eating place when he looked through the window and saw someone sitting at one of the tables.

Frank Lowery gaped in astonishment. The woman, sitting alone and eating a simple sandwich, was Clara Beaufort.

Chapter Seven

Frank Lowery felt his heart beat and his nerves tingle when he saw the girl sitting alone in the cafe. He walked inside and edged his way to the table.

"Miss Beaufort? What are you doing here?"

The girl looked up and her eyes widened in surprise. "Frank? I might ask you the same question. I thought you went to Guthrie." Then she noted the deputy marshal's badge on his shirt and her blue eyes widened even more. "My God, what are you doing, wearin' that star?"

"Do you mind if I join you?"

"No, no," she gestured. When Frank seated himself opposite the girl, Clara Beaufort leaned over the table. "I can't believe this. When did you decide to become a lawman?"

Frank shrugged. "I gave up cowpunching. You remember I told you that I had some business in Guthrie and that's why I couldn't join Bronco Kinney. To be honest, it wasn't my intention to join the law, but I didn't like the man I was supposed to work for down there. His business looked too shady to me. Then Marshal Egan approached me again to join him, and he was mighty convincing, because here I am, a deputy federal marshal."

Clara Beaufort grinned. She had guessed right about this man: apparently, money did not mean that much to Frank Lowery, and he did indeed possess a strong moral fiber that would prevent him from taking up with people whose activities were outside the law. The girl guessed that someone in Guthrie had offered him some kind of illegal work for good pay, but that Lowery had turned the job down, just as he had turned down the offer from Bronco Kinney. She almost laughed. As a deputy, he would probably need a couple of years to earn the kind of money Bronco had given her for a mere few hours atop a horse.

"I suppose I shouldn't have been surprised," the girl said.

"What about you, Miss Beaufort? What are you doing here?" He leaned over the table. "Is your friend Kid Carver with you?"

"Kid Carver?"

"I'll have to tell you, I saw you with him after you left me, so I assumed that he and Kinney put you up to luring me into joining Kinney. Is that right?"

"All right, I admit it," the girl said, lowering her head with a tinge of embarrassment.

A waitress appeared at the table and looked at Frank. "Do you want to order something?"

"Yes," Frank answered, "a ham dinner. It was mighty tasty the last time I had it in here." As the waitress nodded, Frank looked at the girl. "What about you? Something more to eat?" When she shrugged, Frank grinned again. "We'll make it my treat this time."

The girl smiled. "I'm not very hungry; this sandwich is

enough for me." The waitress nodded and scribbled on her pad. "I'll bring you more coffee." When the waitress left, Frank looked at the girl again. "I thought you'd be with Kinney, this Carver, and the rest of them at Ingalls, or someplace like that."

"I left them," the girl answered soberly. "I got to thinkin' about their intentions and I concluded that I didn't want no part o' their ideas. They hinted that they might do somethin' illegal, and that kind 'a business is not for me. I came into Stillwater yesterday and I have a room at Mae's Boardinghouse."

"I used to stay there; nice place." Then Frank frowned. "But what are you doing for money?"

"I got a considerable sum saved," the girl said. "It'll hold me until I find some kinda job." Then she looked hard at Frank. "If you joined the federal law service in Guthrie, what are you doin' in Stillwater?"

"I came here today to deliver a prisoner," Frank said, "but the marshal said I could stay overnight, and I'll likely stay at Mae's Boardinghouse, too. Egan gave me a board and meal card that's good at that boardinghouse and in this cafe, so I'm on what you might call an expense account."

"That's nice," the girl said. Then she held Frank's hand and again the warmth sent a shiver through his body. "We can spend the rest o' the day together, Frank. You wouldn't mind that, would you?"

"No, I guess not," Frank answered.

"And we're stayin' in the same place, so we could also go home together tonight, so to speak."

"I suppose that's also true," Frank said. "After I have my meal, I'll check into the boardinghouse."

The duo continued their chit chat for the next half

hour or more while they ate their meals. Clara munched daintily on her sandwich, but Frank was quite hungry after the long hours on the trail, so he ate ravenously. By two o'clock they had finished and they walked up the boardwalk to the jailhouse where Frank had left his horse. From there, accompanied by Clara, he merely walked the animal for the short distance to the boardinghouse. He tethered the animal and pulled the bell rod. Soon he and Clara heard the waddling footsteps, and the Widow Crawford opened the front door. She was surprised to see Frank standing there with Clara Beaufort, and more surprised to see the deputy marshal badge on his shirt.

"Frank Lowery!" Mae Crawford gaped. "What are you doin' back here, and since when did you become a lawman?"

"Since yesterday," Frank said.

The Widow Crawford looked sad. "I'm real sorry about what happened between you and Sarah."

"It's all done with now," Frank said.

Mae looked at Clara Beaufort and then grinned at Lowery. "I can see that you're over it."

"Her being here is a coincidence." Frank gestured toward the girl. "I'm to stay overnight, and the marshal told me he has an arrangement with you." He showed the widow the card. "This is good, isn't it?"

"It sure is," Mae nodded. "You'll just have to sign for your stay. I bill the marshal once a month." She craned her neck and saw the tethered horse. "You can take your animal to the stable out back. That's part o' the service with Egan."

The girl looked at Frank. "I'm going up to my room. Number twenty-six. I'll change into somethin' more

116

comfortable and then we can take a ride this afternoon, maybe. Is that all right?"

"Sure," Frank said.

After Clara Beaufort went inside and up the stairs, Mae Crawford looked at Lowery. "She's pretty all right; been here since yesterday. I don't know nothin' about her, but she paid a week's rent in advance, and she's real quiet and clean. So, I ain't complainin'. What can you tell me about her, Frank?"

"I met her a couple of times before. I think she came from Kansas and she's lookin' for a job here."

"Well, I'll put you in room twenty-four, two doors down the hall on the second floor. Is that all right?"

"Sure."

"I'll have your room ready by the time you stall your horse."

About fifteen minutes later, after Frank had settled his mount in the stable behind the boardinghouse, he went up the stairs and strode through the hall until he saw room 24. He walked inside, where the smell of the clean linen on the bed invigorated him. He would have liked a bath, especially after the long, almost all-day trek from Guthrie, but he could not accommodate himself on this. However, he took off his pants, shirt, boots and BVD's and gave himself a sponge bath with a washcloth to clean away the accumulated sweat. Then he brushed away the dirt from his shirt and trousers as best he could, cleaned his boots, and washed his hands and face thoroughly. He dressed and combed his hair. And finally, he strapped on his gunbelt, for now, as a deputy marshal, he could not go around unarmed.

Frank sat in the chair for another few minutes, restless, but he finally left his quarters and walked the

117

short distance to room 26 and knocked.

"Come in," Clara Beaufort answered.

At the end of the hall, a short, thin man, perhaps middle aged, watched Lowery walk into the girl's room. The snooper did not say anything, but only stroked his chin and then went downstairs and out the front door.

When Frank entered the room, he eyed Clara with a tinge of admiration. She had clad herself in riding clothes: trousers, blouse, boots, kerchief, and a rawhide stringed hat. The clean attire enhanced her shapely frame, exciting Frank. Her face was clean and smooth, with just enough mascara to accentuate her thin lips, clean skin, and sparkling dark eyes. She had combed her hair, and pins held the strands in place.

"I'm ready, Frank," the girl smiled.

"You sure look pretty, Clara," Frank said. "I hope you don't mind me calling you Clara."

"It's about time you got rid of your formality," the girl said, coming close to Frank and tugging on the lapels of his shirt.

For the remainder of the afternoon and into the early evening, Frank Lowery and Clara Beaufort enjoyed each other's company. Frank hired a horse and shay and the pair trotted out to the open countryside, enjoying the scenery and afternoon warmth. They veered off the road and through a patch of forest to the riverbank, where they sat, rested, and enjoyed mutual small talk. They looked into each other's eyes more than once, acknowledging their mutual desire for each other.

The duo continued their leisurely ride until late afternoon. Then they rode back to town, arriving on Broadway well after dark. The streets were crowded now, mostly with cowpunchers who had come into town to visit the drinking places. Frank stopped at the jailhouse, where the constable told him that all was under control. Harvey Green had gotten his supper and he was now loitering quietly in his cell, not giving Hutchinson any problems.

"I done what you told me, Mr. Lowery," the constable said. "I made sure that two of us was here before we opened the door to feed 'im."

"Good," Lowery answered.

Outside again, Lowery remounted the shay and continued up the wide, crowded Broadway with Clara Beaufort at his side. He drove all the way to the rental stable at the end of the avenue and returned the rig. Then he and Clara walked up the boardwalk and ducked into the Broadway Cafe, somewhat crowded now. A waitress sat them down and they ordered dinner, a steak for Frank and a pork dinner for the girl. They sat there eating for about an hour. Then Frank paid the check and they walked outside.

"I don't know where I can take you now," Frank said. "We could go into one of the saloons, but I'm not a drinker or gambler anymore."

"I know," the girl smiled. "They don't serve coffee there this time o' night."

"Anyway," Frank grinned, "I'm not sure I should take a woman into one of those places. Still, I don't know where else to take you in town."

"To tell the truth, Frank, I'm kinda tired. It's been a long day for me, and no doubt an even longer one for you." She snuggled close to Frank and then peered fervently into his gray eyes. "I'd like to go back to the boardinghouse," she almost whispered. "Would you mind that, Frank?"

"No. I think I'd like that, too."

They walked together up the dark, crowded street, avoiding the mobs of carousing men: cowpunchers, farmers, drifters, laborers, and a host of others seeking diversion. Many of them, already too filled with liquor, eyed the pretty Clara Beaufort lustfully, but made no comments nor attempts to talk to her. They saw the deputy marshal's badge on the shirt of her escort, and they could see the low-slung holster at the waist of the tall, strong Frank Lowery. Whatever these revelers might have thought, they wanted no trouble with this man.

By nine o'clock, Frank and Clara had reached the boardinghouse, and they opened the front door carefully and walked slowly and softly up the front staircase to the second floor. In the near darkness, only a low-wicked lamp offered any light. They continued on until Clara stopped before room 26.

"Will you come inside, Frank?" the girl whispered.

Lowery responded by looking fervently into the girl's admiring dark eyes. Then, without saying anything, he held her and kissed her hard on the lips. As he retreated slightly and stood rigidly, Clara looked eagerly at the tall deputy marshal. She did not speak, but simply took his hand and led him into the room. She closed and locked the door behind her.

Again, at the far end of the hallway, the small middle-aged man had witnessed the mutual affection between Clara and Frank and then their disappearance into the girl's room. He stood for some time, until he was certain the man was not coming out. Then he grinned and walked lightly down the back stairs.

Frank indeed spent the night in Clara's room, but by

daybreak he was dressed and ready to return to his own room.

"Will you go back to Guthrie today, Frank?" the girl asked.

"Right after breakfast, I'd guess," he answered. "I'm going to my own room to shave. I'll be back in about a half hour and we can go out to eat."

The girl nodded and watched Lowery leave the room. Then she too got out of bed to wash herself before dressing.

Frank Lowery had been in his room for about ten minutes and he had just finished shaving when a knock came at his door. He frowned, then opened the door. He saw an elderly man standing there wearing a telegrapher's cap.

"Mr. Lowery? Mr. Frank Lowery?"

"Yes."

"Sorry to bother you so early, sir," the man apologized, "but I got a telegram for you from Guthrie. The wire is from Marshal Fred Egan and I was told to deliver it to you as soon as possible. It's a pretty long message. Mrs. Crawford told me what room you were in."

Frank Lowery nodded. "Thank you." He took the telegram, went inside, closed the door, opened the envelope, and read the contents.

To: Deputy Marshal Frank Lowery: Big robbery at Abajo Springs Mining Company two days ago; office clerk killed and loss in cash and gold estimated at $50,000. Descriptions from overpowered guards hint that robbery and murder carried out by Bronco Kinney. Please remain in Stillwater and investigate. Will send your clothes to

Mae's Boardinghouse by stage today. Wire back anything you find out. Marshal Fred Egan.

Frank Lowery read the message with a mixture of anger and dismay. The Kinney gang had robbed again, and now they had killed. But worse, Clara Beaufort had been with this band. Had she had anything to do with this crime? She'd said she had come into Stillwater two days ago, the day of the robbery. Had she been with the gang, and especially with Carver, on this caper? Frank Lowery had developed a warm, satisfying relationship with the girl, a companionship that had made him forget Sarah Langdon. Would he now end up arresting this girl for complicity in robbery and murder?

Frank Lowery, twenty minutes later, left his room and took the several steps to room 26. When he knocked, Clara opened the door and smiled. She was dressed neatly in a blue two-piece blue-striped blouse with a black skirt and tight bodice belt. She wore boots that fit neatly over her legs, and she had again used just enough makeup to enhance her pretty face. She had combed her hair neatly.

The girl's smile suddenly turned to a frown when she saw the sober look on Lowery's face.

"Frank, is there something wrong?"

"Let's get some breakfast and we'll talk about it," he said.

The girl did not answer, but left the room in silence and accompanied Lowery down the front stairs and into the bright outdoors. Frank remained strangely silent as they walked to the Broadway Cafe. When they got inside, they found a small table in a corner.

Frank looked hard at his companion.

"Clara, I've got to ask you something."

"I guessed that," the girl responded. "When you left my room you were pleased and friendly, but when you came back you wasn't the same man."

Frank pulled the folded telegram from his pocket and waved it before Clara. "This came from Marshal Egan in Guthrie early this morning. There was a robbery and killing at the Abajo Springs Mining Company office two days ago. Preliminary information indicates that one of the culprits might be Bronco Kinney. I've got to ask you, Clara, do you know anything about this? Were you with the gang when they pulled off this caper?"

Clara Beaufort reached over and touched Lowery's hand. "Frank, you remember what I told you yesterday? I heard that Bronco and the others were plannin' to do somethin' that was maybe illegal, and I didn't want no part of it. You recall I said that's why I left them and come to Stillwater."

"I remember," Frank nodded.

"I don't know if Bronco, or Walt Carver, or any of the others were the ones who carried out this crime, 'cause I left Ingalls before they did. I can only repeat—I didn't like the way they talked, so I walked out on 'em."

"That's enough to satisfy me," Frank sighed. Then he grinned. He felt better, certain that Clara Beaufort was telling the truth and was in no way involved in the Abajo Springs robbery. "I'll be here in Stillwater at least another day or two, because in this telegram from Guthrie, Marshal Egan wants me to investigate at the mining company. I'll be riding out there right after we eat to talk to some of the witnesses and to pick up any clues I can."

"That'll be nice, Frank," Clara smiled, "you stayin' here a little longer."

"I should be back this afternoon and maybe we can have supper together when I return."

"I'd like that," the girl said.

"What'll you do all day?"

Clara shrugged. "I don't know; maybe I'll just look around town and see if I can find some work."

Frank Lowery now held the girl's hand. "Clara, maybe you should hold off. Maybe you should come down to Guthrie and try to get a job there. I'm sure they've got something. There's more opportunities, because it's bigger than Stillwater."

"Do you want me to do that, Frank?"

"Yes, I would," Frank answered soberly.

"Then, that's what I'll do," Clara said.

After breakfast, Lowery and Clara walked back to the boardinghouse. Frank left the girl off and went to the stable to saddle his horse, making certain he had ample ammunition for both his six-shooter and his rifle. He then trotted out to the street. Within ten minutes he had left town, and he rode comfortably toward the Abajo Springs Mine, about fifteen miles away. At this moderate pace, he would get there in about two hours. He might spend an hour there and then return. He would be in Stillwater in plenty of time to take Clara to dinner.

The day was cloudy, with the threat of rain. The weather was cooler, and Frank had no poncho. If he ran into a storm he would get soaked. Fortunately, no rain came, and he reached the mining company office without incident.

Lowery found the mine foreman, who explained what had happened. Two men masquerading as prospectors had distracted the guards before two or more accomplices had knocked out the sentinels. The bandits had come just at the right time, because everybody had been down in the mine. The outlaws had not been satisfied simply to rob the safe—they had also killed the office clerk in cold blood.

"But there was something strange," the foreman said. "They didn't use enough dynamite to blow open a safe that strong. We gathered up the casing shreds, and as far as we could tell, the robbers didn't ignite anything more than a small stick. That much explosives would never have blown a safe of that size."

"Are you suggesting that someone here was in with those outlaws?"

"Yes, the clerk himself," the foreman said. "He knew the best time for those bandits to show up here, and he knew when the most money and gold would be in that safe. I suspect he was involved, but the outlaws repaid him by murdering him in cold blood."

Frank Lowery next talked to the two guards for a description of the two men who had posed as prospectors. They told the deputy marshal that one of them had been a big, burly man with a matt of dark hair and light gray eyes. The other man had been tall and slender, with dark hair and dark blue or gray eyes. The descriptions confirmed Egan's suspicion that one of them was Bronco Kinney, and Lowery believed that the second man matched the description of Jim Clayborn, who was known to be a friend of Kinney's, and whose photo Frank remembered seeing on two occasions.

Lowery was unable to develop any more clues, but he was satisfied that Bronco Kinney and his gang had pulled off this caper. When he returned to Stillwater, he would wire Egan to make up more wanted posters on Kinney and Clayborn, and he would ask that posters be made up on Bronco's known associates: Kid Carver, Colorado McGuire, and Rowdy Joe Wheeler, as men wanted for questioning.

On the way back to Stillwater, Lowery detoured a few miles and rode out to the QB Ranch, where he arrived at about two o'clock. He pulled into the big yard before the hacienda but found no one about. However, when he dismounted and tethered his horse, young Billie Stevens, the twelve-year-old son of the ranch foreman, suddenly darted from around the side of the house and nearly ran into Lowery. The boy was carrying a small rifle. Frank grinned at him.

"My God, Billie, where are you going in such a hurry?"

The boy's blue eyes widened and a grin creased his young face. "Mr. Lowery!" he hissed. "I sure am glad to see you again. You comin' back to work here?"

"No, Billie," Frank said.

Billie's face dropped in disappointment and Frank felt saddened. He had always liked the boy who had often sought out Frank when he was working on a fence, or hunting a stray, or doing some other chore around the QB Ranch. Billie had always expressed a desire to be like this ex-QB Ranch hand. The boy had missed Frank during the cattle drive to Wichita, but he had been even more disappointed when he'd learned that Lowery was going to Guthrie.

"How's your Pa?" Frank asked.

"All right," the boy said.

Then, Jed Stevens's bellowing voice echoed from somewhere in the yard. "Billie! Billie! Where are you?"

"I'm here, Pa," the boy answered.

"You're supposed to be gettin' ready to go into town,"

Stevens barked again. He, too, came around the house. He jerked when he saw Frank. "Goddamn! Did you come back to work for me?"

"No, just visiting," Frank said.

Then Jed Stevens saw the badge and gaped at Lowery. "Did you finally take that job with the marshal?"

Frank nodded. "I'm up from Guthrie looking into that Abajo Springs robbery. I just stopped by to say hello to the Barker's."

"Well, if you ain't workin' for me," Stevens grinned, "I can't think of a better man you could work for than Marshal Egan." He looked at his son. "Billie, is the wagon ready?"

"All hitched, Pa," the boy said.

"Good lad," Stevens said, rubbing the boy's head. Then he looked at Lowery. "Well, Frank, maybe we can visit sometime when we've got more time. We can spend a few hours together."

"I'll look forward to that," Frank said, shaking the foreman's hand.

"Good-bye, Mr. Lowery," Billie said.

Frank nodded and watched Jed Stevens and his boy disappear behind the house. He walked to the front of the hacienda and knocked on the front door. Rosie opened it and was shocked to see Frank standing there, and even more astonished to see the badge on his shirt.

"Come inside, Frank, come in."

In the parlor, Moses Barker was equally surprised to see Frank and he gave the visitor a warm handshake. "Goddamn, Frank, you became a lawman."

"Marshal Egan convinced me," Lowery said. "I figured this job would be more necessary than the other job I was considering in Guthrie."

"Well, I'm proud of you," Moses said. "But what are you doin' up here?"

"I brought in a prisoner yesterday and I had to stay over to look into that Abajo Springs robbery. I just got back from there. From the descriptions of the bandits, I got a pretty good idea that they were Bronco Kinney and his gang. The marshal will no doubt form a posse to go after them."

"Then it looks like you'll be spendin' more time in Stillwater," Rose smiled. "You'll have to visit us often if you do. In fact, why don't you spend the rest o' the day with us and have supper? You can even spend the night here."

"I can't," Frank said. "I have to get back and telegraph Egan on what I found out. He might ask me to come right back to Guthrie or maybe stay here and wait for him. I'm staying at Mae's Boardinghouse at the federal government's expense."

"Then there are advantages to being in the law business," Moses grinned. "Do you think you can run down this gang?"

"Marshal Egan is a smart man. We'll run them down."

"At least have some coffee and rolls with us, Frank," Rosie said.

"I guess I can do that."

Lowery spent an hour here, enjoying his stay with Moses and his daughter. They spoke of old times, of Lowery's potential as a lawman, and of activities on the ranch. Not once, however, did they bring up the subject of Rosie and Frank. No doubt, no matter how much Moses liked Lowery, he would not again mention the possibility of any relationship between them.

By three o'clock, Frank Lowery left the ranch,

promising to see them again soon. He needed to wire Egan, but more important, he was anxious to see Clara. Lowery recognized that he now had a feverish infatuation for the girl. In fact, he might even be in love with her.

On the trail, Frank rode leisurely, surveying the countryside and occasionally looking up at the still dreary clouds. He was grateful; at least the rains had not come, and perhaps he would be safely back in his boardinghouse before any downpour. He had just come around a bend in the road when a sudden rifle shot rang out and popped open a wad of dirt on the road. Frank veered his horse as a second shot whizzed by his ear. He quickly ducked into a patch of trees and studied the terrain ahead. He caught a fleeting glance of a hat behind a rock and he knew that someone was up there and trying to pick him off.

Frank tethered his horse and moved stealthily through more trees and up a grade. He had pinpointed the spot where the shots had come from, and he now approached the area. The ambusher, whoever he was, apparently believed that the rider would sooner or later come into the open again and he could try to shoot once more. The sniper had no idea that Frank had already circled around to find him. Within ten minutes, Frank had come cautiously out of the trees, and the rock loomed into his view. He saw a man kneeling behind it, his rifle barrel resting on the rock, while he peered intently down.

Within a minute, Frank had come behind the sniper. "Drop it, mister!"

The man turned and looked at Frank and the aimed rifle. Astonished, he dropped his gun. But then the ambusher took his eyes off Frank and looked behind Lowery. The lawman guessed immediately that this man had an accomplice. His suspicions were right, for he suddenly heard a voice to his rear."

"You drop it, Lowery!"

Frank Lowery turned and saw a man holding a rifle on him. With a quick motion, the deputy marshal raised his rifle and fired. The shot caught the ambusher squarely in the chest and he tumbled forward and fell dead. Frank turned to the second man.

"What the hell is this all about?"

The other man looked at his dead companion in amazement. He had never before seen a man fire so quickly and accurately to kill someone who had the drop on him. He stared in near panic at Lowery.

"Well?" Lowery barked.

"They told us you were fast, but I never believed anybody could be that fast and that good."

"On your feet," Lowery ordered. "You got an awful lot of explaining to do."

Chapter Eight

The would-be assassin rose slowly to his feet, glancing first at his dead companion and then looking at the deputy marshal. He still reflected disbelief when he looked at Lowery, and he still quaked from the memory of the man's fast gun and uncanny aim. When the man stood erect, Lowery yanked the handgun from the ambusher's holster and slipped it into his waist.

"Now, mister, start talking. You know who I am because your partner yelled out the name Lowery. Who paid you to bushwhack me?"

"We was only tryin' to scare you," the man said.

"Like hell you were," Lowery growled. "Fun lovers don't play games with lawmen. Besides, those shots came too close to me, and your partner didn't impress me as a man who could hit a bull's-eye at two or three hundred yards." He gripped the man's shirt collar and shook him. "Talk!"

"Honest, deputy," the man insisted, "we were just funnin' with you."

Lowery looked down at the dead man and then at the prisoner. "Your rifle was fired. If I shot you dead here, nobody could fault me."

"You're a deputy federal marshal," the man answered. "You ain't supposed to do anything like that."

"I'm also a man you tried to kill, and I've got a right to protect myself. If you don't tell me who put you up to this, I'll still be target for whoever hired you, and I won't be safe because I won't know who that enemy is. Your life doesn't mean a thing to me, and if I have to live with something like that, why should I let you live? If people see me bring in two dead ambushers instead of one, why those who hired you, whoever they are, will have a hard time gettin' somebody else to come after me." He leaned closer to the man and grinned. "Won't it look better for me to show up with two dead rattlesnakes instead of one? So, if you value your life, you'd better start talking."

The man gulped and tremors radiated through his body. Yes, this deputy made sense. Why should he die for somebody else? "All right, it was Bronco Kinney who hired us. He wants you dead and so do the rest of 'em. They're afraid you might have found out somethin' when you went to the Abajo Springs mine this mornin' to investigate."

"I was only there a few hours ago. How would Kinney know I went there?"

"He's got friends in Stillwater who keep him informed. He knows you got a telegram early this morning from the marshal in Guthrie. And, since you know what Bronco and some o' the others look like, Kinney figured that once you got a description at the mine, you'd know who helped him to pull off this robbery. Anyway, Kid Carver wants you dead because you've been seein' his girl."

"His girl?"

The man nodded. "That dark-eyed fillie he figures belongs to him."

"You mean Clara Beaufort? She's not having anything to do with Kinney, nor Carver, nor any of the rest of those outlaws. She wisely saw what they were planning at Abajo Springs and she left them; ran out on them."

"Ran out on them?" The man grinned. "She was a part of it. She was their lookout. She rode out o' Ingalls with Kinney and the rest of 'em. From what I hear, she got a good piece of the loot and—"

But the man suddenly stopped when Lowery lashed out at him with a vicious right fist, catching him on the jaw and sending him sprawling to the ground.

The man lay dazed for a moment from the hard blow. He then shook his head, wiped the blood from his face, and looked up at Lowery with yet another grin. "The truth hurts, don't it, deputy? But I told the facts. I was in Ingalls when they came back from the minin' company job. True, the girl wasn't with 'em, but when I spoke to some o' them in the band, they told how Bronco had used the girl as their lookout and then gave her a stack 'a bills from that stolen money before she went on her way."

"You're a liar," Lowery cried, threatening to strike the man again.

"Go ahead, beat me up if you like, or even kill me, but that ain't gonna change the truth. Wishin' I was a liar won't make it so. The next time you see that filly, ask her about it."

Lowery withdrew his cocked arm and then gestured. "Let's go. We'll get your horses, and then I'm taking you and your dead partner into Stillwater."

The man nodded and rose to his feet. Then he led Lowery to the two horses that had been tethered in a clump of trees. After leading the animals into the open, the man helped Frank to drape the dead ambusher over one of the saddles before Frank tied the body tightly. Frank ordered the first man onto his own horse. He tied the prisoner's hands to the saddle horns and his legs to the stirrups. Lowery led both horses and their burdens down the rough hillside and onto the main road to the spot where the deputy marshal had tied his own horse.

Lowery mounted his horse, holding the reins of the two other animals. He started for Stillwater, walking the three mounts. He would need to move slowly, and he would probably not reach town before dark. He turned to the prisoner.

"I expect you to give a full statement on this: how Kinney and the others hired you and your partner to kill me; how you have personal knowledge that they robbed the mine company office; and how you were paid to kill me because I might recognize some of the others besides Kinney."

"Would that include the girl, too?" the prisoner grinned.

"Yes, everything."

"Well, I can't do that," the man said. "What I said to you back there was under duress because you threatened to kill me. Oh, I'll admit we took shots at you, but only because we were funnin'. At worst, they'd only get me on a reckless endangerment charge. If I was to say that the Kinney gang hired me, and that I knew they held up the minin' office, why my life wouldn't be worth a dime. Those fellows or somebody else they hired would sooner or later kill me."

"I warned you," Lowery said, "I might kill you myself."

"No, deputy, you won't kill me; not now you won't. Besides if I keep quiet, the girl won't be involved and that

134

should be to your likin'."

"What makes you think I'd protect the girl?"

The prisoner grinned again. "My jaw is still sore from that punch you gave me back there. No, you don't want to see her behind bars."

Frank did not answer.

"Anyway, you probably already know that Kinney and his boys was involved. And Kinney will also know that we failed to get you. You got the information you wanted, and I won't get killed by them outlaws."

Frank Lowery knew that the man was right. Lowery did not need a statement from this ambusher to implicate Kinney and the others. The descriptions by the guards were clear, and they could easily pick Kinney and Clayborn out of a lineup. And Frank was already quite sure about the others: Wheeler, McGuire, and Carver. Further, Frank did feel a sense of relief in knowing that Clara would not come under suspicion. In a way this made things easy. Lowery could deal with the girl himself, without getting her embroiled on criminal charges.

By dusk, Lowery had reached Stillwater, and again people on the street looked at this second strange caravan with the same curiosity. However, no one said anything to Frank as he stopped before the jailhouse. He and Constable Isa Hutchinson put this prisoner behind bars with Harvey Green. The constable found the mortician to bring the dead ambusher to the funeral parlor, and while he was gone, Lowery spoke to the prisoner.

"Tell me who your dead partner is. We'd like to notify his family if he has any. They might want his body."

The prisoner shrugged. "Melvin Richardson. He has a mother and some sisters down in Waco, Texas. We've rode together for the past couple of years. His mother's name is Adelaide Richardson; at least that's what Mel told me."

Lowery nodded. "I'll send her a telegram."

When Frank finished his business at the jailhouse, he walked to the telegraph office to send off a wire to Waco. He also sent a long telegram to Marshal Egan, indicating that he had pretty much confirmed the identity of at least two of the outlaws in the mining company robbery. One of them was Bronco Kinney and the other was Jim Clayborn. Frank said further in the telegram that he had reliable information that Kinney and his gang were probably in Ingalls at the moment. He also mentioned the ambush incident and how the surviving bushwhacker had claimed they were only funning. And finally, Frank said he would be at Mae's Boardinghouse to await further instructions.

Lowery then rode to the boardinghouse and took his horse in the stable. He unsaddled the mount, fed it hay, and brushed the animal down. He then came up the back stairs and went directly to his room. Here, he found a bedroll on the bed, and when he opened it, he saw a clean set of traveling attire, along with his suit, tie, and shirt. Lowery grinned. Egan had made good on his promise to send his clothes here. Frank knew he was late for his meeting with Clara, but he now wavered on whether to see her at once or to clean and change first. He decided on the former, left the room, walked to her room and knocked on the door.

Clara Beaufort quickly answered and smiled when she saw Lowery: "Frank, you're late. Did somethin' happen?"

Lowery stared soberly at the girl, erasing the smile

from her face. "Somethin' is wrong, ain't it?"

"I'd like to come inside," Frank said gravely. "I got some important business to discuss with you."

"Sure, Frank, sure." But she felt uneasy as she ushered the deputy marshal into the room. Clara sat on the bed, while Frank just stood and stared at her. She had primed herself again, no doubt for him: hair neatly combed, face clean and smooth, spotless white blouse and brown skirt, and again the shiny boots that accented her shapely legs. As she looked at Frank, he wanted to grab her, press her close to him, and kiss her. But he only stared soberly.

"Frank, what's the matter?" the girl asked again.

"I went to the mining company office today as you know, and from the descriptions of witnesses, it appears that Bronco and Clayborn were two of the robbers. I can only suspect that Carver, Wheeler, and McGuire were with them.

Clara nodded. "I was afraid of somethin' like that, so I was right to leave."

"But do you know why I was late getting back to Stillwater? Two men tried to bushwhack me. I killed one of them and the other talked, although unofficially."

The girl did not answer.

Frank leaned close to the girl. "He acknowledged that Kinney paid them to bushwhack me because I might have found out that he and his gang were the culprits of that mining caper. But he also told me something else that disturbs me."

Clara Beaufort only pursed her lips.

Frank Lowery took a step closer to the girl and glared at her. "You were in on the robbery. You accompanied the gang to Abajo Springs. You were the gang's lookout, and you even got a stack of money for your part. Is that right, Clara? Did you lie to me?"

Clara dropped her face in her cupped hands, shook her head, and then broke into a sob. "F-Frank, w-what was I gonna tell you?"

Lowery dropped to a kneeling position next to the girl. "You should have told me the truth, Clara; told me everything."

Clara looked at Lowery, while tears dripped down from her eyes. "Yes, I was with them, and yes I got a stack o' bills. But it wasn't like you think. I didn't want to go with them, but Carver made me," she lied. "He said I knew too much about them, and if I didn't go he'd kill me. At the mine property, I wouldn't go near the office, but they made me wait. Then, when I heard that Walt killed the clerk, I was angry, real angry, and I told them I was leavin' them, and the only way they could stop me was to kill me. Then Bronco just took a stack o' bills and dropped them in my saddlebag. He said if I ever talked, the money would prove that I was with them on the job and I'd implicate myself."

Lowery only listened.

"You got to believe me, Frank. That's exactly what happened. I didn't want no part of it."

"Then why didn't you turn yourself in and hand over that money that Bronco gave you? Why didn't you tell me about it after we became close? I could have helped you. Where's the money now?"

"Most of it I deposited in the Stillwater bank, and I have fifteen or twenty dollars here in my room." Then she looked hard at Lowery, a tinge of panic in her eyes. "What are you gonna do, Frank? You gonna put me behind bars?"

Frank Lowery rose to his feet and walked to the window where he stood motionless and stared into the street. Clara also rose, walked to him, put her arms around his neck, and held her head against his back. "I-I think I l-love you, Frank," she sobbed again. "That's why I was a-afraid to tell you. These past couple o' days h-have been the happiest o' my life. I ain't never m-met a man who was so kind, s-so good, so r-respectful o' me. I couldn't wait for you to come back."

Frank Lowery reached around his shoulder and stroked the girl's hair, while he continued to peer out of the window. The girl gripped his wrist and turned him to face her. "F-Frank, I didn't w-want no part o' this, I swear. I'll do anything for you; just d-don't leave me."

The deputy marshal looked at the girl, at the plea in her dark eyes and the anguish on her face. She had all but broken down, a sharp contrast to that haughty, confident young woman he had first seen in the saloon on that warm morning. Suddenly, he felt sorry for her. Frank did not know a thing about her background, or why she had tied herself to a hard man like Walter Kid Carver. But he also felt piqued. How could she say she wanted nothing to do with this gang when she herself had tried to lure him into it? Yet, since he had found her in Stillwater, alone, there seemed to be some truth to her story of wanting to leave the gang.

Now an agony boiled inside the deputy marshal. If she loved him, as she said she did, he too felt a fervent desire for her, something that went beyond mere lust. He wanted to be with her, as she with him. She had made him forget Sarah Langdon. But, if he was to be true to his oath as a law officer, how could he ignore her activities with the Bronco gang? He held her shoulder and pushed her gently to a sitting position on the bed.

"I don't know what to do, Clara," he said softly. "I'm confused. I can't condone what you did, and I don't want to lose you."

"Just hold me, Frank. Hold me and kiss me."

She rose from the bed and threw her arms around him and pressed him close. He responded with a hard kiss. His desire for the girl had erased everything else from his mind.

Later, Frank Lowery again stood erect at the window and stared into the now dark street. Clara soon came over to him. "Frank, what are you goin' to do?" she asked again.

"I'm going to my room to clean up. Then I'm coming back to take you to supper, like I promised."

The girl smiled.

"Is a half hour long enough?"

"I'll be ready," Clara said. She watched Frank leave before she herself hurried to the water basin to freshen herself before she dressed.

Lowery, in his own room, once more sponge bathed himself with a washcloth and shaved. Then he donned clean clothes—the shirt, tie, and suit that had been among the items Marshal Egan had sent up from Guthrie. He strapped on his gunbelt and pinned on his badge, then gathered up the clothing that he had been wearing for the past two days and carried it downstairs, where he found the Widow Crawford.

"Mae, can you have these clothes cleaned for me? They're awfully cakey, because I've had to wear them for two days."

"Sure, Frank. I'll have them ready by noon tomorrow." Then she studied Lowery. "You're sure dressed to kill tonight, Frank. You must have something important to do."

"Just going to dinner."

"You and Miss Beaufort?"

"Yes."

"She's a right pretty girl," the widow said. "I knew she'd make you forget about Sarah Langdon."

Frank Lowery grinned.

At eight o'clock the neatly attired Frank Lowery and the equally well-dressed Clara Beaufort left the boardinghouse and strode along the crowded boardwalk that was Broadway. Clara had slipped her left arm around Frank's right arm, and she hung close to him as they walked. People threw intense stares at Lowery, eyeing him with an obvious sense of awe. Some even moved aside, keeping their distance from him. However, none spoke and Frank frowned, curious. He did not realize that during the past two hours, between the time he had left off the bushwhacker at the jailhouse and now, he had become a celebrity.

At the jailhouse, while the constable had talked routinely to Harvey Green and the second prisoner, the two outlaws had expounded on Lowery's uncanny talent with a gun. They had electrified Hutchinson with their tales, and he in turn had relayed these tales to some of the townspeople. Most residents had seen Lowery come in twice with the combination of a prisoner and dead men, so they believed what Hutchinson said. These listeners spread the news about town, sprinkling in a little exaggeration as they did. Frank Lowery was now seen as some kind of special man, especially since he wore

141

a badge.

The Broadway Cafe was nearly empty at this late hour, and they easily found a table. The waitress, too, eyed Frank with a look of deep respect as she took their orders. Frank could no longer restrain himself.

"Why is everybody staring at me like I'm some kind of freak?"

The waitress grinned and then explained how the two prisoners at the jailhouse had talked about Lowery's uncanny ability to Constable Hutchinson, and how Isa had repeated the stories to others. And, since most people about Stillwater were aware of Lowery's ability with a gun, they believed Hutchinson.

"Oh," Frank said.

Clara Beaufort looked at Frank and smiled, a warmth inside of her. Lowery was a real man in every way, and she thanked God she was with him. By the time their dinners arrived, however, Clara's thoughts had again turned to her problem with the mining company robbery. Her fears returned and she merely picked at her meal.

Frank looked at the girl in surprise. "I suspect you haven't eaten all day. You must be starved. Why aren't you eating?"

"Frank," the girl said. "What are you gonna do? About me, I mean? About us?"

"I've thought about it. For the time being, I don't intend to do anything. I'll take your word that you didn't have any direct hand in all this. Anyway, it's Kinney and the others that we want."

"Shall I give you the money that Bronco forced on me?"

"No," Frank answered, "that would only complicate things. You just leave it in the bank for now."

The girl smiled, somewhat relieved, and she reached over to hold Frank's hand. "You're sweet. I sure am lucky to be with somebody like you."

"Eat your supper," Frank answered brusquely.

"Sure," the girl said.

Frank and Clara were halfway through the meal when the telegrapher came into the restaurant and hurried to the table. "I'm sorry to bother you, Mr. Lowery, but I've got another telegram for you from Marshal Egan."

"Thank you," Frank said, taking the envelope. He broke the seal and extracted the message: "Wire received; please return to Guthrie. We will form posse to go after the Kinney gang. The expedition will draw supplies here and set off for Ingalls in two days. We'll meet you in the morning on Thursday at my office."

Lowery looked at Clara. "I'll have to return to Guthrie."

"Frank," the girl said, "can I go with you? If you're in Guthrie, I want to be with you. And if it's all right with you, I can draw a little money out of the bank to take with me."

"I won't be in Guthrie long," Frank said, "just long enough to pack and move out with a posse. Maybe you can come down there when I'm a little more settled."

After breakfast the next morning, Frank packed his belongings and bid good-bye to Mae Crawford and Clara Beaufort. Lowery signed the room bill so the widow could claim her money. Clara simply accompanied Frank to the Broadway Cafe, where they ate breakfast together before Frank left.

Frank said little to the girl during the meal, for he was still agonizing over his conflict between his duty as a deputy and his fervent desire for her. He tried to

143

rationalize, telling himself that she was an innocent victim of the domineering Kid Carver. Clara, however, talked openly. She told Frank that she had been orphaned at an early age and had held one job after another, usually as a hotel chambermaid or a waitress, or even as a ranch cook or dishwasher. She had barely eked out a living.

Wherever she went, as she blossomed into full womanhood, she had found that men had only wanted her to satisfy their lust, and she had been half tempted to go into prostitution where she could make good money. But she had found most men crude and harsh and she had almost developed a dislike for the male sex. Then, while working in a clothing store, she had met Walter Kid Carver, a well-dressed, neat, sympathetic, and often considerate man. He had promised her a better life where she would not need to scrounge at hard labor just to survive. He had been quite good to her at first, and she had finally felt that her fortunes had turned for the better.

"But then I found out he was a gunman, a hired killer, who just went off to murder somebody for a good price. I was awful naive not to understand where he got all this money without any kind of real job, but maybe I was so filled with hope that I didn't think straight."

"Then why didn't you leave him earlier?" Frank asked.

"I was in too deep with him by then, and I liked the better life too much. I was starting to get used to money in my purse, nice clothes on my back, and good meals in fine restaurants. And I liked the comfortable beds under me. But I swear, Frank, I left Walt and that gang in a hurry when I learned they killed that clerk. I'm still willin' to turn in both myself and the money."

"Forget it," Frank said.

After breakfast, Lowery and the girl returned to the boardinghouse. He kissed Clara good-bye, promising to see her again soon. Frank rode for several hours and by midafternoon he reached Guthrie, where he went to his room at Howard's Boardinghouse. Here he took an exhilarating bath in Trembley's bathhouse. After he dressed, he walked to the marshal's office.

Inside, Fred Egan grinned when he saw his deputy. "Frank! Glad to have you back. You did a good job in verifying the descriptions of Kinney and Clayborn. Then Egan frowned. "What's this I hear about you getting bushwhacked—twice, I'm told. Somebody tried to get you while you were takin' Green to Stillwater? And then somebody tried to ambush you on your way back from the Abajo Mining Company?"

Frank nodded.

"I can see where some of Green's friends might try to get him loose, but why the hell would those others ambush you?" Egan asked.

"The man in jail will deny it now, but he told me that Kinney had hired him to kill me. Bronco thought I could identify him positively if I got descriptions from the guards, so he wanted me dead."

"The bastard," Egan scowled. "Well, I'm glad nothin' happened to you; and I might say, from what I heard, you took good care of yourself: three dead outlaws that nobody'll miss."

Lowery pursed his lips.

"That goddamn Kinney is sure playin' rough," the marshal continued. He shook his head. "I can't get over how lucky those outlaws were to hit that mining company office at just the right time, when nobody was around and when that safe was loaded with money and gold."

"The clerk was apparently in on it," Lowery said.

"In on it?"

Lowery nodded. "The engineer at the mining company determined that the outlaws had used too little dynamite to blow open that safe—it was too strong for just one stick. He thinks the explosion was just a ruse and the safe was probably already open. The desk clerk apparently told Kinney the best time to hit the place."

"And they paid off the man by killin' him?" Egan gasped.

"It looks that way."

"Well, me and Jack Stone have been workin' hard all day and we've rounded up twenty men for an expedition to Ingalls. We'll take two wagons with supplies and arms, includin' a gattlin' gun. We'll clean out that robbers' roost once and for all. The posse will leave Guthrie at first light tomorrow from our office here, so be ready, Frank. I'd guess we'll be out for two or three days."

When Lowery nodded, Egan leaned forward and pointed at his new deputy. "Frank, we also heard something else about that caper at the Abajo Springs Minin' Company. We heard there was a woman with the gang."

"A woman?" Frank asked. "Nobody at the mine mentioned anything like that."

"No," Egan gestured. "I got this information from some other sources, some informants I use now and then. Are you sure you didn't pick up any clues that a woman was with the Kinney gang? Maybe from a prisoner in Kinney's pay who tried to bushwhack you? Or maybe a rumor around Stillwater?"

"No," Frank Lowery lied.

"Well, no matter," Egan shrugged. "Once we get our hands on that gang in Ingalls, we'll shake 'em down and make 'em talk. And, if there was a woman with them, we'll find out who she was."

Frank Lowery suddenly felt a tinge of panic. If Egan learned of Clara Beaufort, she could go to jail and he would lose her. But worse, if Egan found out that Lowery was lying about the girl, he would dismiss him from the force. And Lowery would not appreciate that, because even after this short stint in the federal law enforcement service, he had already come to like the job.

Chapter Nine

By 6:30 A.M., Friday, Frank Lowery appeared at the marshal's office in Guthrie. He had packed a full bedroll, with a change of clothing for a two- or three-day trek. Lowery found fifteen men loitering here. While most of them were mounted on horses, two of them sat on a wagon whose rear carried supplies of food and a gattling gun. When Frank arrived, he saw Egan moving among the men and issuing instructions.

"We should arrive in the Ingalls area by late afternoon," the marshal was telling his posse. "Then we'll camp for the night and start into that robbers' roost before daylight. We pretty well know that the riffraff in there and those who serve 'em are still asleep by then, because they've either been carousing or workin' through most o' the night. We won't likely meet any opposition, and they ain't likely to even know we came into town."

The men listened.

"When we make camp this afternoon, we'll go over these maps we have of Ingalls," Egan continued. "We'll plan to cover the two exits from town, while we come into Ingalls with the wagon carryin' our gattlin' gun." He looked at the two men on the wagon. "Are you sure you know how to use that thing, Ed?"

Ed grinned. "Me and Isaac," he cocked his head at his companion, "have used that gun plenty o' times when we was in the army trackin' down Apache renegades down New Mexico way. We know how to load it and fire, and we know how to hit only what we want to hit."

"I hope so," Egan said. "I don't want none o' my men killed or hurt by that weapon."

"We ain't never touched one of our men yet with that gun," the man Isaac now grinned.

Egan looked up and saw Frank and his eyes widened. "I'm glad you're here. You can ride along with me, while Jack Stone takes the point. I'm goin' to station you and a couple of the others at the south exit out of Ingalls. With your aim, nobody'll get by you. I hope you don't mind that."

"Whatever you say, Marshal," Lowery said.

Fred Egan now scanned his mounted posse, fifteen of them, including himself and the two men on the wagon. "Now, is everything all set? Did you all bring enough clothes for at least two or three days? You got plenty o' ammunition? Anything wrong with your mounts?" When no one answered, Egan nodded. "Then we're ready to ride." He looked at the pair of deputies standing in the doorway of the marshal's office. "You two will have to keep things calm here while we're gone. Make sure you're both out patrollin' the streets tonight and that you're well armed. We wouldn't want some of them drunken cowpunchers to think this town is wide open just because me and Stone are gone."

"Don't worry, Marshal," one of the deputies said, "we'll take care of things here in Guthrie."

The two men stood in the door and watched the parade move away and out of town. Deputy Jack Stone was in the lead, with Egan, Lowery, and the others behind them. Then came the wagons and the others trailing behind them. A few early risers on 2nd Avenue stared as the posse plodded leisurely toward the open country north of Guthrie, but these spectators said nothing. Most of them suspected that Egan and his posse were going up to the Cimarron badlands to root out the gang of outlaws that had robbed the Abajo Springs Mining Company. They watched until the band of riders disappeared into the distance on the road to Stillwater.

The caravan of lawmen moved northward for nearly four hours on this hot, dusty morning, and before noontime, the town of Stillwater loomed in the distance. However, the marshal did not go through here. Instead, he stopped in a grove of trees along the river just outside of town. Here the cook started a fire, gathered water, and prepared a noon meal of bacon, fried pan rolls, and coffee. The men themselves ambled to the riverbank to wash up, and some of them even stripped naked to bathe in the stream, wiping away the dust and sweat they had accumulated during their long hours on the trail.

By one o'clock, after cleaning the campsite, the men remounted and continued north toward the Cimarron country where outlaws had hidden out for years. The rugged, forested mountains made the task of finding lawbreakers almost impossible. The outlaws often came into Ingalls for diversion, and sometimes, if there was evidence of outside lawmen about, they simply ran off to the hills again.

Deputy Jack Stone, riding point, kept alert for signs of any lookouts along the winding road to Ingalls. In the hills, bands of outlaws often kept someone on sentinel duty to keep an eye out for such posses as this one under Marshal Fred Egan. Or, outlaw gangs often hired men to keep a sharp watch. Because of these tactics, lawbreakers generally avoided lawmen who were looking for them.

As the posse continued on, Lowery turned to Egan. "I heard that these outlaws and their protectors are pretty slick, Marshal. Are you sure we'll be able to surprise Kinney and his gang?"

"If we're lucky," Egan admitted. "Like I said, we plan to go into Ingalls at first light, when the town is still pretty much asleep. Once we do that, why we can seal off the exits and conduct a roundup inside the town."

"They're pretty smart," Lowery said.

"Let's hope not smart enough."

But even as the posse rode northeast toward Ingalls, lookouts in some of the hills spotted them. And the sentinels guessed that this band of men were lawmen. One of the lookouts quickly mounted his horse and galloped swiftly into Ingalls, where he found the constable and his assistants and reported the approach of a probable posse less than ten miles away.

"I'd guess they'll camp for the night and hit the town in the morning," the rider said.

The constable turned to his aide. "Move around town, fast, and spread the word. Anybody in Ingalls who's on a wanted list had best get out of town by morning."

The aide nodded and quickly left the constable's office.

Ingalls, of course, had been a haven for outlaws for years. Although such lawbreakers did not directly pay off the local authorities, the outlaws paid local entrepreneurs about twice the going rate for food, lodgings, supplies, prostitutes, or other needs and desires. In turn, the business people who reaped good profits willingly paid high prices for licenses, permits, taxes, or fees to operate. So officials had ample funds to enrich themselves and to pay sentinels who would warn visitors of approaching lawmen.

By three o'clock, the constable and his aide had spread the word throughout town: a posse was approaching Ingalls. In the saloons, bordellos, and boardinghouses the news prompted many visitors to leave Ingalls by nightfall so they would not fall into the hands of lawmen. Bronco Kinney and three of his cohorts had been playing cards in the local Cimarron Saloon on this relatively quiet afternoon when the fifth member of the gang, Rowdy Joe Wheeler, came inside and hurried up to the table.

"Bronco," Wheeler said, "a posse's 'acomin' to Ingalls, no doubt lookin' for you and Clayborn."

Bronco made a face and slammed his cards on the table, breaking up the poker game. "Son of a bitch!" he cursed. "I was just startin' to have a good time in this town."

"What about me?" Wheeler grumbled. "I was just gonna take a hump with that pretty redheaded whore at Daisy's place when this constable barged into the place and told Daisy to get everybody out 'cause the law was on the way to town. I never did get to lay that little bitch and that goddamn madam wouldn't even give me my money back."

"She's a tough old hen," Jim Clayborn grinned.

Then Colorado McGuire looked at Kinney. "Bronco, we'd best move out in a hurry. We can go to our dugout. Those lawmen will never find us there."

"Colorado's right," Rowdy Joe said. "Ain't no sense

153

hangin' around here to get in a shootout with a posse and maybe get captured or killed. The lookout suspects that the posse won't come in till mornin', but you can never tell. They might be here by dark to surprise us."

"I suppose we'd better move," Bronco nodded, "but at least let's have a few drinks and a good meal. Then we'll go to the general store and get ourselves plenty o' whiskey and other supplies to take with us."

"There's some fellows who already rode out," Rowdy Joe said.

"Like I said," Bronco gestured, "we'll put on a good feed and then we'll go."

The quintet of outlaws now sat at the table and ordered big, juicy steaks, which they could easily afford. They had plenty of fried potatoes, buns, and string beans with the meat, and they washed down the repast with plenty of cold beer, for the Cimarron Saloon maintained its own ice house to keep their beer cold.

Bronco and his men had gone halfway through their meals when a slightly built, middle-aged man, the one who had been observing Frank Lowery and Clara Beaufort at Mae's Boardinghouse, came into the saloon. When he spotted Bronco and his four followers, he came meekly up to their table.

"Bronco?" the man said hesitantly.

Kinney looked up. "Ah, Crandall. Well, what's the news from Stillwater?" When the man hesitated, licking his lips, Bronco grinned. He reached into his pocket for a wad of bills, peeled off a pair of twenty-dollar notes, and handed them to the visitor. "Well, what have you found out?"

"I thank you, Bronco, for this money," Crandall said. "And, o' course, you understand that I need to give some to people who give me information."

"All right, all right," Bronco said impatiently. "Well?"

"I'm sorry to say, Bronco," Crandall said, "but Marshal Egan has come to the conclusion that you and your boys was responsible for that robbery and killin' at the Abajo Springs Minin' Company office. This new deputy, that Frank Lowery, found out about you, just as you feared. He got descriptions from the guards and figured it was you and Clayborn who acted like prospectors. Lowery sent a telegram to Guthrie and told the marshal to make up more wanted posters on you and Clayborn. He also suspects the rest o' your boys, although he ain't got no real proof on them. Still, I believe Marshal Egan will be makin' up wanted posters on them too, for questioning on suspicion o' murder and robbery."

Bronco Kinney frowned. "How could Lowery get back to Stillwater? I had two bushwhackers waitin' for him on the trail. They couldn't o' missed Lowery comin' back from Abajo Springs."

Crandall shook his head. "This Lowery is somethin' you can't believe. He musta got wise, 'cause he killed one o' your bushwhackers and brought in the other one, who is now in the Stillwater jailhouse."

"I don't believe that," Kinney huffed. "Those men were supposed to be the best."

"Not good enough." Crandall gestured. "Not only did Lowery get them, but he was bringin' a prisoner from Guthrie to Stillwater, and he killed a couple o' friends o' this prisoner who also tried to ambush him. This prisoner, a man by the name o' Harvey Green, and your man, has both been talkin' a blue streak on how fast and good this Lowery is, since he got them ambushers even after they had the drop on him."

"The bastard," Colorado McGuire hissed. "Them rumors about him are true."

But Kid Carver scoffed. "Sure, hittin' a few slow draws. That's all them men were, slow draws. I'd like to know what that Lowery would do if he came up against a real gun."

"You mean like yours, Kid?" Rowdy Joe Wheeler grinned. "You think you could take him?"

"Sure I could take him," Carver shrugged. "Like Lowery himself said, he only shoots cats and rattlers and rabbits, who ain't gonna shoot back. And them slow draws," he gestured to Crandall, "ain't much different than a rabbit against somebody like Lowery."

"I don't know, Kid," Jim Clayborn shook his head, "you're talkin' about somebody who avoided two traps and got them ambushers clean."

"Well, there ain't no sense adwellin' on Frank Lowery," Bronco said. "If the marshal identified me and Clayborn, and he's suspicious o' the Kid, Rowdy Joe, and Colorado, we can't hang around here."

"Like I said, Bronco," Crandall continued, "the marshal and his posse are on the way here, and Frank Lowery is with 'em."

"I ain't afraid o' Lowery," Carver scoffed again. "He's got nothin' on me."

"I think he has, Kid," Crandall said.

"What do you mean?"

The small man again licked his lips and then eyed the five outlaws at the dinner table one by one. He finally focused his eyes on Carver. "Your girl, Kid."

"What do you mean? My girl?"

Crandall nodded. "That Clara Beaufort. I seen 'er goin' into her room with Frank Lowery at least twice at Mae's Boardinghouse and they never came out."

Kid Carver did not answer, but his neck reddened.

"I seen 'em in the hall lookin' at each other in a way you wouldn't believe," Crandall continued. "Then they'd go into her room and lock the door. There ain't no doubt what they was doin' in there."

Kid Carver's face flushed with rage and he lashed out to strike Crandall. However, Bronco was a flash quicker, gripping Carver's wrist before the Kid could land a punch.

"Take it easy, Kid," Kinney said.

"The bastard is lying." Carver cocked his head at the visitor. "Clara wouldn't go for no pansy like this Lowery, especially if he joined the law."

"I'm only tellin' you what I know," Crandall said. "You don't have to believe me, Kid. Everybody in Stillwater can tell you that them two has been as close as two peas in a pod. They been together around Stillwater for two or three days, almost day and night. They ride and eat together all the time, and they live in the same boardin' house. They was apart only when Lowery went up to Abajo Springs for a few hours. Then Lowery went back to Guthrie, and I wouldn't be surprised if that girl will join him down there as soon as Lowery is finished up here."

"The little whore!" Carver scowled. "After all I did for her, she does this to me? Shacks up with the likes o' Frank Lowery?"

No one at the table answered.

"I'm gonna get that no-good bastard," Carver pointed,

157

"and then I'm gonna take care o' that bitch."

"Look, there ain't no sense jawin' about Clara right now," Bronco said. "Let's gear up and get the hell outta town." He turned to the visitor. "We're obliged to you for all this information you brought us. You keep it up, 'cause we have to know everything that's goin' on. We'll be headin' for our dugout at Miller Creek. You know where that is?"

"I know," Crandall said.

"Well, as soon as you get any other worthwhile information, you ride out there and inform us."

"I'll do that, Bronco," Crandall promised.

"Now you'd best get outta here," Kinney said. "The Kid is as mad as a wounded mountain cat after what you told him, and he might still try to take you out."

Crandall nodded again. He threw a parting glance at the quintet before he hurried out of the Cimarron Saloon.

By late afternoon, a feverish activity had erupted in Ingalls. Men scurried about in every direction, packing gear, saddling horses, buying grub and liquor. Not only the Bronco gang, but other wanted men, at least a dozen more, were also preparing for hasty departures. Rumors had spread that the posse was carrying a gattling gun. Further, all those in Ingalls knew the reputation of Marshal Fred Egan. He would shoot first and ask questions later.

Throughout the town, the madams, prostitutes, saloon keepers, and other business people watched the frantic movements wistfully. Although the men leaving town represented a small number of those visiting there, the evacuees were the outlaws with the most money to spend. The citizens of the town however, had one consolation.

The posse would come into town, find no wanted men, and then depart. At worst, Egan would bluster and threaten and then leave town empty-handed. Within a few days, the outlaws would return, anxious for luxuries again, and once more spend their money liberally.

By dark, Ingalls was almost deserted, with only permanent residents and those not wanted by the law still in town. There would be less business at the saloons and cafes this evening, and most of the prostitutes would sleep alone in their beds tonight.

Fred Egan pulled his posse into a big clearing amid some dense trees and only a couple of miles from town. Here, he made camp for the night, warning his men that they must be awake and ready before daylight for the ride into Ingalls. The cook again prepared the evening meal for the tired, hungry men who had been on the trail from Guthrie since early morning. The men devoured their meal of beans, bacon, and rolls like starved wolves. Fortunately, Egan had ordered plenty of food to accommodate even the largest appetites.

After the meal, and while the men drank coffee around a campfire, Frank Lowery turned to Jack Stone. "I'm still wondering; will we catch those outlaws in the morning?"

"Maybe yes, maybe no," Stone said. "If they've been warned, any outlaws who were in there are probably out of town by now. We'll go in there and come back empty-handed."

"Warned? Who'd warn them?"

"I thought you knew somethin' about Ingalls," Stone grinned. "Like the marshal said, it's a robbers' roost. Every outlaw in the territory finds a haven there, but they spend good money, and those that run the town keep lookouts in the hills outside Ingalls to warn them of lawmen comin'. Sometimes these lookouts miss us and we're lucky enough to go in there and surprise alot o' wanted men. But, other times they succeed, and the town is empty when we get in there.''

"Goddamn," Lowery grinned.

"We'll know in the morning," Stone said.

Frank Lowery nodded, finished his coffee, and then curled under his blanket. He was quite spent and he soon fell asleep. In fact, all the men in the posse were soon in deep slumber.

Before dawn the next morning, Egan and his men had burst into activity: eating breakfast, cleaning up in the Cimarron River, and then dressing. The first streaks of daylight had not yet emerged over the mountains to the east when the mounted posse again moved toward Ingalls. Once more Jack Stone took the point, but he saw nothing on the sides of the road into the town. When dawn finally arrived, the men were on the outskirts of town, and Egan held them up.

"Jack," the marshal said to Stone, "swing around with two men and take up a blocking position at the north end o' town. Frank," he turned to Lowery, "you take two men and do the same thing here on the south end of Ingalls. The rest of us will go up the main street and then fan out to find as many wanted men as we can. Mostly, we'll hit the boardinghouses and bordellos, because they'll either be sleeping in those places or in bed with a whore. Any questions?" When no one answered, Egan nodded. "Okay, let's move out."

Within the next ten minutes, Jack Stone had taken up his position at the north end of town, while Frank Lowery and his partners settled themselves along the road leading out of Ingalls from the south. Egan led the others, including the wagon with its gattling gun, into the main street, now utterly quiet and devoid of a single soul. But then, considering the nature of the business in this town, not many people would likely be awake at this hour.

Egan left the wagon in the middle of the street with the two men on the gattling gun. They would deal with anybody who came out of any buildings and refused to stop for questioning. Egan and the others, meanwhile, made a quick search through the bordellos and boarding-houses in town. The marshal knew well enough that outlaws staying in Ingalls would have enough money to afford such accommodations and they would not need to camp out.

However, Egan and his men failed to root out a single wanted man among the visitors to Ingalls, and certainly not Bronco Kinney. The marshal and his followers had broken down one door after another, rousting landlords, patrons, and employees out of bed. The searchers found no wanted men. The irritated Egan was especially angry with Daisy Carpenter, the biggest madam in Ingalls. He scowled at the still half-asleep woman and the several young women who came out of their rooms when the commotion began.

"Where the hell are they?" Egan demanded.

"I don't know what you're talkin' about, Marshal," Daisy said.

"You know goddamn well what I'm talkin' about," Egan growled. "There were at least fifteen or twenty wanted men in this town yesterday, including Bronco Kinney and his boys. We both know that your whores don't sleep alone when those kinda men are in town."

"We ain't seen Bronco around here," Daisy shrugged. "Business has been slow this week, in fact."

"Like hell," Egan cried. "Who warned them we were comin'?"

"I don't know what you mean," Daisy insisted. "Like I said, we ain't had but a few customers this week."

"You're a no-good liar." Egan cried. When Daisy did not answer, the marshal glared at the still half-asleep young women who stood quietly behind their madam. "You girls, what happened to all the Johns? Where did they go? Who told them we were comin'?"

But the young women only cowered and retreated slightly, none of them answering. Daisy Carpenter then turned to Egan. "Marshal you got no cause to come bustin' into our place to scare hell outta these poor girls."

"Sure, poor girls," Egan huffed. "I should earn a fraction o' the kind 'a money they're makin' here."

"Like I told you," Daisy said again, "business has been awfully slow this week. Now if you want to hang around town, maybe some o' them men you're lookin' for might come in today or tomorrow."

"You pimp bastard!" Egan cursed. "It's people like you who make it easy for lawbreakers. You don't give a damn so long as you get plenty o' dollars for givin' them pleasure. I'm tellin' you, Daisy, we're going to catch you redhanded one of these days and you'll be spendin' the rest o' your life in woman's prison."

"Look, Marshal," Daisy said, "if a man comes into Ingalls and wants one o' my girls, am I supposed to ask him for credentials? Am I supposed to ask him if he broke the law somewhere? I ain't no lawman, and how am I supposed to know if a man is on the run or merely a cowpuncher lookin' for a good time?"

"No cowpuncher could afford the prices you charge,"

Egan grumbled.

Even as Egan berated Daisy Carpenter, one of his posse members came into the bordello and spoke to the marshal. "Nothin', Fred, not a damn thing. We hit the other bordello in town and the two boardin' houses. We found some cowpunchers, a lotta drifters, and a couple o' drummers, but no wanted men. Some of the boys hit the saloon and they didn't find no wanted men, either."

"You bitch!" Egan still berated Daisy, "all of you got your stories straight, too." He turned to the deputy. "Go find the constable who's supposed to keep law and order in this town. I want to speak to him in his office."

"Sure thing, Marshal."

Within the next half hour, Egan and a deputy were standing inside the small Ingalls' jailhouse talking to Constable Miranda and his aide. The two local law officers denied vehemently that they were harboring criminals in Ingalls, and claimed that they had not been aware of any wanted men in town.

"Miranda," Egan gestured angrily, "do you know what'll happen to you if we find that you've been lookin' the other way while outlaws are runnin' fancy free around this town?"

"I ain't lettin' no criminals run loose in Ingalls," Miranda said, "at least none that I know of."

"Well, we know that Bronco Kinney and his gang were in Ingalls as late as yesterday, and that they've been here for the past week or so. After the Wells Fargo robbery in Enid, we made up and sent out wanted posters on Bronco Kinney to every lawman in the territory. You must have got one." He looked at the wall behind the desk. "However, I don't see one posted there."

"Sometimes the mail is slow comin' up here, Marshal,

163

so we didn't get one yet. But, I promise, as soon as I do, that wanted poster will be on my board."

Egan sighed and then shook his head. "It's no use. Everybody in Ingalls is the same, protecting outlaws to make a lotta dollars. But, I'm tellin' you the same thing I told the others." He pointed threateningly at Miranda. "We're going to catch you cold one of these days and you'll be marching off to jail along with the outlaws we nab."

By nine o'clock Egan and his men had swept through the whole town, without finding any wanted men, especially Bronco Kinney. Similarly, neither Lowery on the south nor Stone on the north had seen anybody leaving Ingalls. The marshal grudgingly conceded that his expedition had been a complete failure. By two o'clock the posse was on its way south again, empty-handed. They would not arrive back in Guthrie from this weary trek until late that night. As they rode, Egan turned to Lowery.

"Frank, I'd like you to stay on in Stillwater, if you don't mind. I'll make arrangements with Constable Hutchinson to let you share his office with him. I want you to spend the next couple of days asking questions in town and in the countryside to pick up Kinney's trail. He and his gang are hidin' somewhere in these Cimarron hills, and if you can get an inkling of their whereabouts, we'll come back to flush them out."

Frank Lowery nodded.

"You don't mind, do you, Frank?"

"No, no," Lowery said.

In fact, Frank was thrilled by the marshal's request. He would again house himself in Mae Crawford's place, where Clara Beaufort was also staying, and again, for at least two days, he would be able to enjoy her company.

Chapter Ten

At their hillside dugout in the remote forests of the Cimarron, Bronco Kinney and his four gang members had been drinking whiskey and playing poker. They had plenty of money now—$50,000 from the Abajo Springs Mining Company robbery and $5,000 from the Wells Fargo job. They suspected that lawmen were scouring the countryside looking for them. The Bronco gang had become a hot item, and even Ingalls might not be safe for them at the moment. So they could only lie low for a while instead of enjoying their money.

Kid Carver's mind was not on the poker game. No, his thoughts had wandered to Stillwater, where he suspected that Clara Beaufort was even now saddling up to the despicable Frank Lowery, that handsome ex-cowpuncher with his fancy talk and his ambition to become a notable outlaw hunter. Twice during the last three hands Carver had not heard the dealer's call to ante up, and on both occasions the Kid had merely thrown in his hand with the blunt comment: "I'm out."

The second time, a curious Colorado McGuire peeked at the Kid's discarded hand and saw a pair of aces. He then berated Carver.

"What the hell's the matter with you, Kid? That pair of aces would have taken the pot."

But Carver only shrugged.

Now Bronco Kinney took the deal, and as he scanned his quartet of fellow card players, he saw that Carver's mind lay far from this hideout. An almost comotose look had settled into the Kid's dark eyes, but Carver's revelries were hardly pleasant. In fact, the more Carver meditated, the hotter the anger boiled inside of him. Still, Bronco said nothing as he dealt hands of five card stud.

A moment later Colorado McGuire opened for five dollars, with Rowdy Joe and Jim Clayborn quickly dropping out. Bronco looked at the Kid, who held his hand mechanically, as though he did not know what he held. "Well, Kid," Bronco said, "are you in?"

Carver jerked, looked at his cards, and tossed them on the table. "I'm out."

Now, before Bronco met the ante from Colorado, he took the Kid's discards and looked—a trio of fours. Bronco gaped and then glared at his companion. "You dumb bastard! You toss away a hand like that?"

"I guess I wasn't thinkin'."

"No, you ain't been thinkin' since we left Ingalls," Bronco huffed. "You're still boilin' over what Crandall said to you. I got a suggestion for you. Why the hell don't you get outta this game; go to your bunk and sleep, or get drunk, or anything to make you forget that girl. With the kinda money you got, you could buy the prettiest whore in the Oklahoma Territory."

"She ain't no whore!" Carver protested angrily.

"I didn't say she was," Bronco answered, "you did. But I don't think you aimed to marry her, and if not, what the hell do you want her for?"

166

"I just wanted her to be my woman, that's all."

"Like Bronco said," Rowdy Joe Wheeler grinned at the Kid, "you can have any woman you want now."

"She's mine!" Kid Carver cried again. "I don't like no goddamn cowpuncher takin' her away from me." He rose from the table. "I'm goin' into Stillwater and kill the bastard."

"Are you loco?" Jim Clayborn said, grabbing the Kid's arm. "Every lawman in the West is lookin' for us, and they're all trigger happy. They'd shoot you down before you got near Frank Lowery."

"They only suspect me," Carver said. "They ain't got no proof to tie me into anything. I'll be safe enough."

"Even if you were safe from the law, would you be safe from Lowery?" Rowdy Joe asked with a grin. "You heard what Crandall said about 'im; how he killed them men who had the drop on 'im."

"I ain't afraid o' him or his reputation," Carver said, "and maybe it's just that, a reputation and nothin' more. Did he ever kill anybody who can really handle a gun? No! Only rattlers, mountain cats, and slow draws. Them kinda men don't look you square in the eyes, darin' you to shoot. Besides, when I kill 'im, that'll be one less lawman to worry about."

"Look, Kid," Bronco gestured, "what you're plannin' is foolish. You got nothin' to gain and everything to lose. Even if you did kill him, then what? Lowery is a lawman now, a deputy marshal, and fair fight or not, the law'll get you. They don't accept somebody killin' one o' their own, even if you don't break no laws doin' it. They'll just ambush you and finish you, and then claim you drew on them. They're wearin' the stars, so who do you think a judge is goin' to believe?"

"I'm gonna get that cowpuncher," Carver insisted.

"Do us a favor, will you, Kid?" Rowdy Joe leaned forward. "Leave your share here, and if you don't come back, why the rest of us can divvy it up."

Now Carver grinned. "I ain't afraid to leave it here. You know why? 'Cause I'll be back. I'll be back with one dead deputy marshal lyin' in a Stillwater funeral parlor, or wherever else I find him. And Clara Beaufort will be ridin' back here with me."

"Suit yourself," Bronco shrugged.

Then, as Kid Carver left the table and headed away, the remaining foursome only watched him for a moment before Bronco looked at the others.

"Whose deal?"

"Mine," Jim Clayborn said.

When Carver left the table he did not go to his cell, but went out of the structure and walked to the dugout stall. Here, he brushed his roan horse, patted its nose gently, and then saddled the animal. He tied the saddle carefully and checked his rifle to make sure it was clean and loaded before slipping the weapon into the long scabbard. He then patted the horse again before he returned to the dugout.

Once inside his cell, one of the several small cubicles within the dugout that served as private bedrooms, Kid Carver shed his clothes. He washed his body from the basin, using water poured from a bucket. After he had cleaned himself, he walked outside, emptied the pail of dirty water, and refilled the bucket with clean water from the creek. He then returned to his cell, rinsed himself off, and shaved. Next, he went once more outside to empty the pail, refill it, and return still again to his cell. The others in the dugout merely glanced at the Kid as he shuffled in and out of the structure, but none of them said anything to Carver.

Again in his cell, Kid Carver folded up the clothes he had been wearing and then tied them into a bundle he would carry with him. He would get them laundered in Stillwater. Then, the Kid slipped on clean BVDs, his clean pair of chino trousers, and his clean laced tan shirt. He put on his socks and then his boots, still sparkling black, since he had not used them in some time. He lifted his gunbelt from the wall, checked the .45 revolver, slipped it back into the holster, and ran the belt around his waist. He buckled up and he tied the rawhide lace of his holster around his right thigh. And finally, Carver set his Stetson hat on his head, looking into the mirror to make certain the hat was tilted just right.

Carver now pulled the burlap suitcase out from under the bunk, untied it, reached inside, and pulled out a handful of bills. He extracted about a hundred dollars in tens and twenties, tossed the rest back into the bag, retied it, and kicked the suitcase under the bunk.

When the Kid emerged from his cell, the others looked at him. Jim Clayborn grinned. "Jesus Christ, Kid, you dressed to go to a square dance? I thought you were goin' to Stillwater to kill a cowpuncher."

"Hey, Kid," Rowdy Joe Wheeler also grinned, "did you leave your money here? Not that we'd steal it, understand, but just in case you don't come back."

"I'll be back," Carver promised.

Bronco Kinney gripped Carver's arm and looked soberly at his fellow outlaw. "Kid, take care of yourself. You never know what them lawmen are likely to do. You're a good gun, and I'd hate to lose you."

"I'll be here again in a day or two."

"Sure," Bronco nodded.

The foursome watched their fellow bandit leave the dugout. A silence then prevailed for a moment, with only the sound of gurgling liquor interrupting the quiet as Bronco refilled the glasses with whiskey. Without speaking, the foursome at the table downed their drinks. Then Colorado McGuire looked at Rowdy Joe.

"It's your deal."

Outside, Carver ambled to the stable and led his horse into the open. He squinted at the morning sun and then nodded to himself. If he moved at a fair pace he could be in Stillwater by midafternoon and have this job over with by sundown. He would then celebrate: eat a good restaurant meal, have some fun in a saloon, and get a comfortable night's sleep on a soft boardinghouse bed. Tomorrow he would find Clara and talk her into coming back with him.

Carver crossed Miller Creek from the open area fronting the dugout and then loped for five miles over the winding trail through the dense forest until he finally emerged from Hunters Trail onto the open Stillwater-Ponco Highway. When he reached the road, he turned south and rode easily: trotting, cantering, walking, and occasionally galloping so he would not tire his mount. Now and then he tapped the animal's nose or slipped the horse a sugar cube.

Kid Carver ignored the heat as the sun rose higher in the sky and throbbed fiercely. The warmth did not bother the man. He had been raised and reared in the hot climate of southern Texas, spending most of his life around Laredo and Brownsville among the Mexicans. He had worked at one job or another since age six, because his drunken father had never brought money home, and his promiscuous mother was always off sleeping with somebody for a few dollars.

Carter had worked on the Brownsville docks, or as a ranch hand, a stable boy, a cafe dishwasher, or at any other menial job he could find to get enough money for food. But he had in his youth once seen a gunfighter who had come into Brownsville, and who wore the best clothes, flashed easy money, and garnered oohs and ahs from people. On that day, at age fourteen, Carver had decided that the superior use of a gun was the answer to having money and respect.

The Kid had bought himself a six-shooter with the next few dollars he had earned and had spent the next half-dozen years learning how to use it. He had soon excelled conspicuously in shooting contests, and on three occasions he had put down three fast guns in man-to-man duels. Wealthy men soon came after him, hiring him to threaten or even kill.

Carver had lost count on the number of men he had killed during the past few years, but perhaps more than a dozen. And he had also lost count of the amount of money he had earned and spent. When Kinney had decided to take up banditry, he had quickly sought out Kid Carver to join his band for easy money. In the meanwhile, Kid had met the pretty Clara Beaufort and taken an immediate shine to her. He had enjoyed her company for some time now. He had treated her well and given her money, so he felt justified in his anger.

Now, the Kid intended to take on this Frank Lowery, kill him, and reclaim his woman.

Actually, the Kid felt little apprehension as he rode southward, despite the rumors about Lowery and Crandall's reports of Lowery's prowess with a gun. He did

171

not really believe that this ex-cowpuncher was as swift and accurate as people said he was, and the Kid was sure he could take Lowery in a face-to-face shootout.

Carver rode on, resting only to wash himself at a creek, water his horse, and refill his canteen. Finally, at about three in the afternoon, Stillwater loomed into view. The Kid loped on for another mile, until he was just outside of town. Here, he dismounted, brushed away patches of dust from his clothes, and straightened his hair. He checked his .45, hitched his gunbelt, and tilted his hat on his head again. He remounted, heaved a deep sigh, and cantered toward town. If Lowery was in Stillwater, he would finish his job within an hour.

Frank Lowery was tired. He had been on the trail with Marshal Egan for two days, and he had then ridden all over northern Pawnee County without getting a single lead on Bronco Kinney's whereabouts. He should have rested today because he would be on the trail again tomorrow, but he had to see Clara.

Frank had only slept for a few hours after arriving back in Stillwater in the late morning. He had simply plopped on his bed at Mae's Boardinghouse, not bothering to eat, change, or clean up. When he awoke at about two in the afternoon he felt seedy, and his face itched from the two-day beard. He wiped the sleep from his eyes and stared out of the window of his room, blinking from the early afternoon sun. Then Frank yawned, stretched, and rubbed the itch on his face again. He hoisted himself from the bed, walked to the dresser to extract a clean set of clothes, left the boardinghouse and ambled to Lin Ching's bath house. He was hungry and thirsty, but he would clean up and keep his meeting with Clara Beaufort at three o'clock.

At the bath, Lowery stripped naked and handed his dirty clothes, including his underclothes, to Lin Ching. "I'd like to have these ready by suppertime, because I think I'll be going out again in the morning."

"You have, Mr. Lowery, you have," Ching promised.

Once in the hot tub, Frank Lowery felt ecstasy. The warm, clean, soapy water soothed his tight muscles, loosened his aching bones, and eased his itchy skin. He soaked for nearly a half hour, more than the usual fifteen minutes. Then Ching personally shaved him, until Frank's face was as smooth as silk.

"You feel better now, Mr. Lowery?"

"I sure do," Frank answered.

After he left the tub and dried off, Frank donned his clean clothes: BVDs, gray trousers, light blue shirt, socks, and then his boots that Lin Ching had polished for him. He also put on his gunbelt. He really felt no need to do so, except that he had been wearing his gun when he left the boardinghouse. Then, before a mirror, Lowery neatly combed his thick mop of sandy hair before he donned his gray hat. He gave Ching a fifty-cent piece, thus tipping the man twenty cents. As he left the bath, Ching nodded vigorously after him.

"Thank you, Mr. Lowery; come again soon."

The wash up, shave, and clean clothes recharged Frank Lowery. He felt energetic and satisfied, and he walked briskly up the boardwalk sidewalk toward the constable's office. He would inquire about a possible telegram from Egan and he would then go on to the Broadway Cafe to meet Clara for some afternoon coffee. Some of the few people and merchants about Broadway on this quiet afternoon greeted Lowery with friendly gestures and smiles as he strode past them. They were happy to see the man working for Marshal Egan, because Lowery had thus far proven to be an asset.

When Frank stepped into the constable's office, he saw Hutchinson at his desk playing solitaire. "Any word from the marshal?"

"No," Hutchinson said.

Lowery nodded. "I've covered all the ground I could in Pawnee County, but I still haven't got an inkling of Kinney's whereabouts. I'm going to the telegraph office to send the marshal a wire."

Hutchinson nodded. "Maybe Bronco and his outlaws have left the county or even the territory. The best we can do now is to send those composites everywhere and hope that somebody somewhere will recognize those bandits."

"I guess so," Lowery said.

"Has Marshal Egan identified them others yet?" the constable asked.

"Only Bronco Kinney and Jim Clayborn for sure, but we're pretty certain that Kid Carver, Rowdy Joe Wheeler and this Colorado McGuire were the others in on those two robberies." Lowery sighed. "After I send the wire, I'm going to the Broadway Cafe for some coffee."

"Coffee?" the constable grinned. "You ain't had nothin' to eat yet, have you, Mr. Lowery?"

"I am hungry, but I'll be having supper with a young lady about five," Frank said, "and I don't want to spoil my appetite. After my coffee, I'm going back to Mae's Boardinghouse, if anybody's looking for me."

"All right," Hutchinson said. "I'll know where you'll be in case the marshal sends a reply to your telegram."

The constable watched Lowery leave the office and then returned to his game of solitaire.

Lowery had only been gone five minutes when Isa Hutchinson heard the neigh of a horse outside. He rose from the chair and stared out of the open jailhouse door, where he saw a tall thin man tethering a roan horse. The constable was surprised by the man's neatness: clean chino trousers, groomed shirt, and sparkling boots. But the gunbelt impressed Hutchinson the most. It hung low, with the holster tied tightly on the right thigh. The lawman almost came around the desk, but the man had already come inside.

"Good afternoon," Kid Carver smiled. "I'm lookin' for a deputy marshal, Frank Lowery. Is he in Stillwater or has he gone back to Guthrie?"

Hutchinson squinted suspiciously at the stranger. "You a friend of his?"

"We used to ride together at the QB ranch," Carver lied. "I was passin' through Stillwater on my way to Guthrie. I heard that Lowery was workin' for Marshal Egan and I don't want to miss him if he's in Stillwater instead of down in Guthrie. I understand he's been workin' around Stillwater."

Hutchinson shrugged. "He's still in town. He just went to the Broadway Cafe for a cup of coffee. It's just up the street and you can probably catch him there. But if he's gone, he said he'd go back to the boardin' house."

"What boardin' house would that be, constable?"

"Mae's place on 10th Street," Hutchinson said. "You couldn't miss it, a big two-story place, painted white, with a sign on the front porch. Mrs. Crawford is always there, but you'll need to pull the bell handle real hard, because she can't hear too well anymore."

"I'm obliged," Carver said, tipping his hat. "Do you mind if I leave my horse outside? I won't be long."

The lawman shrugged. "I guess not." He watched the stranger leave and he then reseated himself to resume his game of solitaire.

Kid Carver ambled swiftly up the boardwalk, his boots literally clattering on the wooden planks. He glanced into the wide dirt street and nodded to himself. There was little or no traffic, all the activity being usually in the morning or after the sun went down. Most people had returned to their businesses, homes, ranches, or farms by now. But a quiet street suited Kid Carver just fine for what he had in mind.

Carver finally stopped in front of the Broadway Cafe and peeked through one of the large front plate glass windows. He saw Lowery sitting with Clara Beaufort at one of the tables, where they both sipped coffee. Inside, Frank frowned, wondering why this man was looking at them through the window. A moment later, Carver came inside and walked up to the table.

"Hello, Clara." Carver looked at the girl. Then he stared at her companion. "And you, too; Frank Lowery, ain't it?"

Lowery nodded, but Clara Beaufort gaped in astonishment and then threw her hands to her face.

"Don't you remember me, Mr. Lowery?"

Lowery frowned and then stared. Carver! The man who had been with Clara in the Star Saloon and then had tried to wheedle him into the Bronco gang—a man who was probably an outlaw, although Frank had no real proof. When Lowery did not answer, Carver leaned forward and grinned.

"Lowery, I don't give a damn what you do, but some

176

things just ain't right—like havin' a time with my woman while I was away on business. You musta known that Clara was my girl. I was told that you even wanted her to move to Guthrie, so's you two could be together." He glared at the girl. "I heard you even went to bed with this man. Is that true?"

Clara Beaufort did not answer, but Frank glowered at the man. "Clara doesn't belong to anybody, not to you, not to me, not to anybody. What she does is none of your business."

"I say different," Carver answered, straightening his lanky frame. "You and me, we got business, Lowery—gun-shootin' business. I'm callin' you out, mister, and when I'm done, Clara is comin' with me."

"Are you crazy?" Lowery said, rising from his chair. "I don't even know you, and Clara can make up her own mind."

"Well, I know you, and I know what you done with my woman," Carver said, again glaring at the girl and then surveying the others inside the cafe: five patrons, the waitress, and the cook, all of whom stared at the trio at the table.

"This man is a louse," Kid Carver shouted to those inside as he gestured at Frank Lowery. "He's a low-down, no-good, connivin', lyin' son of a bitch. He ain't got no business livin', even if some o' you think so." He slapped his holster and looked once more at Lowery. "Well, you coyote, are you comin' outside or ain't you?"

"I have no business with you."

"Scared, ain't you? You're a coward, just like I figured." He looked at Clara again. "Is this the kinda man you took up with?" He looked smugly at Lowery again. "You an' your high talk about how fast you are with a

177

gun," he scoffed. "Maybe you got some people thinkin' you're quick and straight, but you don't scare me. Now, are you comin' out, or ain't you?"

"Walt," Clara screamed, "I told you I didn't want no more to do with you, not with you or with them you run with. I told you to stay outta my life from now on and I meant it. You got no call comin' in here and making such a scene."

"A scene is it?" Carver grinned. "You and this fancy pants makin' out like he's a man, when he ain't nothin' but a mouse?"

"You better calm down, Carver," Lowery said. His voice had calmed and he spoke softly and deliberately. "You're not asking me, but I'll give you some advice anyway. Get out of here and ride back to wherever you came from. And stay away from Clara. She told you she wanted nothing more to do with you, and she has a right to do as she pleases."

"Like goin' to bed with a coyote like you?"

"That's enough," Lowery warned. "I suggest you leave here before you get yourself into real trouble."

"Why, tin star man?" Carver scoffed again. "You gonna arrest me for callin' you out? Are you tryin' to hide behind that badge?"

"He's just tryin' to talk some sense into you, Walt," Clara said.

Kid Carver heaved a deep sigh. Then, without an inkling of warning, he lashed out at Clara, slapping her hard across the face so viciously that she fell backwards in her chair and onto the floor. Frank Lowery instinctively dropped next to her, held her cheek, and then saw the blood on his hand.

"There was no reason for that," Frank said.

But Kid Carver only grinned again. "If you want to do anything about it, why I'll be waitin' outside. I'll wait one minute, and if you ain't out by then, I'll know I've been talkin' to the biggest louse and coward in the territory. You hear that?" the Kid screamed at the stunned patrons and employees in the cafe. "This man is the biggest louse and coward in the Oklahoma Territory. That's what he is!" He pointed emphatically at Frank Lowery. Then he darted out of the cafe.

Frank Lowery carefully hoisted Clara Beaufort to her feet, took out a handkerchief, and wiped away the blood from her cheek. "You wait here, Clara; I'll be back."

"No, Frank, no!" Clara gripped his arm anxiously. "He's a gunman; he kills as a profession. You can't believe how fast he is. Don't go out there."

"You wait here," Lowery answered soberly.

As soon as Frank left, a clattering din erupted inside of the eating place. Tables, chairs, and silverware thudded and clanked as the five patrons, the waitresses, and even the chef rushed headlong to the front of the Broadway Cafe and peered anxiously out of the two big plate glass windows or the open door. They stared in silence, looking first at Kid Carver standing alone in the middle of the street, and then at Frank Lowery, who walked diagonally away from the cafe before he too stopped in the middle of the street and turned to face Carver, some fifty yards away.

Clara Beaufort, however, only sat silently at the table, her head buried in her hands while she sobbed alone in distressed solitude. She feared the worst for Frank Lowery. While she had heard of his ability with a gun, she knew positively of Carver's swift draw.

"Anytime you're ready, louse," Kid Carver cried.

"You did the calling, mister," Frank Lowery answered, placing the fingers of his right hand only inches from his holstered gun. As Carver took a pace forward, Frank also advanced, until they had come within thirty yards of each other. But now, Kid Carver licked his lips. He saw no fear in his adversary's eyes, no anxiety; only a calm, steady stare. Suddenly, it was Kid Carver who was not sure of himself. He glanced about the street where a dozen people and shop owners now stood immobile, like wax statuettes, while they stared in fascination at the drama in the middle of the street.

Kid Carver looked again at Frank Lowery, but the same stoic expression remained in Lowery's gray eyes and on his face. Carver felt a nervous twinge inside of him. Perhaps he had made a mistake, but he knew he could not back off now.

"I'm waiting, Mr. Carver."

The Kid glanced once more at the awed crowd and then reached for his gun. He had barely whipped the weapon out of his holster before two quick shots echoed through the quiet thoroughfare. Two bullets struck the Kid squarely in the chest in rapid succession. One slug hit the heart and the other his right lung. Kid Carver's body snapped backwards in two tandem jerks and he fell full length to the ground, flat on his back with his arms and legs spread-eagled. His unfired gun lay beside him. Frank Lowery came forward and looked down at the instantly dead Kid Carver. Then he scanned the crowd.

"Somebody get the mortician."

Chapter Eleven

Shortly after the gunfight in Stillwater, Constable Hutchinson took it upon himself to report the incident to Marshal Egan in a telegram. When Egan read the wire on the shootout, he fumed in anger and he sent a quick telegram to his deputy, ordering Lowery to return to Guthrie in the morning. Still, despite the apparent reproof in store for him, Lowery still took Clara to the evening meal at the Broadway Cafe. They said little to each other. After the repast, Frank and Clara walked back to Mae's Boardinghouse, where Frank would pack his things to leave town the next day. Clara hooked her arm through her companion's crooked elbow.

"I'm real sad about this, Frank," the girl said.

"It wasn't your fault," Lowery answered.

"Yes, it was," Clara said. "If I hadn't been tied to Walt, there wouldn't o' been no need for that gunfight." She looked sympathetically at Frank. "And now I got you in trouble with the marshal. What'll he do to you Frank? Will he fire you?"

"I don't think so," Lowery said. "He'll probably give me a good tongue lashing, and I suppose I'll have it coming. I'd guess this kind of thing won't sit well with those people in Washington who run the Federal Marshal Service. And I suppose there'll be a lot of talk around Stillwater; me getting into a gunfight in a row over you."

"I'm sorry it happened, Frank," the girl said. "I know how much you love this new job."

When Frank and Clara reached the boardinghouse, Frank stopped only momentarily at room 26, while the girl looked up at him. "Do you want to come in?"

"I've got to pack," Frank said, "and then I'll need to get some sleep. I'll have to leave early in the morning." The girl nodded and watched Frank Lowery walk into his own room.

The hour was already late, past nine o'clock, and Frank was tired as well as rattled from the confrontation with Kid Carver. He had been out for two days, covering a radius of twenty-five miles of territory, while he looked for a lead on the whereabouts of Bronco Kinney and his men. He had ridden through the northeastern and northern areas above Stillwater, talking to nearly twenty people as he sought a hint of the hiding place of the outlaws. He had spoken to ranchers, trappers, and even a few drifters, but none of them had seen anyone answering the description of Bronco Kinney or Jim Clayborn. Frank had even stopped at the QB Ranch for a short visit with Moses and Rosie Barker and with foreman Jed Stevens and his son Billie.

Frank had found those at the ranch quite warm and friendly, and happy to see him. Still, he had declined an invitation to stay on for supper or to stay overnight, again claiming that he needed to return to Stillwater to send a telegram to Marshal Egan in Guthrie.

The last thing Frank had needed after galivanting all over the territory for two days was a gunfight with Kid

Carver in the waning afternoon.

Now, Frank washed up with water in the basin and then stripped down to his BVDs. He was about to climb into bed when a knock came at the door. Lowery opened it and saw Clara Beaufort standing there. She was clad in a long nightgown that reached to her feet, and she wore a smile on her face.

"Frank," she whispered, "can I come in?"

Lowery pursed his lips and opened the door wide to let her inside. Here, after Frank closed the door, she moved close to him. "I can see that you're ready for bed, too." She threw her arms around him and kissed him. "I don't want to be alone tonight," she whispered. "I'd like to curl up with you to keep me warm and comfortable."

Frank and the girl spent the night in his room.

When Lowery awoke at daylight, he peered through the window. He hoisted himself out of bed and hastily dressed. He had just finished when Clara herself awoke, slid out of bed, and smoothed out her nightgown so it hung over the full length of her body. She walked up to Frank and kissed him on the back of his neck as he was washing. Frank jerked and then turned.

"I'm going to my room to dress, Frank. Then can we go to breakfast?"

"Sure," Frank said. He opened the door and peeked into the hallway. "Nobody out there." The girl nodded and left the room.

By seven o'clock, after breakfast at the Broadway Cafe, they returned to the boardinghouse. Clara stood in the back yard as Frank led his packed horse from the stable. She only stared as he climbed aboard the animal and then reached down to squeeze her hand. "I don't know when I'll be back from Guthrie, but I'll keep in touch,

I promise."

Clara nodded and watched Frank clod out of the yard.

Three hours later, in Guthrie, Frank walked into the marshal's office. Egan met the deputy with a mixture of eagerness and anger. "I'm glad you're here, Frank, but I must tell you, I was shocked when I got that telegram from Constable Hutchinson tellin' me you were in a shootout. That's the last thing we want from one of our deputies: a gunfight in the middle of the street. What possessed you to do anything like that, anyway? That kinda thing don't look good for our office, but worse, you coulda been killed."

"He didn't give me any choice," Frank said. "I told Carver I didn't want any trouble, but he kept pushing me into a fight. If I didn't take up the challenge, our reputation could have been hurt real bad."

"Why the hell would he want a gunfight with you, anyway?"

"Frank's got a fast gun," Jack Stone suddenly said with a grin, "and I suppose there will always be those who want to challenge him."

Lowery sighed in relief. Stone's assumption had freed Lowery of the necessity of telling Egan the truth—that the fight had been over a girl, whose own reputation was suspect.

"Well, Frank," Egan said, "let's hope it don't happen again." Then he gestured. "Now, did you get any clues on the Bronco Kinney gang?"

"I must have rode over a hundred miles during those two days. I talked to all kinds of people, but nobody saw Bronco; nor had they any idea where the gang might have gone from Ingalls. Kinney and his men must be holed up somewhere in the Cimarron hills, but God only knows where."

"Well, I don't think there's any use of going in there now," Egan said. "We'll wait until we get a lead on their whereabouts. Anyway, we could use a little rest, especially you, Frank, since you've been ridin' all over hell for the past few days."

Marshal Fred Egan would not wait long for a new lead on the Kinney gang, for they were already planning a new robbery from their Cimarron hills hideout on Miller Creek. The man Crandall had called on Bronco at the dugout on the same day that Lowery had returned to Guthrie. Crandall reported the astonishing death of Kid Carver in his shootout with Frank Lowery, and he told Bronco that the Stillwater Farmer's Bank had received $40,000 in payroll money, while Lowery himself had returned to Guthrie.

"There ain't no law around Stillwater right now except for that old constable, and that bank'll be easy to take."

"He's right, Bronco," Rowdy Joe Wheeler said. "Besides, I'm gettin' tired o' holin' up here with nothin' to do but play cards."

"But we've already got plenty 'a money," Jim Clayborn said, "and now we've even got Kid Carver's share."

"Listen," Rowdy Joe pointed out, "if we take that bank with all that money, why we'd have enough cash to last all of us a near lifetime. We could break up the gang and go our separate ways, and we could lose the law forever. For myself, I'd go to San Francisco, where I'd sure get lost in that big town and no marshal would ever catch up to me. You fellows could go to some other big towns, like

185

Chicago or even New York to get lost; change your names, and nobody would ever find you. There's all kindsa places now where you can change your appearance. There's McCarthy's place in Enid, and there's another place in Wichita."

"Rowdy Joe's right," Bronco Kinney said. "He makes a lotta sense. We could be set for life with the cash in the Stillwater bank added to what we already have. I say we hit the bank in the morning."

"I say we ought to do it," Colorado McGuire now spoke. He looked at Clayborn. "Well, Jim, don't this make sense?"

Jim Clayborn sighed and then nodded. "All right, I'll go along."

The four outlaws left their hideout in the Cimarron hills before dawn the next morning. By the time they'd gone fifteen miles, the sun had risen over the hills behind them. Jim Clayborn squinted up at the sky before he studied the wide plain that stretched from the Cimarron River and all the way southward to Stillwater. Then he looked at Bronco Kinney.

"Ain't we movin' a little too slow?"

"No," the leader answered. "We want to get there about ten. The heavy mornin' bank business will be over by then, and we won't likely see too many customers in the place. The streets themselves will be as busy as a hive and nobody will even notice us come into town. Like Crandall said: he studied the bank and figured that ten o'clock was the best time to hit it. If all goes well, we'll be outta town before anybody even knows the bank was robbed."

"Unless there's shootin'," Rowdy Joe said.

"If we do this right, there won't be no shootin',"

Bronco answered. "We'll have no need to shoot. Them people workin' in those banks don't want to get killed for somebody else's money."

The group moved on and by nine o'clock they could see the town of Stillwater ahead. Bronco Kinney motioned to the others; they followed him off the road and into a clump of trees to rest and to review their plans. They had eaten breakfast earlier, devouring a meager fare of salted beef jerky, coffee, and biscuits. They dismounted, tethered their mounts to the branches of trees, and then gathered in a circle.

"Now," Bronco gestured, "I hope everybody knows what to do. We can't have no mistakes. Is there anybody who's not sure?"

Jim Clayborn frowned.

"What's the matter?" Kinney asked.

"I don't like the idea of robbin' sodbusters and miners who have money in the bank. They work hard, and it don't seem right."

Bronco Kinney grinned. "Christ, you're worryin' about that now? You agreed to come along. Anyway, we ain't stealin' much from them, so to speak. That bank don't usually have more'n a couple thousand dollars on deposit from miners and farmers. All that money in there belongs to the Pawnee Mining Company, like Crandall said. If they lose it, why they'll only get some more for wages. It'll only mean that those workers will need to have a delay before gettin' paid."

"Bronco's right." McGuire now spoke. "Those miners won't be the losers in this heist, only the minin' company. As for the sodbusters, most of 'em don't have but a few dollars in that bank, and they won't be out much. Besides, it'd serve 'em right. This is cattle and minin' country, not farmland."

When none of the others spoke, Bronco continued. "We'll go over this one more time and make sure there ain't no mistakes. Colorado will go in first, like a cowpuncher to deposit money. Jim and me will come in next, and we'll lock the door after us and pull down the shades. Rowdy Joe will stay outside with the horses near the tether post in front of the haberdashery shop. That won't draw no suspicions."

Wheeler screwed up his face. "I don't like bein' outside. I'd rather come into the bank with the rest o' you."

"Somebody's got to stay outside," Bronco pointed out, "and you're quite good at handlin' horses. Besides, you got eyes like a cougar. You can spot anything suspicious in a second, and that's the kind o' man I want as a lookout." He stared at the others. "Remember, we don't want nobody even hurt, much less killed. Stealin' is one thing; killin' could bring the whole territory down on us."

The others listened.

"Now," Bronco continued, "once inside the bank and we make them understand that this is a hold-up, we get the chief cashier to open the vault. He'll likely be at the desk to the left o' the teller cages. We'll also have to make sure there ain't nobody in the private office behind the chief cashier, somebody who could get out the back door and get help." He looked at McGuire. "Don't waste no time. You got to gag and tie up anybody inside in a hurry and then leave 'em flat on the floor behind the teller cages."

McGuire nodded.

"That's all we'll do to anybody inside," Bronco waved

his arm emphatically, "nothin' more. Once we get the vault open, me and Clayborn will clean off the shelves. When we leave, we'll split up, ridin' off in two groups and meetin' back at our hideout sometime tomorrow."

"It's pretty clear, Bronco," Colorado McGuire said.

"Okay, let's go," Kinney said. "We should be gettin' into town at just about ten o'clock."

The four riders mounted up and again loped slowly toward Stillwater. If there was any uneasiness among any of those in the gang, none showed any fear or uncertainty. Colorado McGuire did reach into his saddlebag to make sure he had the gags and the pieces of rope to tie up whoever was inside the bank. Bronco, meanwhile, checked his own saddlebags to make sure he had the sacks in which to stuff the money they expected to take from the Stillwater Farmers Bank. All of the gang members checked their kerchiefs, making certain they could quickly cover their faces once inside the bank.

As the riders came down Broadway, they could not help but notice the bustle on Stillwater's main thoroughfare. General stores were doing a good business as merchants loaded supplies on wagons for surrounding sodbusters and cattlemen. Men on horseback, in pairs, groups, or singly, cantered along the wide main street. Ambling along the wooden sidewalks were men going about their business, women with shopping baskets, other men in their neat business suits. Some of the saloons were already open, and drifters, cowhands, and others were already at the bars drinking or sitting at tables to play cards. The cafes were also catering to customers, although early morning business had long ago abated.

Soon, Colorado reared his horse in front of the

haberdashery shop a few doors up from the bank. Bronco Kinney, Jim Clayborn, and Rowdy Joe Wheeler came over to McGuire before the four men dismounted, Wheeler taking the reins. They loitered there, waiting until Rowdy Joe had a good grip on the reins before Kinney, McGuire, and Clayborn strode onto the boardwalk and walked slowly toward the bank.

Three people came out of the bank and moved up the boardwalk just as Colorado McGuire reached the door of the building. The outlaw appreciated this exodus by the trio of patrons, because it meant there might be fewer people inside the bank. He entered the building, glanced about quickly, and half nodded. He saw only two customers there, along with a teller behind the cage and a man sitting at the desk to the right of the cages. Then, astonishingly, Colorado also saw the door to the vault wide open.

McGuire pulled his bandana over his face, stopping just below the eyes, and he then pulled down the brim of his hat. Quickly, he walked to the right of the cages to the man at the desk behind the railing.

"Just sit right there, mister." He brandished his gun at the chief cashier.

The three others in the bank gaped at the pointed weapon and stood immobile for a moment. Only seconds later, Bronco Kinney and Jim Clayborn came into the bank, pulling up their bandanas as they came through the door. This twosome also aimed guns at the startled group inside. Bronco gestured to Clayborn who swiftly yanked down the dark shades on the two front windows and the door. He then snapped up the lock hasp, but he had done so too quickly and carelessly, and the hasp had not caught. Unknown to the outlaw, the door had not locked.

Bronco advanced deeper into the room with Clayborn and he too gaped in elated surprise when he saw the vault door open. The job would be a hundred percent easier. Bronco stood put momentarily, while McGuire spoke again.

"We want everybody behind the cages and on the floor, and we'll shoot the first one of you who utters a sound. Now move it!" he barked.

No one resisted, nor did anyone scream or shout. Without hesitation, the two bank employees and the two customers, fearfully staring at the pointed weapons, moved behind the counters. Bronco, meanwhile, looked at the door marked private beyond the desk. He then came behind the cages and scoffed at the chief cashier.

"Who's in there?" he demanded.

"N-nobody," the chief cashier stuttered.

"Don't lie," Bronco said, raising his weapon in a threatening gesture.

"That's Mr. Crawford's office, but he isn't in there this morning. He's gone to Enid on business."

"I'm tellin' you somethin', mister," Bronco said. "If anybody comes through that door, we're gonna shoot him dead and then shoot you dead. Now, are you still sure there ain't nobody in there?"

"N-no, sir, honest," the man insisted.

The teller nodded vigorously in agreement, so Bronco Kinney was satisfied. "Okay," he gestured to McGuire, "gag them." Then he cocked his head at Clayborn. "Let's get in that vault."

Quickly and efficiently, Colorado McGuire forced the four onto the floor, flat on their stomachs. Then, methodically, he took his prepared gags and ran them around the mouths of the prisoners, tying them on the napes of their heads. Just as quickly, he tied the two foot pieces of cord around the wrists of the foursome behind their backs. McGuire half grinned, pleased at his quick work.

In the meantime, Bronco and Clayborn had entered the vault where they now grabbed the bound packs of bills and stuffed them into bags. The money was mostly in ten- and twenty-dollar denominations, and this pleased Kinney quite well. These small bills would enable them to dispose of the loot with a minimum of difficulty. However, the job required more time than they had planned on, necessitating the use of four sacks instead of the expected two. Still, without stopping to ogle at the huge haul, the two men worked quickly, and within three minutes they had cleaned off the shelves inside the vault. When they came out, Kinney glanced at the four bound people on the floor and then turned to Colorado McGuire and Jim Clayborn.

"Okay, let's go."

They moved swiftly across the floor toward the front entrance. But before they reached it, the door suddenly swung open. A man and a boy had come innocently into the bank. The man was the foreman of the QB Ranch, Jed Stevens, and the boy was his son Billie. The pair stood in utter shock when they saw the three masked bandits, all of them aiming guns and two of them carrying sacks of money. The boy gaped at McGuire, apparently recognizing him, despite the bandana over his face. Billie Stevens could not mistake the man's deep-set, penetrating hazel eyes.

"Mr. McGuire? What are you doin' here?" the boy gasped.

Now, Jed Stevens also peered hard at this man holding

the gun, and he too recognized the former QB Ranch hand. "My God, Colorado, have you takin' to robbin' banks? Is that what you've been doin' since you left the QB Ranch?"

Colorado McGuire felt the perspiration dampen his face and he felt a shudder jerk his entire body. He looked at his two cohorts, who only stared at him, and McGuire could see the ire in their eyes. They were obviously upset and angry because the two unexpected visitors to the bank had recognized him. Colorado's companions stood motionless, too shocked to move.

"McGuire?" Jed Stevens said again.

Colorado took a deep breath, straightened, and then aimed his .45 at Jed Stevens and his son. Then, without a word, he simply fired in rapid succession, four shots, two slugs striking young Billie in the chest and face and the other pair of bullets hitting Jed Stevens in the abdomen. The sudden burst of gunfire shattered the near silence inside the bank, and prompted those bound and gagged prisoners behind the cages to stir uneasily. Were those bandits now going to kill them all?

The close-range hits on young Billie had thrown the youth backwards, as though he had been struck with a huge sledge hammer. The boy slammed against the bank door as spurts of blood suddenly covered his face and chest, as though saturated with a heavy torrent of deep red paint. He bounced off the door and crumpled to the floor, killed instantly.

Jed Stevens fared no better. The two slugs that hit him blew away tatters of his coat and white shirt before heavy smears of blood quickly covered his torso. He staggered backward, but not as far as the door, before he too collapsed. His eyes rolled into marbled orbs before he fell

193

to the floor, dead.

McGuire's companions stared in utter dismay. There was to have been no shooting on this caper, no killing, and especially not a twelve-year-old boy as one of the victims. Further the men now realized that the four shots might draw people to the bank, if only out of curiosity. They remained rigid, however, uncertain. But then McGuire shoved the body of the boy away from the door and turned to the others.

"Let's get out of here."

Colorado opened the door and darted outside, the others following him. McGuire rushed up the street toward the haberdashery shop and leaped quickly atop his horse as Rowdy Joe Wheeler eyed him curiously.

"What happened back there?" Wheeler asked. "I heard shots."

But McGuire could already see people coming toward the bank, people who had obviously heard the shots and now hurried to investigate. Without a word, McGuire kicked the flanks of his horse and seconds later he was in a full run. Rowdy Joe stood uneasily, wondering why his outlaw companion had dashed off in near panic.

But Bronco Kinney and Joe Clayborn had been right behind McGuire, also dashing full speed toward their horses in front of the haberdashery shop, carrying the bags of money. Rowdy Joe now hesitated no longer. He mounted his horse as the other two shoved the money bags into their saddlebags and clambered atop their horses.

"What happened? What was the shootin' about?" Wheeler asked.

"That dumb asshole McGuire," Bronco cursed. "I'll tell you about it later. Right now we've got to get the hell outta here."

Wheeler never hesitated. He reared his horse and quickly followed Kinney and Clayborn who sped up the street, scattering the crowds: men with wagons, pedestrians, and men on loping horses. A dozen merchants and their customers had ducked out of business places to stare at the trio who galloped swiftly past them, leaving a cloud of dust on Broadway.

The four were well out of town before several townspeople came into the bank and gaped in astonishment at the bloody corpses on the floor. They advanced further when they heard the struggles and muffled moans of the others behind the teller cages. Three men quickly untied and ungagged them, while one of the rescuers turned to a fourth man.

"Get Constable Hutchinson."

The man nodded and darted out of the bank. He ran swiftly up the street, while others filtered into the bank. The courier soon reached the jailhouse and burst inside. The constable was leisurely scanning some papers at his desk and he looked up.

"Isa," the visitor panted, "a gang of outlaws just robbed the bank and left two people dead."

"What?" Hutchinson barked, bounding to his feet.

"They're a bloody mess." The man shook his head. "The bandits just tied up the others. I don't know why they'd kill them two: one a man and the other one just a kid."

"Oh my God," Hutchinson hissed.

Within two minutes, Constable Isa Hutchinson had waddled swiftly to the bank and waded through the crowd of some twenty-five to thirty people who were now jammed inside the bank. The constable first peered down at the two bloodied corpses and then gestured to the crowd.

"Somebody get these bodies to the undertaker and then we'll clean the floor." He waited a few moments until six willing men picked up the bodies of Jed Stevens and his son Billie and carried them out of the bank as the spectators stared. Then Hutchinson sought the two employees of the bank and the two patrons who had been in the place at the time of the robbery. He looked at the chief cashier, who had now returned to his post behind the desk.

"What happened?"

"They worked as smooth as silk," the chief cashier said. "They just came in, pulled down the shade, and bound and gagged the four of us behind the cages before they cleaned out the vault."

"Four of you?" Hutchinson asked. "What about the two dead?"

The cashier shook his head. "That was shocking, Isa, real shocking. I have no idea why they killed them. Jed Stevens and his son must have come into the bank accidentally because the bandits didn't lock the door like they was supposed to. The outlaws must have panicked and shot them. They could've killed us, too, and we feared they might do just that after we heard those shots. But I don't think they wanted to hurt anybody, much less kill somebody."

"You're probably right about that," the constable nodded.

"Generally, these kinds of bandits never want to cause harm, because they know what killings mean," the chief cashier continued. "It means that lawmen will hunt them down with a vengeance. I just don't understand why they'd want to kill Jed Stevens and his boy."

Hutchinson shook his head. "I better get right over to the telegraph office and wire Marshal Egan."

Chapter Twelve

When the telegram from Constable Hutchinson reached Fred Egan in Guthrie, the marshal read the message in horror. The robbery itself was bad enough, but to kill the ranch foreman and his son in cold blood was an absolute outrage. Egan could not understand the killings, since the bandits had taken the time to carefully bind the two customers and the two bank employees without harming them. Why would they kill these two innocents, who had inadvertently walked into the bank during the hold-up? Why hadn't they simply tied up the man and his son as the bandits had tied up the others?

After Egan himself read the wire from Stillwater, he allowed his deputies to read it. Jack Stone was shocked, but Frank Lowery was absolutely stunned. Lowery had always liked Stevens and his boy and their cold-blooded murders aroused an almost uncontrollable rage inside of him.

"I want to go after those killers right away, Marshal," Frank said.

"Take it easy," Egan answered. "I understand how you feel, but going off like a madman isn't going to do any good."

"At least, let me go to Stillwater. I'll ride hard and pick up their trail. Somebody had to see them leave town, and maybe they can tell me which way they were headed."

"We can't go off half cocked," Egan insisted. "I'll ride up there right now and talk to those people who were in the bank; see if I can't find out who those bandits were."

"I'd like to go with you. Please, Marshal, let me come."

Egan pursed his lips and then nodded. "All right, Frank. Get some gear packed and meet me here in an hour." Then Egan turned to Stone. "Jack, get another posse formed. You can start out tomorrow morning at first light and you should be up in Stillwater about noon tomorrow. Tell the men they might be on the trail for two or three days, same as last time. I'll meet you at the Stillwater jailhouse."

"Don't worry," Stone answered, "we'll be there."

By noon, Marshal Egan and Deputy Frank Lowery had saddled their horses and packed bedrolls with extra clothes and other paraphernalia. They planned to stay overnight at Mae's Boardinghouse and then on the trail for two or three days. After they loped out of Guthrie and moved north, they traveled at a rather swift pace, trotting the horses most of the way, galloping for short distances, and walking the animals only minimally. By dark they reached Stillwater.

Egan quickly found the chief cashier and the teller, who accompanied the pair of lawmen to the now closed-for-the-day bank. Inside, Egan and Lowery found the premises quite clean, for some volunteers had cleaned away the bloodstains and put the area back in order. The bank vault was closed. While Lowery studied the interior, Egan spoke to the bank employees.

"Am I right to assume that Jed Stevens and his boy

were not in the bank when the bandits came in?"

"That's right, Marshal," the cashier said. "They came in when the robbers were getting ready to leave. I think the bandits miscalculated in not locking the door and the QB Ranch foreman surprised them."

Egan sighed. "They could have tied them up and left them with the rest of you. Were the bandits wearing masks?"

"They were," the cashier nodded.

"Then I don't understand." The marshal shook his head.

"I'll tell you why, Marshal." The teller suddenly spoke. "I think Stevens and his son recognized one of the bandits. I was lying on the floor behind the cages, true, and I didn't see nothin'. But, I did hear because I have good ears. I heard the boy cry out the name o' one o' them robbers. Then I heard Jed Stevens repeat the name. He said somethin' like 'are you robbin' banks now? Is that what you've been doin' since you stopped cowpunchin'?' Next, I heard four shots."

"The name? What name?" Egan asked anxiously.

"I didn't get it clear, Marshal," the teller said. "The boy called the robber Mac somethin', and then Mr. Stevens called him Mac somethin', too. He was the one who said somethin' like 'did you quit ranchin' to take up bank robbin'.' Somethin' o' that nature."

Egan stroked his chin. "Mac; Mac."

"Like I said," the teller repeated, "Mr. Stevens and his boy knew the bandit. I'd swear to it."

Now Frank Lowery frowned and looked at the marshal. "Jed was the foreman of the QB Ranch. If he and his son recognized one of these bandits behind a mask, they knew him very well. Jed and the boy didn't come into town too often, so it couldn't have been someone from town. It had to be somebody they knew at the ranch."

"But Mac something; who the hell would that be?"

Frank Lowery concentrated and stared up at the ceiling as he fell into deep thought. He knew most of the hands at the QB Ranch, and he repeated their names mentally to himself as fast as he could remember them. Then, paying especial attention to Mac, his eyes suddenly widened and he pointed to Egan.

"I think I know who it was. He left the QB some time ago." He looked at the bank teller. "Would the name have been McGuire? Colorado McGuire?"

"That's it, deputy, that's it! McGuire!"

"Frank," Egan said excitedly, "he's one of the suspected members of the Bronco gang—Colorado McGuire."

"Yes," the teller repeated, "I remember Stevens callin' the name McGuire."

"Damn it," Lowery scowled, "that means it was the Bronco gang who held up this bank today."

Egan sighed. "They probably went to some hideaway in the Cimarron hills. I'd like to catch them before they leave the territory, but that posse won't be here until tomorrow."

"Let me start after them right now," Lowery said.

"No, we'll have to wait for the posse." Then Egan looked at the chief cashier and teller. "I want you to come to the constable's office tomorrow and give statements. If you know who those others were in the bank with you, I'd like you to bring them with you. Either my deputy or myself will be at the jailhouse during all of tomorrow morning."

The bank employees nodded.

200

Egan and Lowery left the bank. The marshal turned to his deputy. "Frank, I'm goin' to the telegraph office. I'll meet you in the jailhouse in about a half hour. Go there; ask Hutchinson if he has any other information. You might talk to a few people around town to see if they can tell you anything."

Lowery nodded and turned. But as he walked toward the Stillwater lock up, the rage boiled inside of him again. Jed Stevens and his son were dead, victims of the Bronco gang. He had already taken Carver, and by the time he reached the jailhouse, he had made up his mind to go after the other four at once, even if he had to go alone. He was not about to wait until Jack Stone got here tomorrow from Guthrie. The outlaws' trail might be cold by then, and the gang could get clear out of the territory.

When Lowery reached the jailhouse, he found Constable Hutchinson there, making out a report. The two prisoners were still inside the cells while they awaited trial. Hutchinson looked up and grinned at the visitor.

"Good evenin', Mr. Lowery."

"Constable," Frank said, "do you have any idea where those outlaws might have gone after they left the bank?"

"No," the lawman answered. "They just lit outta town, from what I was told."

"But what direction?" Lowery asked again, emphatically. "Didn't you question some people in the streets or in the shops who might have seen them ride away?"

Hutchinson stroked his chin. "Well, now that you mention it, seems that a couple o' storekeepers told me those bandits rode north; maybe toward Ingalls or Enid."

"Nothing more specific?"

"No, nothing at all," the constable said. "That's all I

201

could find out."

Frank Lowery left the jailhouse and strode about town, questioning a few people in the shops on Broadway and asking the same question: did they know where the bandits might have gone when they left town? But they could only give the deputy marshal the same information they had given Hutchinson: the robbers had apparently gone north, probably into the Cimarron badlands where they would be impossible to find.

Lowery then decided to stop into the Broadway Cafe, but he had barely reached the door when he heard a cry: "Frank! Frank!" Lowery turned to see Clara Beaufort hurrying across the street, weaving past the horses and wagons on the thoroughfare. Frank did not even speak when the girl reached him. Clara wore a sober look on her face.

"I suspected you'd be back in Stillwater right away," the girl said. "I've been kinda waitin' for you. I'm glad to see you."

Frank did not answer.

"I'm sorry about what happened at the bank today. Mae Crawford at the boardin' house told me the man and his son were good friends of yours."

"I must admit, I was shocked," Frank said.

"I wish there was something I could do, but I know there's nothin' I can say to make the hurt easier, short o' tellin' you where to find those killers."

Frank nodded.

"Come inside, Frank. Let me buy you some coffee."

"Why not," Frank shrugged.

On this early evening the cafe was a little crowded, but they found a table. After the waitress took their order for coffee and rolls, Clara looked about the place, studying the patrons there. Then her eyes locked on a man sitting alone at a corner table and eating a ham dinner. He was a small man, middle aged. The girl frowned, certain she knew him. She leaned from the table to take a closer look and then gaped.

"Clara? What's the matter?"

The girl gripped Lowery's wrist and stared hard at him. "Frank, maybe we can find out where those murderers went." Lowery frowned, puzzled. "That man sittin' in the corner: I know him. I've seen him talkin' to Bronco Kinney on a few occasions at the Cimarron Saloon in Ingalls, and I remember seein' him at Mae Crawford's Boardinghouse. Frank," her eyes widened, "he musta been the one who told Walt Carver about you and me, and he must be the one who's been feedin' information to Kinney."

Frank glanced at the small man and then turned to Clara. "Damn, I remember seeing him around the boardinghouse, too."

"His name, I believe, is Crandall; Marvin Crandall," Clara continued. "It wouldn't surprise me if he told Kinney that the Stillwater Farmers Bank was loaded with that payroll money."

"Sure," Frank hissed. "Why else would Bronco pick today to hit that bank, especially when he knows that Egan is out looking for him. But then, Kinney must also have known that I was recalled to Guthrie, and only Constable Hutchinson would be around today. He's the only man who could have known that, except the man at the telegraph office. This Crandall apparently pumps people around Stillwater for information that he brings back to Kinney."

"And if Kinney is not in Ingalls. . . ."

"Then this Crandall must have talked recently to Kinney at Bronco's hideout in the Cimarron hills."

"So it seems," Clara said.

"No doubt, Kinney headed for this hideaway as soon as he robbed the bank, and that man at the corner table knows where the place is located."

"What are you goin' to do, Frank?"

"Talk to him." Clara did not answer as Frank left the table and walked over to the small man, dropping into the chair opposite. The diner looked up, surprised, but he said nothing. Crandall stared at the deputy marshal's badge pinned on Frank's shirt.

"Is your name Crandall? Marvin Crandall?"

"What if it is," the man answered with forced bravado. But Frank could see the nervousness in his eyes and the uneasiness on his face.

"Do you know that Bronco Kinney and his gang are responsible for this recent killing and the robbery of nearly forty thousand at the bank today? And that they pulled off those robberies and the killing at Wells Fargo and the Abajo Springs Mining Company?" The man only pursed his lips, and Frank leaned over the table. "And I'm sure you know that I had a shootout with Kid Carver who came looking for me because he said I stole his girl. Now how could Carver have known that when he was holed up in Ingalls or some other hideout since the Abajo Springs robbery?"

"I-I d-don't know," Crandall stammered.

"Well, I recall now that you're staying at Mae's place, and I suspect you saw me and the girl there. I'd also guess that Carver learned about me and Clara from you. I'd also suspect that you told Bronco Kinney about the payroll money in the bank here and that I had left town."

"I d-don't know what y-you're talkin' about," the man fidgeted.

"Mister," Frank pointed menacingly, "all I have to do is to make a few inquiries around town: the bank, the telegraph office, the constable, or some of the business places. I could learn quick enough if you got answers to some of these questions. People may agree to keep quiet if you slip them a dollar or two, but they'll open up real quick to avoid getting involved in murder. I might say the same thing about you, Mr. Crandall. Do you want complicity in murder?"

"I had nothin' to do with murder, deputy," Crandall said anxiously.

"There seems to be some circumstantial evidence to indicate that you gave Bronco Kinney information to help him pull off this robbery today. That makes you an accessory to murder. We can hold you for twenty-four hours on mere suspicion, and that will give me plenty of time to check into your activities for the past week or two." He again grinned at the man. "You'll be in jail, while Kinney and his boys are free. Would you like that?"

"I didn't have nothin' to do with murder or robbery, I swear," Crandall said again. "All right, I'll give you information on Bronco Kinney, but I didn't know he was gonna rob a bank nor kill somebody."

"I could believe you and let you go," Frank gestured, "but only if you're willing to tell me the whole truth."

"The whole truth?"

"We know you didn't speak recently to Kinney in Ingalls, because he ran out of there when the posse showed up. No, you spoke to him after he skipped out of that town, and it had to be somewhere in the Cimarron

205

hills. Now, if you tell me where that is, why I might let you go."

"I-I don't k-know."

"Okay, if you want to lie," Frank shrugged. "I'll just have to take you over to the jailhouse and lock you up. I guarantee, by this time tomorrow, I'll have plenty of evidence on you to bring accessory to murder charges against you. And even worse, if Kinney finds out why you've been locked up, why he'll make sure you're dead before you can talk to the law."

"No, no," Crandall said. "All right, I'll tell you."

Frank took a pad and pencil from his pocket and handed it to Crandall. "You draw me a map, and start with the road north of Stillwater."

Crandall nodded and carefully drew a map: several miles northward out of Stillwater on the Stillwater-Ponco Road, then left at Belson's Bend, and four miles over Hunters Trail through the dense Cimarron forests, then across the Cimarron River, near a large boulder, then two more miles over the winding forest trail to Miller's Creek, a clearing across the creek, and then Kinney's dugout into a hillside.

Frank took the map. "Remember this, Crandall, if you're lying, your life won't be worth a nickel. No matter where you try to run, I'll find you, and you know what I can do with a gun."

"I ain't lyin', deputy, I swear. The map is as accurate as can be. You'll surely find Kinney, McGuire, Clayborn, and Wheeler all in that dugout."

"I believe you," Lowery said, rising from the chair. He folded and slipped the map into his shirt pocket. When he got back to his own table, he grinned. "I got all I need to know," he told Clara, "and I'm going after that gang."

"Right now?" the girl asked in surprise.

"First thing in the morning. If I leave at daybreak I can probably reach Kinney's hideaway by noontime."

"Please Frank," Clara gripped his wrist, "don't do it. Don't try to go in there alone. They'll kill you."

But Frank Lowery was not even listening. He had been enraged since he'd first learned of the cold-blooded murders of Jed and Billie Stevens. And now, he knew where these killers were. Perhaps he was somewhat irrational over the incident, but he was unwilling to wait very long before going after Kinney and the others.

Clara Beaufort now regretted her identification of the man Marvin Crandall, for Lowery could be a dead man before she saw him again. She continued to plead, imploring Frank to calm down, but he would not listen. He told Clara to go back to the boardinghouse and wait for him. He would seek permission from Egan to leave town the first thing in the morning, and then he would come to Mae's place.

When Lowery left the tearful Clara Beaufort standing alone in the street, he hurried to the jailhouse. Inside, Fred Egan was talking to Hutchinson, and when the marshal saw his deputy, he straightened. "Frank, where the hell have you been? I told you to meet me here a half hour ago."

"I'm sorry, Marshal," Lowery said.

"Well, I suppose it don't matter," Egan shrugged. "I've telegraphed Jack Stone and he's already sent me a reply. He said he would start forming a posse tomorrow, at least a dozen men, but he can't start for Stillwater until the first thing in the morning the day after tomorrow. As soon as he gets here, we'll start right out after those killers."

"Marshal," Frank Lowery said soberly, "I got an idea where Bronco Kinney and the others are holed up."

"What?" Egan gasped.

"I met a man who knew something about Kinney and I got him to draw me a map to Kinney's hideout, a place where this man had talked to Bronco a couple of times."

"You mean he was an accessory?" Egan barked. "Where is he? We'll put him in."

"No," Frank grinned, "I kind of promised him he wouldn't be arrested if he gave me directions to Kinney's place in the Cimarron forests. The man agreed, so I'd appreciate it if you left him alone."

"But will he run off to warn Kinney?"

"Not a chance. He's too scared."

Egan nodded and then read the rough map that Crandall had given Frank. "It looks pretty clear. We'll start out as soon as Stone gets here with that posse the day after tomorrow."

"Marshal," Frank said, "I want to leave at first light tomorrow morning. I can reach Kinney's place by about noon. We'll make a copy of this map and you can follow me with the posse."

"Are you crazy, Frank? Go in there alone?"

"If I start out early, I can be at the dugout while they're still there. I can keep an eye on them; keep them under surveillance. If they move out, I'll know where they went. I promise, I won't do anything foolish; just watch them."

"I don't know," Egan balked, stroking his chin.

"Please, Marshal."

"All right," Egan said, "but I'm givin' you a long purple ribbon. You're to leave a piece on the trail to that outlaw dugout, so we know where you went, understand?" He looked at the map. "Put a piece here, and then at this turn, especially, do you follow me?"

"I'll do that," Frank said.

"Let me draw a copy of this map so we'll know where we're going," Egan said. "We'll meet you here, on the bank of Miller's creek, sometime the day after tomorrow. And remember," Egan gestured. "Don't try to take those outlaws alone."

Frank nodded.

"After we copy this map, we'll go straight to supper and then get a good night's sleep," the marshal said. "We'll both need to get up early. I want to do some more investigating around town, and you'll have to be on your way. But remember," the marshal added, "I'll tell you again. Don't try to take those killers by yourself. Just keep an eye on them."

"I understand," Frank said.

But Lowery knew he was lying. He had every intention of taking them on, either one at a time or all four at once. Lowery was bent on vengeance, and he would waste no time in capturing them or even killing them, if necessary. He vaguely realized that his anger might well be dulling his common sense, and that he could get killed, no matter how fast and accurate he was with a gun. But he didn't care.

Chapter Thirteen

Marshal Fred Egan had already left Mae's Boarding-house by the time Frank awoke at dawn. As Lowery started to wash up and shave, Clara Beaufort knocked on the door. When he answered, she looked at him still in his BVDs and smiled. She was holding a hot iron in her hand.

"Let me help you get started, Frank," she said.

Frank nodded at the girl and ushered her into his room. He unabashedly took off his underclothes and put on clean BVDs, while the girl ironed the clean riding clothes that Lowery had brought with him from Guthrie. He dressed in a neat tan shirt, dark brown trousers, clean boots, and his ten gallon hat, and Clara packed the clothes she had ironed neatly in his bedroll. She had brought other items with her, which she also packed in the bedroll. She finished these chores just as Frank strapped on his gunbelt, the holster low on the hip, and tied it on his thigh. He surely looked like a lawman, or even a gunman, with a determined mission.

"I'll walk to the stable with you, Frank."

Lowery nodded.

They went down the back stairs and into the rear barn,

where Frank patted his horse and put on the saddle. He then led the animal to the street, Clara following him. Then he tied the packed bedroll behind the saddle and adjusted the rifle in its scabbard.

"I put three cans o' beans and some coffee, and a pack o' jerky in your bedroll," Clara said. "I hope you don't mind."

"I appreciate that, Clara." The girl did not answer, but only watched Lowery take the rein before he mounted his animal. Then, she reached up and gripped his wrist.

"Be careful, Frank; please be careful. They're murderers and they won't care who they kill." A tear dripped out of her eye. "Y-you will be careful?"

"I won't do anything foolish," Frank promised. "I hope I have more sense than to do anything rash." The girl nodded and stood immobile as Frank loped away.

By early daylight, Lowery had come well north of Stillwater, alternating between walking and trotting his horse. The sun had begun to rise in the east and a breeze had come up, leaving Frank comfortable as he rode. Occasionally, he referred to his map, making certain he traveled in the right direction.

Soon he passed the long, straight wagon lane that led to the QB Ranch. He was tempted to stop here, but thought better of it. No, his presence at the ranch would only remind Rosie and Moses Barker of what they had suffered through with the brutal murder of Jed Stevens and his son. No doubt, the Barkers were even now planning for a funeral tomorrow, or they might have already had it. This was not the time to come calling. Besides, he would be bombarded with questions about the case of Kid Carver, and Lowery wanted to forget this gunfight and hoped that others would forget it, too.

As Frank continued on, he could see the cattle meandering about the extensive QB grasslands. The stock seemed peaceful enough, and no doubt Barker would have another big, fat herd to send north to the railroad in Wichita. Lowery could see two riders near the herd, men loping about leisurely in their routine vigil duties. Frank could not identify them from this distance, but he suspected that one of them was Jesse Meade or Swede Anderson.

After riding another hour, Frank Lowery finally reached Belson's Bend. Here, he stopped to study his map. If he had calculated correctly, he would reach the outlaw dugout within two or three hours, for the map indicated that Bronco's Cimarron place was only about ten miles away. He put the sheet away and loped into the depths of the trail, riding slowly in the gloomy forest while he reminisced. Lowery thought of Jed Stevens and his boy, he thought of Clara, of his gunfight with Carver, of his future as a government lawman, and of Bronco and the other outlaws. He wondered if he would catch up to the lawbreakers. He stopped his meditating when the echoing caws of crows and the sweet chirps of thrushes echoed in the forest.

Lowery loped about five miles along Hunters Trail and stopped only long enough to tie a new length of ribbon on a low branch of a tree. He then veered on through the depths of the dim forests, again riding easily for about an hour to avoid any snags, holes, fallen limbs, rocks, or other obstructions that might injure his mount. Finally, he reached the north stretch of the Cimarron River, and here he rested himself and his mount for about a half hour. He untied his bedroll, took out the blanket, and spread it out in a clearing near some trees.

Lowery gathered some wood and built a campfire. He heated some jerky and beans in a pan, and heated water in a pot for coffee. He felt hungry, and the simple fare tasted as good as a thick steak. He grinned to himself, thankful that Clara had packed the food in his bedroll. After he finished, he cleaned the campsite, repacked his bedroll, and tied it behind his saddle.

Meanwhile, only a couple of miles away, inside Bronco Kinney's dugout, the four outlaws were fully awake. After they had eaten breakfast, two of them sat at a small round table. Bronco Kinney played solitaire, while Jim Clayborn only loafed in a chair and nursed a bottle of whiskey. They watched their two cohorts, Rowdy Joe Wheeler and Colorado McGuire, who moved briskly about the premises, packing gear as they prepared to leave. Wheeler and McGuire had been shuttling swiftly between their dugout sleeping quarters and the small stable, carrying their gear and money to store in their saddlebags and bedrolls. By ten o'clock both men had finished and they slumped into chairs at the table.

"Goddamn," McGuire sighed, "I ain't used to doin' all this runnin' so early in the day."

"Me neither," Rowdy Joe Wheeler panted, "but at least I'm all packed and ready to go."

"There ain't no need to rush off this fast," Bronco Kinney said. "Ain't nobody goin' to find us here. Anyway, you'd be better off if you waited another week or two until things cool down."

"I'm gettin' outta here as soon as I can," Wheeler grinned. "I got me close to twenty-five thousand in gold and bills inside my saddlebag. I'll ride as far north as Wichita, change my name, grow me a beard, change my hair, and then take the next train to San Francisco. With hat kind 'a money, ain't nobody who can stop me from avin' a good time for the next four or five years, and naybe even longer."

"It's Denver for me," Colorado McGuire said. "I'm idin' to Enid, change my appearance in that McCarthy Hair Saloon they told us about in Ingalls. Then I'll ride he stage all the way to Sante Fe and from there I'll take a rain to Denver. With all this money," he patted his ulging saddlebag, "I can buy myself a nice cattle ranch n Colorado. I'll be home again. I'll be a rich and respected rancher, and I'll live the good life from now on."

"If it wasn't for you," Bronco Kinney glared at McGuire, "we wouldn't need to split up and go off in four lirections with identity changes."

"I couldn't help it, Bronco," McGuire said. "That boy nd Jed Stevens recognized me. If I didn't kill 'em, they'd lave identified all of us and every lawman in the West vould have been after us."

"Didn't that bother you? Killin' them two?" Jim Clayborn asked. "After all, you worked for that Jed Stevens and you musta known his boy. Didn't you feel nything when you shot 'em?"

"Sure, I felt real bad about it," Colorado said, "but I'm ike everybody else. I got to think o' my own self-preservation first. The truth is, Jim, you and Bronco are he only ones they know for certain. They ain't sure bout me and Rowdy Joe, and I want to leave it that way."

"You're mistaken," Clayborn pointed. "The last time Crandall talked to us he said the law was suspicious of ou and Joe and they're makin' up wanted posters on you wo as well as on me and Bronco."

"But only for questioning," Rowdy Joe said with a grin. "They got no real proof that we were in on them

215

robberies. Even if they was to take us in, they got no witnesses who can really identify us. They'd have to let us go."

"I wish Crandall would get here," Bronco Kinney said. "I'd sure like to know what's goin' on in Stillwater. I'd guess there's already a posse formed to come after us. Crandall could tell us if they have any idea where we are or if they've already started after us."

Wheeler leaned over the table and grinned again. "Then you ought to be movin' out right away, Bronco, the same as me and Colorado. Why take chances by stayin' here? Christ, you got a lot 'a money, includin' Kid Carver's share." He turned to Clayborn. "Same thing for you, Jim. What the hell do you want to hang around here for?"

"I ain't in no hurry," Bronco Kinney shrugged. "I might even go back to Ingalls for a while and have a little time there before I decide what to do."

"You must be crazy," Colorado McGuire said. "Why, after what happened in that Stillwater bank, they won't give you no shelter nor nothin' else in that town, especially if Marshal Egan shook 'em up when he went in there and talked to Daisy and the others."

"I ain't worried," Bronco said.

"Me neither," Jim Clayborn said before he downed another shot of whiskey from the bottle in front of him.

"Well, I'll be on my way now, Bronco," Colorado McGuire said. "It was nice workin' with you boys. It sure gave me plenty o' money. I couldn't have had this kind 'a cash in my saddlebag if I worked on a ranch for the next fifty years, and I never spent a dime o' my wages. I got to thank you, Bronco, for talkin' me into joinin' up with you."

"Sure," Kinney answered mechanically.

"Well, if I don't see either of you again, good luck to both of you," McGuire said, extending his palm and shaking hands with Kinney and Clayborn. The two men at the table remained indifferent and watched their fellow outlaw leave the dugout.

Now Rowdy Joe Wheeler looked at Bronco and Clayborn. "I guess I'll have to say good-bye, as well. I'd also like to thank you, Bronco. You figured out them three jobs real well and you made me rich. I'm sorry about the killings, though. I didn't figure on anything like that, although I suppose I can't worry about them dead people for the rest o' my life." He extended his arm and shook the hands of Kinney and Clayborn. "So long, boys. I doubt if we'll ever see each other again, so I can only wish you the best o' luck. I know I'm gonna have me a goddamn good time in San Francisco."

"Take care of yourself, Rowdy Joe," Clayborn said.

"You needn't fret about that," Wheeler grinned. "I'm gonna take real good care o' myself." The two men remaining at the table said nothing as Rowdy Joe also left the dugout. They stopped and straightened only when they heard the neigh of horses outside and the clod of hooves from the same mounts. When the sounds had diminished, Clayborn turned to his companion.

"Well, they're gone."

Bronco Kinney only shrugged.

Rowdy Joe Wheeler and Colorado McGuire had enjoyed a bit of luck that morning. Neither man had suspected that Frank Lowery was less than an hour away from them. They had taken the shortcut trail along Miller's Creek to reach the highway instead of riding over Hunters Trail. Thus, they had missed a possible meeting

217

with the resolute deputy marshal.

As the two outlaws were riding off, Frank Lowery, still deep in the forest trail, again looked at his map, remounted, and crossed the Cimarron River, where he once more tied a strip of ribbon, this one on a tree branch hanging over the riverbank. Fred Egan could not miss it once he reached the river. Frank continued on and soon enough he heard the gurgle of water, obviously Miller's Creek. He dismounted and led his horse carefully and slowly toward the creek, hoping that no one saw or heard him. Finally, he tethered his mount to a tree and crouched warily on until he saw the narrow, swiftly flowing, shallow creek. He squinted to both sides and then saw the dugout beyond a small clearing, built into the side of the hillside.

Frank Lowery had found Kinney's hideaway in the Cimarron hills.

Lowery walked back to his horse and extracted his rifle from its scabbard. He checked both the Winchester and his holstered six-shooter before he sighed heavily, straightened, and started for his target.

When Lowery reached the bank of Miller's Creek, he moved stealthily through the trees until he got to a point directly opposite from the dugout. He now had a clear view of the adobe structure set into the side of the hill, the slightly sloping patch of clearing in front of it running from the dugout to the bank of the creek. The low, squat building had two windows and a doorway. To the right was a small lean-to, also against the side of the hill, obviously used to stall horses.

Frank peered hard but counted only two animals in the stall. He scowled. Two of the outlaws had apparently left. Still, Lowery was grateful he'd come out as soon as he had, because at least two of the bandits were still there. If he had waited to come with the posse, he might have lost all four outlaws. Frank Lowery had hoped to take all four of the wanted men, and he now hoped to take alive whoever was inside the dugout so he could find out where the others had gone.

Lowery walked himself and his horse slowly across the shallow creek to avoid any sounds of sloshing water that might arouse suspicion. When he reached the east bank, he tethered the horse in a patch of trees. Then he crouched down and stepped lightly toward the north end of the clearing. Here Frank again checked his weapon, then stepped out from the trees and into the open, and suddenly cried out:

"You in there, whoever you are, come out with your hands up! Your hands up!"

When Lowery's voice echoed into the dugout, the two men stiffened in astonishment. Bronco stopped in the middle of his solitaire, holding a card aloft in his right hand. Jim Clayborn pressed his whiskey glass to his lips, as though trying to muffle his own voice. Neither man spoke.

"You hear me? Come out of there!"

Kinney and Clayborn looked at each other, their eyes widened into startled orbs. Neither of them believed that the demand from outside was real. No one had ever found this dugout, so who was the man with the threatening voice? How did he know they were there? How had he gotten there?

Lowery cried out again. "This is the law out here, Bronco, if you're one of them still inside. You and whoever else is with you had better come out."

"Son of a bitch!" Bronco cursed in a low, hissing

voice. "Who told that man out there where to find us?" Then he scowled. "Crandall! That bastard Crandall! The law must have got an idea that he knew something about us and they scared him enough to talk."

"What are we gonna do, Bronco?"

"I'll take a peek," Bronco said. He rose quietly from his chair and moved toward one of the front windows, peering outside and studying the terrain. He caught a glimpse of Frank Lowery standing at the edge of the clearing with a rifle in one hand and his other hand near his holstered gun. Bronco could also see the star on the intruder's shirt, since the badge blinked in the morning sunlight. However, Kinney saw no one else around, not another soul. He moved back from the window and turned to Clayborn.

"There's only one man out there. I can't believe that a single lawman would come out here alone."

"One man?" Clayborn asked in surprise.

"That's all I see."

Jim Clayborn almost bounced out of his own chair and rushed to the window himself. Clayborn also saw the armed deputy standing at the edge of the clearing, and he also failed to see anyone else in the area or in the trees on the opposite side of the creek. He turned to Kinney and frowned.

"Who the hell is he? Did he expect to come here alone and take four of us?"

Bronco Kinney stroked his chin and shook his head. "I don't know who'd be dumb enough to try somethin' like that." He grimaced. "No, there must be others out there, a whole posse."

"But we didn't see nobody else."

"They must be hidin' real well."

"Do you hear me, Bronco?" Lowery's voice again echoed into the dugout. "If you've got any sense, you'll come out of there with your hands up."

Bronco Kinney rushed once more to the window and now shouted from the structure. "Kiss my ass, mister! If you want us, come inside and get us."

"Don't be foolish, Bronco," Lowery answered. "I won't need to come in there. All I have to do is to drive off your horses and you'll die out here without mounts. And maybe I can light a couple of torches and smoke you out or burn you right down to the bone in there. Now get your hands up and come out."

"My God, Bronco," Clayborn gaped, "that man could do just that, and I ain't got no desire to burn or suffocate to death. Maybe we ought to call him out. Hell, there's two of us. We could take him easy."

Kinney frowned. "I wonder who the hell he is. There ain't no doubt that he's a lawman, but who? Where did he come from?" He stroked his chin again. "I got an idea, Jim," he half whispered to his companion.

"Are you coming out?" Lowery cried again. "I'm running out of patience."

Bronco again walked to the window and shouted. "I'll come out, mister, but I ain't comin' out unarmed."

"Suit yourself," Lowery said, "but I'm only giving you one minute. If you aren't out by then, I'll drive off your horses and burn you out."

Bronco Kinney shied away from the window, grabbed his hanging gunbelt, and swiftly strapped it around his waist. He checked his six-shooter and looked at Clayborn. "Jim, you go to the window with your Winchester. That lawman ain't likely to shoot me the minute I get out there. But, as soon as I get his attention you let him have it with a couple of thirty-thirty rifle slugs."

"But suppose there's others out there?"

"We didn't see any," Bronco said. "Besides, we'd best worry about one thing at a time; take care o' this bastard before we take the next step." Kinney again shouted from the window. "All right, mister, I'm comin' out."

Frank Lowery stepped back two paces and waited alertly as the pine board door opened slowly and the hulking figure of Bronco Kinney stepped out of the dugout and into the sunlight. He wore only a pair of dark rumpled pants, heavy socks, and no shirt or boots. The top of his long johns showing above the waist of his pants. Bronco wore a gunbelt, with a black-handled Colt protruding from the holster. A growth of beard covered much of his big, round face. He peered hard at his adversary. Lowery guessed that Kinney had been simply lolling idly about the dugout since the Stillwater bank robbery, and that he had made no effort to keep himself clean.

"That's far enough, Bronco," Lowery said. "If I were you I'd just put up my hands and come toward me so I can disarm you."

"You're crazy, lawman," Bronco grinned. "Do you think I'd simply let you take me so's they can swing me from a rope? Anyway, who the hell are you? And where's that posse you're braggin' about?"

"The posse is on the way. I'm the advance point."

"Shit, you're alone here." Bronco grinned again. "Somebody who's tryin' to make a name for himself, but who's only gonna lay here dead, if you don't throw down them guns. Who'd be crazy enough to do what you're doin'? What's your name? I'd like to know so's I'll

222

remember who it was I buried out here."

"My name is Lowery, Bronco; Frank Lowery."

Bronco Kinney stopped dead in his tracks. His mouth flew open in a wide, astonished gape. An electrifying fear stung every nerve in his huge body, and his eyes marbled in horror. His bearded face twisted and his fingers began to tremble. He was too shocked to say anything.

"Maybe you heard of me, Bronco, just like I've heard of you and seen you and admired you when you were doing honest work on the rodeo circuit. Too bad you decided to take up robbery and murder. There was no cause to kill Jed Stevens and his boy, none at all." Bronco stood silent and immobile, like a stunned deer ready to be devoured by a wolf, and Frank continued. "If you don't come ahead and give me your gun, why it might simply be you who's buried in these Cimarron badlands. Believe me, it wouldn't bother me one bit to kill you, but I'm willing to take you in alive, you and whoever else is inside there."

"A-ain't nobody i-in there; only me," Bronco stammered.

"You're a liar," Frank said. "There's two horses in the stall."

"Honest, mister," Bronco said, "that's an extra mount. I use it in case one o' my horses goes lame. The others are all gone, all of 'em: Wheeler, Colorado, and Clayborn. They've all been gone since yesterday."

"Maybe," Frank said. "You just come forward so I can disarm you."

"Sure, sure," Bronco said, grinning and raising his arm. "I don't want no trouble with you, Lowery, none at all. I'm comin' with my hands up, as you can plainly see."

But Lowery's observations were keen, and he caught the shift in Bronco's dark eyes as the outlaw inadvertently glanced in the direction of the dugout window. Then Frank caught sight of an obscure outline and the tip of a rifle barrel at the window, revealing to the deputy marshal that somebody was there, waiting to hit him. Lowery tossed his own rifle from his left to his right hand and then raised the Winchester.

"Hey, deputy," Bronco cried, "what are you doin'? I'm givin' myself up without a fight."

But Lowery ignored Bronco and fired twice at the window. The first shot struck Clayborn's rifle barrel, knocking the weapon free from his hand and down to the ground outside the dugout. The second shot splintered a piece of window casing only inches from the second outlaw, prompting Clayborn to suddenly vanish.

"Your partner can't help you now, Bronco."

Kinney lowered his arms slightly and rolled his tongue around his thick lips. He once more stood motionless and stared at Lowery. The deputy tossed his rifle to the ground and lowered his right hand toward his gunbelt holster. "You've got two choices, Bronco. Either keep coming with your hands up or try to take me." Bronco Kinney, however, continued slowly to lower his hands, preparing to stop if he saw Lowery go for his gun. But, since Frank made no such move, Bronco's hands were soon at his side.

"Well, Bronco?"

Now the outlaw took a deep sigh and straightened. He wiped the perspiration from his face and then brought his hand close to his holstered gun.

"You ain't takin' me in to hang."

"Don't be foolish," Frank said. "You'll get a fair trial."

A second later, Bronco Kinney went for his gun. But his fingers had not even reached the handle of his Colt before Frank's own right hand had extracted his own six-shooter, aimed it, and fired twice. Both shots struck Bronco squarely, tearing away strips of his upper long johns before a twin spurt of blood exploded from his chest. Bronco staggered backwards for two steps, turned, and then collapsed to the ground—dead.

Frank Lowery only glanced at the fallen outlaw as he walked toward the dugout with his six-shooter still in his hand. When he reached the structure, he flattened himself against the wall next to the door and shouted.

"Whoever is in there better come out! Now!"

"D-don't shoot, d-deputy," Clayborn whimpered from inside the building. "I-I'm comin' out and I'm unarmed."

"Move it, move!" Lowery cried. Frank then heard the banging and thumping of rude furniture intermingled with the sounds of hurried footsteps before someone reached the door.

"D-don't shoot," Clayborn pleaded again. "I'm comin' out right now."

"I'm waiting."

Seconds later, Jim Clayborn eased out of the door with his hands raised over his head. He too was clad only in trousers and socks, his upper long johns exposed. He wore no gun.

Lowery studied him. "Are you Jim Clayborn?"

The man nodded vigorously.

Then, without warning, Frank Lowery lashed out with

his left, backhanding Clayborn across the face and knocking him to the ground. Clayborn wiped away some of the blood that the vicious slap had drawn from his cheek. He looked up fearfully at Frank Lowery, who now leaned down and gripped the man's underwear.

"Clayborn, you better have a lot of answers for me."

Chapter Fourteen

Jim Clayborn shifted his eyes between the tall figure of Frank Lowery leaning over him and the slain Bronco Kinney lying like a huge broken doll in the clearing in front of the dugout. Clayborn felt a dread fear in the presence of this deputy marshal, for he had now seen for himself the awesomeness of Frank Lowery. If anything he had heard about him seemed exaggerated, he now believed that Lowery's skills, in fact, had been underrated. He still trembled from his own recent ordeal: two quick shots from fifty yards away, one that had neatly picked the Winchester out of his hand, and the second that had come within a whisker of killing him.

Suddenly, a horrifying fact struck the outlaw: Lowery had deliberately fired the second shot to frighten him and not to kill him. This man wanted him alive! Not for a simple reason like taking him back to Stillwater to a hangman's noose; no, Lowery could not have cared less whether Clayborn lived or died. This deputy wanted information from Clayborn, and the outlaw suspected that if he did not satisfy his captor, he would be as dead as Bronco Kinney.

Lowery brandished the barrel of his six-gun in

Clayborn's face and then spoke. "All right, where are the others?"

"T-the others?"

"I've got no time to play games, Clayborn. We both know that four of you held up that bank in Stillwater and killed an innocent man and his son. The four of you rode out here. But Wheeler and McGuire are gone. Where are they?"

"I don't know," Clayborn said.

Lowery shrugged. "Then you aren't any good to me, and there's no sense in wasting time taking you all the way to Stillwater. I may as well bury you along with Bronco Kinney before I go back."

"You'd k-kill me in cold blood?"

"You didn't have any qualms about killing an innocent man and his young son in cold blood. And you didn't have any qualms about killing me from ambush."

"T-they left," Clayborn stammered. "They lit out as soon as we come here."

"Like I said," Lowery said, "if you can't help me I see no reason to let you live. Who'd fault me for gunning down a member of a killer gang that tried to pick me off from a window?"

"No, no." Clayborn gestured frantically. "I'll talk."

"I'm listening."

"Rowdy Joe and Colorado left the dugout less than an hour before you got here. They both went with nearly twenty-five thousand each in their saddlebags. Rowdy Joe is headin' for Wichita, where he'll take a train to San Francisco, and Colorado said he was goin' to Enid to take the overnight stage into Sante Fe. Then he'll ride a train to Denver. He said he was gonna buy a ranch up there." He looked anxiously at Frank. "I swear, that's the truth.

228

That's just what they told me and Bronco before they rode out."

"How come I didn't see them on Hunters Trail?"

"They used the shortcut," Clayborn said, "the old Indian path along the creek that'll take 'em to Eagle's Bluff five miles north o' here. It saves a few miles to the highway instead o' followin' Hunters Trail all the way to the Stillwater-Ponca Highway."

Lowery pursed his lips. "Eagle's Bluff?"

"Yes," Clayton nodded.

"Then Wheeler will keep going north to Wichita and Colorado will veer west on the road to Enid."

"I'd guess so," the frightened outlaw answered. "They'll probably split up at Eagle's Bluff."

Lowery brandished his revolver. "On your feet and back in there."

Jim Clayborn nodded and rose to his feet, then led Lowery into the structure. Lowery forced the outlaw to bring out the loot they had taken from the three robberies, four bags that held both Clayborn's and Kinney's share of the loot, nearly $50,000 in gold and bills. Clayborn dropped the bags on the table. As Lowery stared at them, Clayborn shuttled his glance between the money and the deputy marshal. The outlaw grinned.

"There's a lotta money in them bags, deputy. If you'll let me go, why I'd be glad to share this with you, give you half of it. No," he gestured, "I'll give you all the money and one bag o' gold, and I'll just take one bag 'a gold. I'll be long gone and nobody'll know we made this deal."

"Are you crazy?" Frank scoffed. "I can take it all. But, three people are dead because of this loot, and two of them were real good friends of mine. Do you think I could enjoy any of that blood money, knowing that Jed and Billie Stevens are fresh in their graves this morning?''

Clayborn gestured again. "I didn't kill that man and his boy, I swear it. We didn't want no shootin'. Colorado did it. We didn't know why he just shot them, but then we found out that they knew him.''

"Yes,'' Frank nodded, "Colorado McGuire used to be a hand at the QB Ranch. He left there just before I signed on.''

"What are you goin' to do with me, Lowery?''

"I don't know,'' Frank said. "I'd like to start out after those two right away, but I'm burdened with you and that stolen money. The posse won't be here until at least tomorrow afternoon, because they won't be leaving Guthrie until tomorrow. I guess I'll have to take you and the money with me and leave a note behind for Marshal Fred Egan.''

"Take me where?''

"To Enid, to put you in the jailhouse there; or maybe even take you along with me until I catch up to McGuire and Wheeler before they get away.''

"They'll be goin' in opposite directions once they reach Eagle's Bluff,'' Clayborn said. "You can't follow both of 'em.''

"We'll see,'' Frank said. "First, we'll stretch out Kinney's corpse in one of the sleeping cells you've got in here. We don't have time to bury him. Then we'll saddle your horse and leave on the same trail along the creek.''

Lowery forced the outlaw to help him carry the body of Bronco Kinney into the dugout and place it on a small bed in one of the cells. Next, Lowery and Clayborn gathered grub—coffee, canned beans, flour, and a bottle of whiskey—and put them in the saddlebags of Clayborn's horse. Then Lowery ordered the outlaw atop his mount and tied Clayborn's feet to the saddle stirrups. He also tied the outlaw's forearms together, leaving the hands free to grip the saddle horn. And finally, Frank took the reins of the bandit's horse and tied them to the saddle of his own animal.

"Now you can balance yourself atop that mount, because I intend to move pretty fast." Clayborn sat motionless on the animal while Frank loaded the two bags of bank notes and two bags of gold into his own saddlebags. Frank wrote a note and pinned it on the door of the dugout, then ripped off a piece of ribbon and pinned it to the same door. He mounted his own horse. When Egan got here tomorrow he would find the message.

"I'm telling you," Lowery pointed to Clayborn, "don't try anything on the trail, and if I catch up to one of your friends, don't try to warn him. If you do, I'll just shoot you dead. After all, you gave me the information I wanted, and I don't need you now. Anyway, even if you go to trial, you might only serve a jail term and not hang for murder if you can prove you weren't directly involved in those killings. So, I'd suggest you behave yourself."

"I wasn't responsible for them killings, I swear," Clayborn insisted. "It was Kid Carver who killed that clerk and Colorado who killed them others in the bank. Me and Bronco and Wheeler didn't want no killings, none at all. If you find Rowdy Joe, he'll swear to it."

"Then it would pay you to cooperate," Frank said. "You'd best hang on to that horn, because I'm in a hurry."

The two men left the clearing and soon disappeared

into the trees to the north. They followed the gloomy path along Miller's Creek. He often jogged the mounts in a brisk trot, hoping that McGuire and Wheeler were moving at a slow pace, not only to keep their mounts fresh, but also because they were certain that no one was after them. The pair of riders continued on for about an hour and finally stopped to water their horses. Frank took a drink himself and offered a drink of water to Jim Clayborn.

"I'd sure like some o' that whiskey we packed."

Frank nodded, then took out the bottle and held it while his companion took a big swig. Lowery then put away the bottle and squinted through the dense trees. "How much further to Eagle's Bluff?"

"About a mile."

"Are you sure?"

"I've been on this trail enough," Clayborn said. "This is the way we usually ride to Ingalls and back to the dugout from Ingalls."

Frank nodded again and remounted his horse.

Meanwhile, as Lowery had hoped, the other two outlaws had moved along the creek at rather a slow pace, and they had come into the clearing at Eagle's Bluff only ten or fifteen minutes ahead of Frank Lowery. When they reached the main Stillwater-Ponco Highway, the two men brought their horses to a stop. Colorado got his canteen and took a long drink of water, but Rowdy Joe pulled a whiskey bottle from his saddlebag and gulped down several heavy swigs before he recapped the bottle and slid it back into his saddlebag.

"Ah," Wheeler said. "That sure hit the spot."

"Don't you believe in water?"

"Not when I got good whiskey to quench my thirst."

Colorado McGuire squinted at the sun that had now risen high in the sky. "Well, Joe, looks like this is where we part company. I'll be in Enid by early afternoon, have a good meal, sell my horse and saddle, buy some new clothes, get a new hair job at McCarthy's, and then take the night stage to Sante Fe. It'll get me there in a couple of days and I'll take that long, comfortable train ride north to Denver. My name will be Edward McCann when I get on the stage, and that's what my handle will be from now on. Nobody'll ever be lookin' for me again."

"I guess I'll be doin' the same thing," Rowdy Joe said, "only I'll be doin' that in Wichita. Then, it's an even longer ride for me, a train all the way to San Francisco." He peered at the trees behind him. "I wonder what Bronco and Jim Clayborn will do."

"Probably go into Ingalls to find a whore, and that's just where Marshal Egan is likely to catch up to 'em. But, them two ain't very smart."

"Colorado," Wheeler said, leaning from his saddle and extending his hand, "this is good-bye. I doubt if I'll ever see you again, 'less you come to San Francisco, 'cause I sure as hell won't come to Denver."

"No," Colorado answered, pumping Wheeler's hand in a firm hand shake. "I'd say this is the last we'll see of each other. You take care of yourself, Joe. Remember, them whores and gamblers in San Francisco are a lot smarter than these in the Oklahoma Territory. If you ain't careful, why they'll steal every last dollar and nugget from you before a month goes by."

"Ain't nobody gonna steal this fortune from me," Wheeler grinned, patting his saddlebag. He then tipped his hat to Colorado, wheeled his horse, and continued north up the main Stillwater-Ponco Highway. Colorado

233

McGuire waited until horse and rider disappeared aroun
a bend in the road. Then he too whirled his horse an
loped westward toward Enid, about two hours away.

Colorado McGuire had barely disappeared up the roa
when Lowery emerged from the same brake of dense tree
and into the open at Eagle's Bluff, still hauling Claybor
behind him. When Frank reached the highway, h
dismounted and walked his horses while he studied th
dirt pavement. He easily saw the fresh hoofprints, one se
leading north and the other going west on the road t
Enid. He looked up at Clayborn. "They left here less tha
a few minutes ago."

"I told you I was tellin' the truth, deputy."

"Well, whoever went north can't be too far ahead o
me," Frank said, "and neither can the man going west
Colorado McGuire: isn't that what you said?"

Clayborn nodded. "He plans to take the night stage t
Sante Fe."

"That means I'll have time to catch up with Wheele
before I double back and go after McGuire. Even if
reach Enid late this afternoon, he'll still be there."

Frank Lowery tied the reins of Clayborn's horse to
tree. He took another piece of rope and firmly tied th
outlaw's hands. Clayborn stiffened with anxiety. "M
God, Lowery, you ain't gonna leave me here like this, ar
you?"

"I won't be gone long."

"But suppose somethin' happens to you and you don'
come back," Clayborn complained. "I could die ou
here."

"You should have thought of that before you decide
to join up with Bronco Kinney to rob and kill."

Jim Clayborn squirmed in his saddle and watche

234

apprehensively as Frank mounted his own horse, checked his Winchester, veered his horse, and started north. The outlaw fidgeted hard, trying to loosen his legs from the stirrups or to untie his hands and arms, or to jerk the tied reins from the tree. But Lowery had done a good job, and Clayborn could not come close to freeing himself. He could only sit and hope, praying that Frank Lowery would quickly catch up to Wheeler, bring him back, and then rescue Clayborn.

Frank Lowery moved up the Stillwater-Ponco Highway at a rapid pace. He trotted his mount most of the time, and even galloped him for short distances, even though the mount was tired, since the animal had been on the go since early this morning. However, Lowery had only gone about four or five miles, traveling less than an hour, when he saw a horse and rider go ahead. The man was probably Rowdy Joe Wheeler, and Frank quickened his strides. The man himself was only walking his horse and was obviously unaware that someone had been following him.

Soon, however, Rowdy Joe heard the clods behind him and he turned to look. When he saw the man coming on, Wheeler's first instinct was simply to stop and wait for the stranger. However, he suddenly remembered that he had a small fortune in his saddlebags. He was disinclined to become a possible victim of a highwayman. And then, something worse: Wheeler saw the sparkles reflecting from the chest of the oncoming rider, and he guessed at once that the man behind him was a lawman.

Rowdy Joe kicked the flanks of his horse and broke into a gallop. Frank Lowery whipped his own horse to catch up to the outlaw, extracting his Winchester from its scabbard. Even at this gallop Frank fired twice, popping out small clumps of earth on the road only a few feet from the galloping legs of Wheeler's horse. These near misses from a man firing while at a full gallop panicked the outlaw, and he veered off the road and into the jumble of rocks.

Wheeler had miscalculated quite badly. Had Rowdy Joe continued on, he would no doubt have escaped Lowery, since Frank's horse was quite spent, while Rowdy Joe's mount was still relatively fresh. Now Wheeler forced his mount up a steep, craggy patch of terrain and ducked behind a huge boulder. Here he dismounted, grabbed his rifle and set the barrel atop a big rock. A moment later, as Lowery loomed into view, he fired twice at his pursuer, but missed by a wide margin. Shooting straight was not one of Wheeler's talents.

Lowery turned his horse into the same jumble of rocks and quickly dismounted. He tied the mount to some scrub brush and avoided two more shots from the outlaw as he continued to crawl upward. He came within forty or fifty yards of the outlaw, then stopped and shouted. "Wheeler, this is the law! Come out of there with your hands up!"

"Suck my ass, lawman!" Wheeler shouted back. "If you want me, you come up here and get me."

"You haven't got a prayer in there, Wheeler. The rest of the posse will be here within an hour," Lowery lied. "We'll flush you out; maybe kill you, or let you starve to death up there. Make it easy on yourself and come out with your hands up."

Wheeler did not respond this time, only fired his rifle again, twice. Both shots richocheted harmlessly off some rocks. Lowery responded with a shot of his own, and the deputy marshal's slug skimmed off the top of the rock behind which Wheeler cowered. The close call prompted the outlaw to cower deeper, allowing Lowery to come closer to his quarry. Soon, Frank was no more than thirty yards away, and also crouchng behind a rock.

"Don't be a fool, Wheeler; come out of there."

But once more Wheeler responded with two shots from his rifle, both of which, while coming close to Lowery, again hit some rocks harmlessly.

"You're making a mistake, Wheeler," Lowery cried.

"I'm on the high ground, lawman." Wheeler answered. "You have to come up here and get me."

"I've got all day," Frank said. "I can wait for the posse to join me."

Rowdy Joe Wheeler peeked over the rock behind which he hid, and he squinted hard to the south. He saw no sign of riders on the road over which he had just come. He did not know if Lowery was lying about the posse, or whether more lawmen might still arrive. And now Rowdy Joe no longer heard a sound in the nearby rocks below him. He fired two more rifle shots, but this time Lowery did not respond. Frank said nothing and did not fire. Rowdy Joe wiped away the sweat that had beaded his pudgy face and thick neck.

After two minutes of near total silence, Wheeler fired still another pair of bullets. But still, no sound came from Lowery. "Hey, lawman," Rowdy Joe cried, "are you still down there?"

But the outlaw got no reply. He did not know that Frank Lowery had been advancing through the rocky terrain, inching his way upward without the slightest sound until he reached a spot almost even with his quarry.

Wheeler cried out again. "Lawman? How come you

ain't talkin' no more? What are you waitin' for? I don't see no posse comin' this way. You're a goddamn liar about that. Why ain't you babblin' now? You scared? You a coward?" But still Wheeler got no reply, and frustration gripped him. "You son of a bitch!" he cried. "Make a move! I dare you to make a move!"

Frank Lowery continued on until he reached a point above Rowdy Joe Wheeler only fifteen yards away. He peeked over a rock carefully and saw Wheeler still looking frantically downward, or throwing a glance at the road that ran straight south. The outlaw's gun barrel lay atop the rock.

"You bastard!" Rowdy Joe cursed again. "Why don't you come and get me?"

Frank Lowery rose full to his feet and stared down at the outlaw. "All right, Wheeler, drop it! You're under arrest!"

Rowdy Joe whirled and stared up at Lowery in astonishment. How could this man have worked his way to this advantageous position without making any noise? For several fleeting seconds the bandit squatted in a frozen position, gaping, while his rifle remained balanced on the rock. Slowly, Wheeler moved his fingers toward the trigger of the weapon.

"Don't be a fool, Wheeler. I'd rather take you back alive."

"Lawman, you ain't gonna take me," Wheeler said. He slowly lifted the rifle and turned to fire. But a quick shot by Lowery knocked the weapon out of the outlaw's hand.

"That slug could have gone right through your head," Lowery said. "But, as I said, I'm willing to take you in alive."

Almost instinctively, Rowdy Joe reached for his

238

holstered gun. However, he had not even brought his hand halfway down when Lowery reacted spontaneously and unleashed another rifle shot that struck the outlaw in the upper torso, ripping open his shirt and saturating the man's chest with blood. Wheeler bounced backwards against the rock from the force of the close-range hit and then slid to a sitting position before his eyes marbled and his head fell almost to his shoulder. Lowery had killed the man almost instantly.

Frank spent the next half hour bringing the hefty body of Joe Wheeler down from the rocks and onto the highway. He also brought down the man's horse and slung the body over the animal's back. Then Frank replaced the outlaw's rifle in the saddle scabbard and jammed the man's six-shooter into his own waist. He searched the saddlebags, pulling out the bags of gold and bills and transferring them to his own saddlebags. Finally, Frank remounted his horse, took the reins of the second animal, and walked the two animals at a mild pace back to Eagle's Bluff where he had left his prisoner tied up.

When Jim Clayborn saw the horses coming toward him he sighed in relief. But then he saw the draped body of a man over the trailing horse and he knew that Frank Lowery had killed Rowdy Joe Wheeler as he had earlier killed Bronco Kinney. Clayborn stared at Wheeler's corpse as Frank reached him, and the outlaw then stared at Lowery.

"Did you have to kill him? Rowdy Joe wasn't bad or mean. He never murdered anybody."

"He didn't give me any choice," Lowery answered. "I told him to come out of those rocks with his hands up, but he wouldn't do it. He just kept firing his rifle at me, trying to pick me off."

"Yeah." Clayborn nodded. "He always was a stubborn man."

Lowery spent the next several minutes preparing to move out. He untied Clayborn's hands so he could again hold on to the saddle horn to balance himself. He made sure that Wheeler's body was properly secured and he then tied the reins of Wheeler's horse to the saddle of Clayborn's horse, and the reins of Clayborn's horse to his own mount. When he completed these tasks he mounted his horse and moved out with his strange caravan at a slow walk, veering left, onto the road to Enid.

"When we reach that town, Clayborn, I'll turn you over to the deputy marshal there and bring the corpse to the mortician. Then I'll find McGuire."

"He's the man you want most, ain't it?" Clayborn grinned, "because he's the one who killed that ranch foreman and his son. So, it's four down and one to go. Is that it, deputy?"

"Only doing my job."

"Sure," Clayborn sneered, "but you ought to know one thing, deputy. Colorado McGuire won't be as easy to take as the rest of us were."

"We'll see," Lowery answered.

Clayborn did not answer. He turned and looked at the draped body of Rowdy Joe Wheeler as he, the deputy, and the dead man continued toward Enid.

Chapter Fifteen

Colorado McGuire, about an hour ahead of Frank Lowery, reached Enid around two o'clock in the afternoon. He thus had four hours before he needed to board the night stage to Sante Fe. McGuire had already made up his mind to come over some back streets and ride directly to the McCarthy Tonsorial Parlor, since he knew that the deputy marshal maintained a small jailhouse and office in town. He stopped two young boys and asked directions on how to reach the place.

McGuire had learned in Ingalls that for the right price, McCarthy could transform a man's appearance: darken or lighten the hair, change its style, shave a beard or apply a beard, and even tint the face to change a complexion from dark to ruddy or vice versa. McCarthy would ask no questions and he would give no answers to anybody, not even to probing lawmen. The shady barber also had an associate who made up those new identification cards with a photograph on them. In McGuire's case, such a card would name him Edward McCann, of Denver, Colorado.

When McGuire finished these chores, he would buy new attire, a suitcase, and his ticket to Sante Fe. He would then take the train north to Colorado, where he would be free forever.

But, James Colorado McGuire had not guessed that a dogging, determined lawman was close on his heels.

After directions from the youngsters, Colorado veered left down a narrow avenue and then right on Blair Street. He trotted slowly on until he reached a small structure with a fading "McCarthy's Tonsorial Parlor" painted on a sign above the door. He dismounted and tethered his horse, took his bag of money and bag of gold out of the saddlebag, and ambled to the door of the establishment. A rather small, bald-headed man eyed McGuire thoroughly, especially his dusty clothes and the bags he held in his hand.

"What can I do for you?"

"I want a new look," the visitor said. "A man by the name of Marvin Crandall told me you could take care of it."

The man nodded. "I can help you, but it won't come cheap."

"I understand," McGuire said.

McCarthy studied the potential customer again, more carefully this time. "We'll cut your hair short, and since you've got light-colored eyes, we can dye the hair to a sandy light brown and part it in the middle. I don't think it'll matter if you have a clean-shaven face. I've got a rack of suits in the next room with ties and shirts. You can pick one out that fits. I'll also furnish you a traveling suitcase so's you can carry your extra clothes and valuables."

"That'll be fine."

"We'll give you some spectacles and you'll look like a merchant. When we're finished here, I'll send you to a man two doors away. He'll take your photograph and make up one of those identification cards that a lot of people are carrying around these days. You just tell him what kinda name you want."

McGuire nodded. "How long will this take? I've got to catch the night stage to Sante Fe."

"You'll make it in plenty o' time," McCarthy said. "And I can see that you can use a small valise," he pointed to the two bags. When McGuire did not answer, the man ducked through a door and came back a moment later with a small piece of black luggage. "Put those bags in here."

"How much?"

The man shrugged. "We'll settle when we're finished."

"That'll be fine."

"Right now," the man said, "go around the corner to the bathhouse on Main Street and get cleaned up. You can leave the valise here."

"I'll take it with me, if you don't mind."

"Whatever you say," McCarthy said.

"What about my horse and saddle? Can I sell them? I sure as hell don't want to take them with me."

"I'll have a livery man take a look at them while you're takin' your bath. He'll give you a fair price. When you come back, I'll get to work on you."

McGuire nodded.

The outlaw left the place and walked to the corner, up a small lane, and onto Main Street to the bathhouse several doors from the intersection. A Chinese man greeted him with a smile and a bow, helped him out of his riding clothes and settled him into a hot tub. McGuire felt exhilarated from the warm, soapy water, and he soaked with relish. While Colorado cleaned himself, the Chinese man took his clothes, dusted them off, and cleaned them with dry goods benzine. He then ironed them. By the time McGuire got out of the tub and dried off, his clothes were quite neat and fresh.

Colorado put on a new pair of BVDs that he bought from the proprietor and discarded his old pair. He slipped on his trousers, his rawhide shirt, his socks, and his boots, which the man had also cleaned. Next, he strapped on his gunbelt and put on his hat. He handed the man a dollar bill, and the attendant grinned and bowed again.

McGuire left the place quite pleased with the service. When he got a new suit from McCarthy, he would pack these clothes and the other things from his bedroll into the new suitcase he would buy from the barber. However, he would carry his money and gold in the small black satchel. He promised himself never to leave the valise out of his sight. When Colorado saw a sign a few doors up the street, Enid Saloon, he decided to go inside for some beer and perhaps a beef dinner. He was thirsty and hungry after the many hours on the trail.

The outlaw had made a fatal mistake.

Colorado had barely ducked into the saloon when Frank Lowery loped up Main Street with his burdens, a man tied to a horse and a corpse strapped over a second animal. He headed directly for the deputy marshal's office, where he alighted, dismounted his prisoner, tethered the animals, and ordered Clayborn inside. A few curious people looked at him, and Deputy Marshal Vic Gray came out of the jailhouse and grinned at the visitor.

"You must be Frank Lowery."

Lowery nodded.

"Frankly," Gray said, "I don't think I believed

Marshal Egan when he wired me to keep an eye out for you."

"Marshal Egan?"

Gray nodded. "I got a telegram late this morning. He said there was a possibility that one of his deputies, Frank Lowery, might come into Enid with some prisoners, either dead or alive. I guess he was right—one dead, one alive."

Lowery grinned. Egan had been quite perceptive. The marshal had not fully believed that Frank would simply stay near Bronco Kinney's dugout, he'd guessed he would try to take the gang alone, if the opportunity presented itself. And, if he did take prisoners, he would bring them to Enid, the nearest town from the location of the outlaw's hideaway.

"Egan also told me that if you got here, to keep you in Enid and for you to wait for him. I got an extra bunk in the rear of the jailhouse where you can sleep tonight," Gray said.

"I'd appreciate that," Frank answered. He then pushed his prisoner into the jailhouse. "This is Jim Clayborn, a member of the Bronco gang. I'd like you to lock him in one of your cells, and the marshal can decide what to do with him. The dead man is Joe Wheeler, another member of the band. I had to kill him when he tried to shoot me instead of surrendering peacefully."

Gray led Clayborn into the cell, locked the door, and turned to Frank. "What about the rest of the outlaws?"

"I got Bronco himself at the dugout when he also tried to shoot me instead of giving up. I left his body there along with a note for the marshal. He'll know I'm here and I'd guess we'll see him in a couple of days."

"I know what happened to that Kid Carver, and I'm sorry it took place. But that's only four. Where's the last one, this Colorado McGuire, who was supposed to be the one who killed the ranch foreman and his boy?"

"You're pretty well informed, deputy," Frank said.

"Egan keeps all of his deputies informed. He sends more telegrams than anybody I know. Now, what about McGuire?"

Frank looked soberly at Vic Gray. "He's right here in Enid. Came here maybe an hour ago. From the information I have, he plans to take the night stage to Sante Fe."

The Enid deputy marshal looked at his wall clock: 3:10. "That'd be about three hours from now."

"What do you suppose he'd be doing here for all that time?" Frank asked.

"Eat, drink, clean up, get new clothes, and anything else he figures he'll need for that stage trip."

"Where do you suppose I can find him?"

"Well," Gray said, "if I'd been on the trail since this morning, I'd sure be hungry, thirsty, and dusty. I'd want a cool drink, some food, and a hot tub—in that order."

"Deputy," Frank said, "I'd like to make sure that McGuire doesn't make that stage. I'll go out and start looking for him now, but if I don't find him, you should be at the stage station."

"Start looking in the Enid Saloon," Gray said. "They have cold beer and good meals. I never met a traveler yet who didn't make that his first stop when he came to town. And if McGuire isn't there, why try the Main Street Restaurant, and if he's not there, he'll probably be at Ming's bathhouse." He leaned closer to Lowery. "Are you sure you don't want me to go with you?"

246

"If I find him, I can handle him."

Deputy Gray nodded. "From what I've heard about you, I'm sure you can. Anyway, I'll be here if you need me."

"Thank you, deputy."

"Wait." The Enid lawman suddenly gripped Frank's arm, "I just thought of something else. If McGuire's face is on a wanted poster, he might also try to change his appearance. I've never been able to prove it, but I think Kevin McCarthy, who has that tonsorial shop on Blair Street, is suspected of helping wanted men to change their appearance. Was this McGuire ever in Ingalls?"

"Yes."

"Well, then he'd surely have learned of McCarthy's place in that robbers' roost, and he'll go there. So, if you don't see him in the saloon, the restaurant, or the bathhouse, the chances are he's in McCarthy's getting his face and hair taken care of. All of these places are almost next door to each other, but McCarthy's Tonsorial Parlor is over on Blair Street. You can leave that dead man," Gray gestured, "I'll get him over to the mortician."

"I thank you," Frank said as he left the jailhouse. He ambled up the street, weaving past the few pedestrians about, some of whom eyed this deputy marshal with curiosity. Who was this visiting lawman? What was he doing here? Was he joining Vic Gray in some kind of special assignment? Lowery had walked along the boardwalk for only several minutes when he saw the sign that said Enid Saloon, and he peered inside over the swinging door entrance.

Frank saw only a few people here on this early afternoon, but he spotted Colorado McGuire sitting alone

247

at one of the tables, drinking cold beer and gnawing on a thick roast beef sandwich. Frank recognized the man from the wanted posters that Marshal Fred Egan had had made up. Lowery adjusted his gunbelt, walked inside, and ambled slowly up to the table. He reached the outlaw just as McGuire finished off a tall glass of beer to wash down some of his food. The man stopped and stared at Lowery, mainly at the deputy marshal's badge pinned on the intruder's shirt.

"Are you Colorado McGuire?"

The outlaw grinned. "You made a mistake, deputy. I never heard of anybody by that name. I'm Edward McCann, from up Denver way."

"You sure look like McGuire to me," Frank said. "I'm afraid I'll need to take you in until we can prove who you are."

"I told you, deputy, you made a mistake."

"All I know is that McGuire came into Enid today and you look exactly like him. I'll have to arrest you on suspicion of murder. If we made a mistake, why we'll surely let you go on your way."

"You're crazy," Colorado huffed. "I ain't goin' off to no jail for somebody else." He started for his holstered gun, but Lowery gripped his wrist.

"I wouldn't try anything so foolish."

By now, the few people about the place, some customers, the bartender, and two harlots loitering near the bar, were staring intently at the two at the small table. McGuire shuttled his glance between these spectators and Lowery, and then the outlaw shrugged.

"All right, deputy, I'll go with you," McGuire said, rising from the table. Frank relaxed just enough for the outlaw to make a quick move. Colorado threw a hard right into Lowery's stomach and the surprised deputy marshal doubled over. Then the outlaw unleashed a left to the jaw that sent Frank sprawling to the floor. Before Lowery recovered, Colorado darted out of the saloon.

Frank rose to his feet, wiped the streak of blood from his jaw, and hurried out of the saloon. The spectators bounded from their chairs and rushed to the swinging doors to peer outside, where they watched Lowery disappear up the street. Frank was only a hundred yards behind the fleeing outlaw, who tried to whirl off Main Avenue and into an alleyway. However, the lawbreaker almost got run down by a horse and wagon, and he fell to the pavement as he jerked backwards and twisted away from the vehicle.

"Hold it right there, McGuire!" Lowery cried.

But the outlaw bounded to his feet and cried back. "You ain't takin' me anywhere, mister." He then backtracked several paces and lowered his right hand toward his holstered six-shooter.

"Don't be a fool, Colorado," Lowery shouted.

The loud exchange between the two men and the obvious confrontation triggered excitement in the street. Several men riding horses or wagons veered out of the way and to the side, while pedestrians on the boardwalks stopped and stared. Business people and customers came out of shops. A quiet descended on the normally busy street as people looked into the suddenly abandoned main thoroughfare of Enid where McGuire was moving backwards and Frank Lowery was inching toward him.

"Give it up, Colorado," Lowery cried. "That's the smartest thing to do."

"Go to hell," McGuire shouted back. Then he stopped and stood erect, glaring at the advancing Lowery.

"Deputy, you'd be wise to stop right there. I don't want to kill you; I just want to go on my way peaceably."

"The law is not inclined to let cold-blooded killers go on their way peacefully," Frank answered.

"You can't prove that."

"And you can't prove you're innocent unless you give yourself up."

"I told you, deputy, you'd best stop right there or you'll be a dead man."

But Frank Lowery continued forward, walking slowly and deliberately. The spectators on the boardwalks adjacent to the street now stared in awe. The mob swelled as more people congregated to view the drama. They had rightly guessed that a shootout was imminent and that one of the two men facing each other would probably be dead before another minute passed. The onlookers stiffened in anticipation as they awaited the climax of this spectacle.

The end was not long in coming.

Colorado McGuire stood stiffly, his legs implanted firmly on the dirt pavement. He wiggled his fingers, now but a few inches above his holstered gun, as Lowery stepped ominously toward him. The time for talk had obviously ended, and only the weapons would settle the issue.

Frank Lowery had come within twenty-five or thirty yards of the outlaw when McGuire reached for his gun. But he had only extracted the weapon halfway out of its holster before the deputy marshal drew his own gun, aimed, and fired twice. The two slugs hit Colorado squarely in the abdomen. McGuire bounded backwards and spun around before he doubled over, grimacing, as he held his bleeding body. Then, he crumpled to the round, facedown and dead.

Lowery walked slowly to the slain man and kicked the body over on its back. Then, with an uncontrolled rage, still smarting over the death of Jed and Billie Stevens, Frank fired two close-range shots into the fallen outlaw. He might have fired his remaining rounds, but Vic Gray suddenly gripped his wrist. The Enid deputy had rushed out of the jailhouse when someone had told him that a gunfight was about to happen. The fight was over before Gray got there.

"You crazy, Lowery?" Gray scolded Frank. "It's done! It's finished!"

Frank dropped his head. "I'm sorry."

Gray motioned to some spectators who now gathered close to him, Lowery, and the dead Colorado. "Get this body over to the mortician."

Several men quickly complied.

Lowery now told Gray that the slain outlaw had been carrying a good deal of stolen money, and the two deputies began a search. They started at the Enid Saloon, where one of the harlots gave Gray the bag that McGuire had brought in with him, which he had left behind when he had scurried out of the place. The prostitute gaped in astonishment when Frank opened the small valise to expose the bag of gold and the bag of bills.

"I think this is the last of the stolen money," Frank Lowery said.

Deputy Marshal Vic Gray nodded.

Frank Lowery remained in Enid for the next couple of days. He had just finished breakfast on the second morning at the jailhouse when Marshal Fred Egan,

Deputy Jack Stone, and two volunteers from the posse dismounted in front of Vic Gray's jailhouse. The other members of the posse had apparently decided to return to Guthrie. Deputy Gray greeted Egan and Stone with warm handshakes and ushered them inside. Here, Egan found Lowery sitting in a chair, and he eyed his deputy with a mixture of pride and irritation. He pumped Lowery's hand in a strong handshake, but then he shook his head.

"Frank, you've given me more goddamn fits during the short time you've been with us than any of my other deputies. You were supposed to keep that dugout under surveillance, and now I learn you took on the whole Bronco gang alone. Your note was clear enough, but can't say I appreciate the way you handled this, even if you did come out all right."

Jack Stone did not speak, but he looked at Frank with an admiring grin.

"It was my intent merely to watch the place, Marshal," Frank said, "but when I reached the Bronco hideaway, I found that two of the outlaws were gone and the other two might leave at any moment. If I had waited for you to show up, those two still there might have left as well."

"You could've been killed."

"But if I didn't act," Lowery defended himself, "those four outlaws could have scattered themselves all over the country and we'd have never caught up to them and recovered the money."

"The money?"

"That's right, Marshal," Vic Gray grinned. "We got back every last gold nugget they stole, and almost all of the bills from the Abajo Springs, Wells Fargo, and the Stillwater bank jobs. I've got all of it locked in my safe."

"I'll be damned," Egan said. "Frank, maybe you did do the right thing."

"I'd like to go back to Stillwater, if I can," Frank said.

Egan's face sobered for he knew that his deputy was anxious to see this girl, Clara Beaufort. "Frank, sit down. I've got to tell you something." He ushered the deputy into a chair and then sat down himself before he leaned close to Lowery. "We know about you and that Clara Beaufort and how close you were. She came to me and confessed that she had been with the Bronco gang at the Abajo Springs hold-up, although she denied taking any active part in the thing. She also admitted that Bronco Kinney gave her a thousand dollars from that robbery, almost all of which is still in the Stillwater Farmers Bank. She wanted me to know that you had no knowledge of this, but she thought it best if she came clean, so's not to get you into any trouble."

Frank Lowery's heart sank.

"I don't know whether you were aware of her activities or not," Egan continued, "and I'm not going to ask. Her coming in to me on her own makes it unnecessary for me to do so." When Frank frowned, Egan gripped his wrist. "If it's any consolation, I can tell you that I'd have found out about her anyway, because a man named Marvin Crandall also paid me a visit at the Stillwater jailhouse a few hours later to tell me about Miss Beaufort's association with the Kinney gang. I guess he thought he might get some reward money. So, the girl did herself a favor by comin' to me first. She's in the jailhouse now, and my guess is that a judge will go easy on her. With good behavior, she might be out of woman's prison in a year."

Frank Lowery nodded.

"Now," Egan gestured, "I've got what I hope is some good news for you. I've finally got authorization from Washington to open a new deputy's post at Stillwater. I need somebody there, because it's a long way from Enid to Guthrie. If you have a mind to, Frank, I'd like you to assume this post. A lot of people in that area will be glad you're there. For the time being, you can share the jailhouse with Constable Hutchinson. I'm stayin' in Enid until tomorrow to finish up a few things and to go over some items with Vic Gray. We'll stop in to see you on our way back to Guthrie."

"I'd like to leave right now," Frank said.

Egan nodded. "You do that. Constable Hutchinson is expecting you."

By late afternoon, after more than ten hours on the trail, Lowery arrived in Stillwater. He rode straight to the jailhouse. When he tethered his horse, he hurried inside to find Hutchinson sitting at a desk and Clara Beaufort lying on a cot in a second cell. The constable rose from his chair and grinned.

"Hello, Mr. Lowery. Are you gonna take that new deputy marshal job here?"

Frank nodded.

"Congratulations. It'll sure be nice to have you in Stillwater to keep law and order. I'm gettin' a little old to do it all by myself."

"Constable," Frank said, "I'd like to talk to the woman prisoner."

"Sure thing, Mr. Lowery," Hutchinson said.

When Clara saw Lowery her eyes widened eagerly. She leaped off her cot and rushed to the cell door bars. "Frank, thank God; I'm so glad you're all right."

But when Frank entered the cell, the glee on Clara's

254

ace changed to soberness. She had noticed that Frank had pursed his lips in obvious agony because she was behind bars. However, after he sat on the cell bunk next to her, the girl forced a grin.

"Frank, this was for the best. I have no regrets, and I'm ready to pay for what I done. Anyway, I just couldn't let this thing hang over you, protecting me when you swore to uphold the law. Neither one of us could o' lived with somethin' like that for very long."

Frank Lowery said nothing.

"The marshal told me that I might be outta prison in a year," Clara continued. "That ain't so long, and if you still want me by then, why we can be with each other for a long time with a clear conscience, and with nothin' but a happy future ahead of us." She looked hard at the visitor. "Will you wait for me, Frank?"

"You know I will." Frank Lowery finally spoke. "Egan just put me in charge of a new deputy marshal's post here in Stillwater, and this is where I'll be when you're free again."

"That's great, Frank, just wonderful; you waitin' for me will surely give me somethin' to look forward to while I'm away."

Frank Lowery nodded, but the distress remained on his face.

"Please, Frank, don't feel bad."

Lowery sighed as the girl gently kissed him. He squeezed her hand before he left the cell. Frank continued to visit Clara daily for about a week, until the circuit judge arrived in Stillwater to hear Clara's case. There was no trial or jury, since Clara had pleaded guilty to consorting-with-criminals charges and the possession of stolen money. The judge sentenced her to two-to-five

255

years at the territorial woman's prison. Indeed, with good behavior, she might be out in even less than a year. Frank Lowery personally bid her good-bye before she climbed into the prison wagon for the ride to the penitentiary. He stood outside the jailhouse, staring until the wagon had disappeared.

"She sure is a pretty thing," Constable Isa Hutchinson said. "I hate to see a girl like that go to prison."

Frank Lowery did not answer. He only hoped she was still as pretty when or if he saw her again.